Edvil–Ed—a minion of Hell, is Lucifer's best soul-taker. Stationed in New York, he's very good at what he does. However, all his plans go by the wayside when Hell's accountants tell the overlord that they're two souls over. There's a balance, and that balance between souls up and souls below must be preserved at all costs. If the balance doesn't hold by the end of each year, then the world will be destroyed, and the rulers of Heaven and Hell will have to start the whole process of evolution all over again.

Ed is given the task of helping two souls go topside. His assistant is Millie, a Halo—angel—and together, they have an almost impossible task. Furthermore, Ed's chief rival, Markus, decides to sabotage Ed's efforts for reasons of his own.

Undeterred, Ed and Millie press on with their mission, and along the way they find out that they're much more into each other than they want to admit. After numerous setbacks, Ed discovers Markus' ultimate plan and has to do everything in his power to stop the final apocalypse from happening.

And The Devil Take Ye
Copyright © 2023 J.S. Frankel
ISBN: 978-1-4874-4039-8
Cover art by Martine Jardin

Published by eXtasy Books Inc

Look for us online at:
www.eXtasybooks.com

AND THE DEVIL TAKE YE

BY

J.S. FRANKEL

DEDICATION

*For my wife, Akiko, for my sons, Kai and Ray, for all the support-
ers out there — readers and writers — my greatest thanks. Sara,
Emily, Harlowe Rose, Eva, Gigi, Paul, and so many others, I thank
you as well for your friendship and support. And to my late sister,
Nancy Frankel, who supported me through thick and thin, this
one's for you.*

A GLOSSARY OF ANGEL'S AND DEVIL'S POWERS

Angels and devils have the power of teleportation, although their powers are confined solely to the realms of Earth, Heaven, and Hell. While on Earth, devils can teleport up to a range of a thousand miles. Angels can teleport a little farther than their counterparts can. No one knows why. Maybe it's the wings.

Angels and devils can manipulate matter to a degree. They can fashion food out of the air, create implements, and they can construct most objects. However, they cannot create that which has not been already created.

Angels have backed the New York Yankees since nineteen-twenty-three. Devils have backed every other team. The Yankees have won the most World Series. Now you know why.

Angels say a prayer when someone is injured. Devils curse your name when you suffer an injury and hope to hell it hurts.

Angels and devils can shape-shift when necessary. They can also block their appearance from anyone they choose, save their brethren.

Angels cannot read minds, but they are far more sensitive to another person's emotions. Devils also cannot read minds, but they are quick to pick up on gestures and use them to their advantage.

Neither angel nor devil can control the minds of mortals. They can, however, influence those whose minds are easily swayed. That explains the success rate of those down below.

CHAPTER ONE: EASY PICKINGS

New York City. One AM. June seventh, 2032. An alleyway in the Bronx.

Hunter vs prey. That was the law of the jungle, and even though the alleyway was far from the continents of Africa, or India, or South America, it was still a jungle, albeit an urban one.

Ed — the hunter — knew that. He also knew that he was different from the average person. Gazing into a store window as he walked by, he saw his reflection, that of a young male, lean, muscular, and in perfect physical condition, like a decathlete, only more so.

He wore a pair of high-toned slacks along with a made-to-measure tailored long-sleeved shirt. That seemed totally out of place in the hot and steamy summer weather. His sharply defined features and short black hair, along with his gaze — deep and penetrating — made him stand out from the rest of humanity. After getting into position, Ed waited in silence, scarcely breathing. A fly landed on his arm. He quickly flicked it away and watched as his quarry made his way into the alley.

Heat notwithstanding, he took no notice of the weather and paid scant attention to his surroundings. He was after something more important than a cool room in which to relax.

Ah, his prey had made his appearance, a tall, skinny cat burglar in his late twenties named Billy Crate. Ed had followed his target for the past three days, ever since Crate

1

obtained his parole from prison.

Billy made his way into the alley, and Ed stepped into the shadows, blending with them. It was his skill set that kept him hidden. Special abilities, one might call them.

However, they were endowed abilities, and they didn't come from the one above. They came from the one below. Point of fact—Ed was a demon, and demons could shield themselves from human eyes.

He watched as his target crept along the alley with quiet, careful steps. It was a game, really, to see who was better at stalking. Ed knew that Billy was out to steal something.

Tirelessly, he'd trailed his human target as he went from his flophouse of an apartment to roaming the streets in search of a score. He'd watched Billy's every move, and listened in on his telephone calls to a fence named Winger.

Ed knew that Billy would use his cat-burgling skills to try and steal some cash or jewelry to fence. Only now, he, as a hunter-demon, would strike first.

For his part, Billy gazed at his surroundings, spat on the ground, and uttered his verdict. "What a dump."

Call that a spot-on assessment. The alleyway was narrow, filled with discarded boxes and crates. Every apartment house had violated the building codes long ago. What held them up was spit, substandard metal, and wood, and most of all, luck.

Urban blight didn't half describe this area. However, the greedy owners, not to mention the city officials, had let things slide. Call it bureaucracy—business as usual.

Ed watched as Billy quietly made his way down the alley. It was only a hundred feet long, and there was a chain-link fence at the end.

After looking around to make sure no one was around, he spat on his palms and jumped up to scale the fence with little difficulty.

Ed teleported a bit closer, taking up a position in the shadows from which to observe his target. He watched as Billy jumped to the other side, not bothering to look around. As far as he was concerned, he was alone. In reality, he wasn't.

He must have also thought that he wouldn't be caught or that no one was following him. He was incorrect in that assumption, as well.

Billy had already served two stints in prison, and while it should have shown him the error of his ways, he was of limited intelligence. He also happened to be stubborn, two extremely negative traits that indicated he'd never rise above his station in life.

Ed knew that tonight Billy wouldn't rise above anything, and a grim smile coated his lean features. He watched as the cat-burglar climbed to the third floor of an apartment building and quietly entered through the open window.

Five minutes later, he emerged, clutching a gold watch, eighty dollars, and a bag of weed. "High quality," Billy murmured with satisfaction.

He descended to the ground to do a funky pirouette in celebration of his score. In addition to his dance, he also zipped his fly down to take a leak. Some people would say he was marking his territory or leaving a puddle of urine as a final insult.

Enough is enough, Ed thought as he emerged from the shadows. He could have gone straight over to Billy, but that would have been too obvious and not as dramatic.

This situation called for something dramatic, and so, he hid himself from human eyes. The show would begin soon.

From the invisible void he'd entered, Ed watched as Billy swiped away the sweat with his free hand and cursed the weather once more. "Damn, it's hot," he muttered and sniffed the air. A moment later, he recoiled, as a smell of sulfur slammed into his nostrils. A heavy, cloying smell, it overrode the horrid stench of garbage and animal droppings.

"What in the hell is making that damned smell?"

His question was partially answered when a manhole cover blew off its moorings ten yards ahead in a blaze of blue fire and smoke. The cover, solid iron, went straight up and smashed into the ground about fifteen seconds later.

"Jesus!"

Billy Crate's veneer of manliness shattered, and his output immediately dried up. Now he was spooked, and he wasn't the type to spook easily. Hastily, he zipped up his jeans.

Smoke billowed in the air, obscuring his vision. He coughed and swatted the air in front of him, blinking away the acrid grayish-blue cloud that caused his nose hairs to wilt.

At that moment, Ed chose to come face to face with Billy. "Some light show, mister," Billy said with a tinge of respect. "You with a movie company or something?"

"No."

Billy's eyes grew round as he examined him more closely. "You . . . you look like a kid. What kind of crap is this? Some kinda television show?" He looked around in confusion as if looking for someone with a camera working.

With a sigh, Ed shook his head. No one was around. No lights, no cameras, but there would definitely be some action. "It's not crap, and no, I'm not with a movie company or something."

His tone, calm and yet challenging, seemed to spook Billy even more, and his body visibly deflated as his courage leaked away. Still, bravado overrode common sense. "Mister, you want some trouble? I'll give you all you want."

Ed was well aware that Billy could fight. Demons carried background knowledge of their prey. It made their job so much easier. He knew that Billy had gotten into his share of brawls growing up, learned a few more dirty tricks while in prison, and also carried a switchblade. Mr. Blade had settled more than a few conflicts.

Still, with a little finesse, it probably wouldn't come to an all-out brawl, if Billy was willing to listen to reason. So, Ed made his pitch. "What I want is something you're probably not prepared to give."

That set Billy off. He balled his fists. "You got a name, pal?"

"It's . . . Edvil. You can call me Ed if you like."

"Edvil, what kind of name is that?" Billy's anger peaked, then. "Mister, are you trying to take over my turf? You got another thing coming. I got a blade, and I'll carve you up like a Thanksgiving turkey, if that's what you want."

This time, a brief smile flashed across Ed's lean visage. "I'm not trying to take over anything. I *am* taking over. In fact, I've already taken over, but you, pal, you're just too stupid to realize it."

Billy spit out a few epithets. "You're asking for it, mister. All right, let's get it on." With that, he threw a right hook, one aimed to mash Ed's nose in and send him down for the count. It didn't connect. Instead, Billy's momentum carried him into the wall. When he turned around, he found Ed grinning at him. "What the hell?"

"Now you're getting it," Ed said. "Try again?"

Thoroughly pissed off, Billy threw a series of lefts and rights, missing each time. Ed had uncanny reflexes and twisted and turned a split-second before the punches connected.

Panting now and seemingly discouraged, Billy stopped his attack. "You're not even gonna fight back? What are you, yellow?"

After giving an almost inaudible sigh, Ed curled his hands into fists. Some people simply wouldn't listen to reason. "If you insist." He proceeded to unleash a lightning-fast attack, jabbing, hooking, and pounding Billy about the head and torso. Billy tried to cover up, but every single shot got through, and soon he fell back, bleeding from his nose and mouth.

"Had enough?"

Ed's calmly asked question caused Billy to spit out a small river of blood, and he yelled, not caring if anyone heard, "Who are you? What the hell are you?"

Ed shook his head. He knew that not a hair was out of place, and not a bead of sweat appeared on his smooth, un-lined forehead. "At first, I thought you were the most igno-rant person I'd ever met. You're not even close."

"Huh?"

"You talked about Hell. That's the first thing you've gotten right, buddy. In fact, it's the only thing you've gotten right. Hell is the operative word here."

Billy stared as if unable to process the obvious. Then, rea-son left him, and in a quick, practiced move, he reached into his pocket and took out his handy-dandy switchblade.

One press of the button on the side, and the six-inch blade sprang out. That seemed to give Billy courage, and he waved it in Ed's face. "You want some? I'll give you all I got!"

Ed didn't budge and repeated his earlier statement. "What I want, you're not prepared to give."

Now, Billy's fury went incandescent. He'd already gotten his ass kicked. His pride had been shattered. And he looked mad enough to kill. "Hey, do you know who I am? Man, this is *my* turf. I rule this place. I rule! I'll give you everything, you punk. I'll give you anything and everything I got on me, and . . ."

Zap! A blue bolt of hellfire emanated from Ed's left forefin-ger and incinerated Billy in his tracks. Nothing remained ex-cept a few scraps of smoking clothing and a scorched smell that hung in the air. The area was quiet, and the air was still.

The only difference between now and seven seconds ago was that before, there had been two people. Now, there was only one, and the one that remained could not be considered a person in any way.

Ed pulled a black notebook and pen from his pocket, muttering, "Foolish" as he did so. He noted the day, the time, and the location of the incident, carefully jotted everything down, and then he stowed his notebook away.

In life, there was always death. Ed remembered his master's explicit instructions. "This is not someone we want. Don't bring him to us or send him to them."

Ed had followed the instructions to the letter. As he reflected on this evening's sojourn, he thought that the master would be pleased. Yes, indeed, he would.

CHAPTER TWO: PARTY

Five months later. Manhattan. December twenty-sixth. Evening.

"You're hosting the party this year," Frank said with a hint of anticipation. "Aren't you?"

Ed tried to ignore the question as he and Frank stood on the sidewalk outside Ed's apartment building, watching people stream around them in a ceaseless flow. Citizens, rich and poor alike, black, white, Asian, mixed, whatever religion — it didn't matter. They're like ants, Ed thought. Just like ants.

Although it was cold and snowing lightly, neither individual noticed it. It was one of the perks of being a demon. Immunity to cold or heat, rapid healing factor, immunity to death unless it was at the master's hand — as a demon, unlife was good.

Unfortunately, with every good thing came something bad, and in Ed's case, the bad was the party he had to throw. His friend repeated the question, this time with the broad hint that he wanted an invitation. Frank wasn't the type that demons — much less people — said no to.

With a sigh of resignation and knowing there was no way he could weasel out of this situation, Ed answered, "Yeah, guess it's my turn."

Being a party-meister had to rate as the worst job around. Thankfully, it was only once a year. Every demon who headed up a major city had to host a year-end bash. As New York was Ed's domain on Earth, and as he was the chief soul-taker there, he had to invite no less than five other demons. That was it.

Furthermore, everyone else, if they weren't hosting a party, they had to attend at least one shindig. *"It promotes solidarity."* So said Lucifer, and his word was law.

In reality, it promoted boredom and divisiveness, although no one ever mentioned it aloud. In Ed's case, he'd have rather given up all the souls he'd taken to get out of putting this get-together together, but the rules had to be followed.

The previous year, he'd attended Pern's party in Alaska. Pern, who was reputedly Finnish in descent and therefore had absolutely no sense of humor, moped from start to finish, and the party was a bomb, even by demonic standards.

Everyone had stayed for an hour, listened to Pern grouse about being stationed in Alaska, the backward attitudes everyone had, the inclement weather, and then, one by one, they made the usual BS excuse of having to attend to some other tasks and departed.

Pern was a decent demon and a hard worker. He got his share of souls, but he could be a real buzzkill at times. From the moment Ed stepped into his large, log cabin house, with its distinct lack of a homey atmosphere and a cold fireplace that could have been lit by a blast of hellfire but wasn't, he felt the waves of Pern's discontent, and he couldn't wait to have his one drink and leave.

Pern's discontent stemmed from his position in a backward area — his words — and the fact that demons' voices were often ignored. *"We should all have a say,"* he often uttered and then reiterated his statement when no one backed him up.

"Dangerous words," Ed replied, knowing that Lucifer was the one and only voice in Hell. Talk like this could get a demon in trouble. Lucifer heard everything. There was no way he couldn't miss this. *"Our master, well, you know."*

"All I'm saying is, we're the pawns, and sometimes pawns want a little more of the pie, y'know what I'm saying?"

Pern went on to talk about unionizing, and a few of the guests privately muttered something about socialism and how it would undo Hell. Lucifer was the only power down there. Call it a dictatorship—and it was—it worked, and it worked very well.

Not wishing to bring on any more bad feelings, Ed had nodded, rejoined the party, and then excused himself a few minutes later, teleporting back to Manhattan and the safety of his own digs . . .

"So, I'm invited?" Frank asked, bringing Ed back to the present. "Can I bring a guest?"

Probably one of his girlfriends, Ed thought. Frank had a lot, or so he said. "Yeah, of course, you're invited. You, Nebulazar, and a couple of others."

Frank glowed. "Solid!"

With that, he took his leave, strolling off into the crowd and vanishing among the throng. After he left, Ed heaved another half-sigh and then stopped himself from going all the way. That was a trope. He hated tropes, and furthermore, there was no choice in the matter.

Still, he took a certain amount of pride in this past year's doings. He'd taken many souls, more than anyone else. The accountant downstairs would total up the takings, and then let the celebrations begin. And, of course, he had to throw the obligatory party.

It was a rare occasion, as the demonic horde ate and drank and reveled both upstairs as well as downstairs. In Hell, the damned were given a day off to recuperate.

Preposterous? Not really. Those were the orders of Lucifer himself. *"They're here for eternity, unless my, ahem, maker, decides to intervene on their behalf."*

For him, as well as for his disciples, it didn't matter. They expected a ceaseless flow of souls in. It had always been that way, it would always be that way, so why worry?

And, if those above decided to swoop in at the last second

of that sucker's life on Earth and snatch up their soul, well, those down below didn't sweat it.

After all, the difference would be made up sooner or later. All accounts would be settled by year's end. The balance, as always, would hold.

It wasn't as if either side didn't try to gain an advantage, but for some unknown reason, they always ended up even on December thirty-first at midnight. And then the whole soul-taking, soul-saving routine would begin again the following day.

"Forget about that for now," Ed murmured to no one in particular. "You've got a party to plan."

Custom demanded that everyone bring their own booze and eats — or conjure them up — in addition to the host or hostess providing quality grub.

In Hell, demons didn't have to eat unless they wanted to, but on Earth, in mortal form, demons got hungry, so Ed bought only the best. That meant going to the finest import stores in Manhattan, and he enjoyed shopping. It relaxed him. Even demons suffered job burnout from time to time.

Money was no object. Demons always had access to money, and even if they ran short, they could always get some from mortals. A few well-chosen words, and voilà, the cash would be theirs.

Or they could simply run an electrical charge through an ATM, but Ed had never done that. For him, it was a matter of pride to pay for everything without having to steal it from a machine.

Likewise, he could always conjure it up, but that wasn't his style. Conjuring up clothes, though, or a new DVD, well, that was acceptable.

As he laid out the buffet table, he marveled at the quantity, as well as the quality of the food. Quantity-wise, it filled the nine-foot-long table, almost to overflowing.

Quality-wise, it was the best. Black caviar from Russia, smoked salmon from Canada—he favored a small store in Toronto that sliced the fish and prepared it in an elegant floral pattern—and the finest of fruits, meats, and vegetables from every corner of the globe filled the table.

Oh, and there had to be beverages. Finely aged whisky, wine from the best wineries worldwide, champagne, beer for Frank—the senior demon didn't care for anything else—and enough spirits to satisfy the most die-hard of alcoholics.

As he looked around his eighth-floor apartment, Ed couldn't suppress a grin. If he had one weakness, it was this place. Call it materialistic, call it snobbery, he loved his earthly abode.

Located in the Upper Westside of Manhattan, near Ninety-Sixth and Broadway, his place, the Royal Heights, a twenty-year-old apartment complex, lay in the heart of that great area, and he couldn't have been happier.

A beautifully designed two-bedroom affair, it had been built with an Art Deco motif, and in addition to offering privacy and security, it had a kitchen that would have made a gourmet chef green with envy.

Moreover, it had all the accouterments of someone with wealth and power and privilege—built-in stereo, voice-activated light switches, finely tuned air-conditioning—the works.

Best of all, the view was incredible, a vista that showcased the beauty of the city. Ed often spent his evenings simply gazing at the landscape below him.

How a teenager on the cusp of adulthood could get in and out would have raised suspicion from anyone, but a simple shape-shift into the form of an older man allayed any suspicions.

To those passersby on the street who didn't know Ed, they

saw him as a preppy teen who wore the latest in brand-name clothes.

To the doorman, Milton, a proper gentleman in his late sixties, and to the other occupants of his building, they saw him in the guise of Edward Anderson, a wealthy businessman in his early thirties.

He had the necessary documents, the apartment had been bought and paid for, and no one asked any questions.

All was ready, and now, since the clock had struck seven, he only had to wait until his guests arrived. They'd be coming in soon, fashionably late.

While waiting, he snapped his fingers, and Alanna, his voice-activated computer control device, called out, "Yes, sir?"

"Put on some music, please."

Her tone was sweet. She'd been programmed that way. "Which selection, sir? We have KPop, JPop, classical, rock, heavy metal, and many more. Please make a selection."

Options, he had plenty of options, and he mentally ran through them before deciding on something light and airy. "Put on KPop, C-Gals Best Selection, and then E-Beat."

Instantly, the sounds of a Korean girl's group filtered through the air, something upbeat and catchy. KPop had hit North America about twenty-five years ago, and there seemed to be no shortage of new, young singers, all manufactured by the Korean music companies.

Their voices, high yet womanly, got him into the spirit of things. Christmas, which he loathed, was over. Boxing Day was also over and done with, so the only thing left was to finish off the year on a high note. It was time to enjoy things with friends — except for Frank, the rest were acquaintances, really — and greet the New Year with a smile.

Ed thought about who was coming. Most of the other demons had other parties to attend, but he'd asked a few people he respected, and they'd agreed.

Besides Frank, there was Lars. Lars had a demon wife. It proved out Hell's adage—the family that preyed together, stayed together.

As for Nebulazar, Ed had no idea what he was up to. He was a quiet sort from somewhere in Mongolia, originally. A good worker, he ran the south-west Asian contingent, although Frank controlled Tokyo and most of Japan.

Matombo and Laban both hailed from the African continent. Always busy, they said that they'd pop in for a quick drink. It was better than nothing.

While he waited, Ed walked over to the window to observe the evening sky. A streak of red had appeared, and it seemed to split the night. It was clear, the stars were bright, and all seemed well until a sudden tremor shook his apartment.

A tremor? In New York? It had happened once before, but that was due to an earthquake happening elsewhere. New York had never been the epicenter of one, not that he knew about.

Checking the news, the announcers confirmed that a tremor had occurred only a minute ago, it was minor, there was no damage, and please enjoy the holiday and New Year's season.

"Holiday season," Ed echoed. "T'is the season to take—and take."

He hadn't snatched up any souls since the middle of December, but he felt sure that he was in the lead. Could a promotion to director of North American acquisitions be far behind? It was almost too much to hope for, a dream come true . . .

A whiff of burnt ozone filtered over to his nostrils, and he turned around to see Frank and a young Asian woman standing five feet away.

In his true form, Frank was exceedingly ugly, with fangs, red and black leathery wings, a massive torso, cloven feet, and a tail—in short, a nightmare.

Now, due to being on Earth, he'd assumed his mortal form, that of a man in his late thirties with a linebacker's body and a swarthy face with coarse features. He was casually clad in jeans and a lumberjack shirt.

In contrast, his girlfriend couldn't have been more than twenty. She also wore jeans and a long coat that partially covered a flowery blouse, and she had a pleasant smile on an oval, pretty face.

A bag hung over her shoulder, and Frank immediately took it along with her coat and laid the items carefully on a nearby couch while the woman adjusted her blouse.

In a completely unselfconscious move, she tossed her head back, and a mane of long and lustrous black hair flowed behind her. Ed wondered what she'd think if she saw Frank in his true form, and then he decided that it was none of his business.

Frank straightened up and greeted Ed effusively, extending his hand for the obligatory shake. "Hi, bud, thanks for the invitation. You're looking good."

"I can't complain."

The young woman walked over to bow politely. "My name is Mariko Inagawa," she said in heavily accented but grammatically correct English. "It is nice to meet you."

"Same here," Ed acknowledged, offering a friendly smile. "Is this your first trip to New York?"

She bobbed her head. "It is my first trip anywhere. Frank and I flew in last night. We are staying tonight at the Harleton Hotel."

They'd flown in, not teleported. Well, demons couldn't teleport that far, anyway, at least, not on Earth. Their powers were limited, after all. "I hope you had a good trip."

She nodded. "It was exciting."

After some more small talk, Ed asked them to sit at the

table and help themselves. "Some spread you put out," Frank said with admiration as he filled his plate. Mariko took only a few items, saying that she was on a diet.

"Only the best," Ed replied and then he excused himself as another pop of ozone signaled a new arrival. It was Lars, with his wife.

Mariko looked up, but she didn't seem surprised in the least at someone popping in from the ether. Frank offered a wink. Obviously, his girlfriend knew who and what he was, and just as obviously, the fact that her boyfriend was a demon didn't seem to matter.

"Happy year's end," Lars said in a thick accent. A big, burly man with a shock of reddish-brown hair and equally reddish-brown skin, he'd been born in Sweden around five centuries ago and retained the appearance of a man in his late thirties.

Lars headed up the Scandinavian section. It was a position of great responsibility, and he dealt with everything in a quiet, reserved manner.

His wife was as tiny as he was large, roughly the same age, with bright blue eyes and a head of short brown hair. She hugged Ed and greeted Frank and his girlfriend with hugs and kisses.

"Big hugger, my wife is," Lars said as he took a seat and grabbed a bottle of vodka. "That's why she's so good at her job. People trust her."

Ed knew his wife—Seritte. Getting a hug from her wasn't so bad. She reminded him of the mother he never knew. Seritte managed the Scandinavian area along with her husband.

"Oh, and Nebulazar gave me a message to give to you," Lars continued. "He can't make it. The boss wanted him to stay downstairs this year. The other guys told me that they couldn't make it, either. They had business to take care of, and the boss let them off the party hook."

Ed received the news with a sense of equanimity. Sure, it was disappointing, but not unexpected. Lucifer had his plans, and the big man was not the sort to oppose in matters like these — or any matters. "No problem," Ed replied. "Enjoy the meal."

He sat down and helped himself to a good portion of the food, and the meal and conversation flowed effortlessly from that point on. Frank had always been a loquacious sort, crude at times, especially when discussing the virtues of Asian women in bed, but tonight, he was on his best behavior.

He had his beer, he had his girlfriend, and he laughed along with the rest of the jokes people told, mainly about conquests. Conquests didn't refer to sleeping around. No, they had everything to do with how many souls each of them had gotten.

Ed didn't believe in shop talk, but this was a holiday treat, after all, and he had good reason to celebrate. He rarely drank, but when he did, he enjoyed a glass of good champagne, and he had fourteen bottles of the best on the market.

Upon his command, Alanna switched the music to an easy listening selection, and the mood became mellow, although it took a slight downturn when Lars got drunk.

It took a lot to get him drunk, mainly fifty bottles of vodka over a period of an hour, and he started singing an incredibly dirty song that caused Mariko's mouth to drop open, as well as Frank's.

Lars only stopped when his wife chided him. "Husband! This isn't the time! You big goof, you're ruining Ed's party. Let's get you home."

Immediately, Lars started to argue, saying that he didn't want to leave, but his wife's eyes blazed a fiery red, a clear signal that she was beyond angry. "Uh-oh," he said quietly, suddenly sober. "I guess it is time to go. See you soon, Ed."

They vanished, and the meal went on. In the middle of it, though, Ed had a thought. Nothing he could pin down, merely a disquieting feeling that something bad was about to happen.

What could happen, though? New York had always been a city of tension, where business and romance and everything in between seemed to tread a fine line between calm and madness. He'd been living there a long time. Tempers often soared, stress was high, but now, a new, unnerving feeling hit, and he got up to look out the window.

The red streak he'd seen before had spread into a haze that covered the sky, almost blanking out the stars. *What is going on here?*

Another pop in the air interrupted his thoughts. Turning around, Markus stood in the center of the room, a senior demon who'd assumed the guise of a young man in his late twenties.

Blond, blue-eyed, with milky-white skin and chiseled features, he could have passed for a male model — or a Teutonic noble.

His companions were also extremely photogenic. A man on his right looked to be in his forties with a beard, a styled haircut, and a practiced look of boredom on his face.

Markus' other companion was a woman in her early thirties. Both visitors were striking, with blonde hair, blue eyes, and chiseled features, much like his.

It figured. Markus liked people in his own image, the image he projected on Earth, as well as below. Perhaps that was what he looked like in his previous life, although Ed had never asked him about it.

Markus was one of the older demons, older than Lars, and he always came across as being aristocratic, almost aloof. He also happened to be one of the best soul snatchers around.

No one liked him, though, a rarity among demons. While they respected him for his ability to track down and grab any soul he wished, his manner of speaking in an arch, brittle German accent, which sounded simultaneously condescending and commanding, turned everyone off.

"Ah, Ed, how nice to see you," he said, throwing his arms around his companions. "I see we've come to the right place. Parties are always a good thing, don't you think?"

If someone had decided to toss cold water on the proceedings, Markus couldn't have done a better job. Ed stifled the urge to simply toss him through the window. Dead was dead, so a little more pain wouldn't hurt.

However, he didn't act upon his impulses, as he didn't want to make a scene in front of his friends. This was supposed to be a time of enjoying one's unlife, not a time for rancor.

Frank glowered and got up. "Markus, you weren't invited."

The other demon took his arms away from his consorts and waved off the other demon's objection. "Oh, Frank, don't be a pill. There's enough room for a little hedonism in every situation, don't you think?"

He nodded at Mariko. "I can see you've already got a head start. Why not make it a quintet with us?"

Frank stepped out from the table. If it came to a simple fist fight, Frank had the edge in strength and fighting skill. If it came to using their powers—mainly tossing bolts of energy, in addition to teleportation—then Markus would win.

A master strategist, he was Hell's unofficial chess champion. Even Lucifer had never managed to defeat him. In numerous matches they'd had over the decades, they'd battled to draw after draw, but everyone had the feeling that Markus was simply toying with the overlord. If he actually checkmated Lucifer, who knew what would happen?

Ed decided to put a stop to this idiocy and got between them, pushing Markus back. While there would eventually be a reckoning, it wouldn't happen today.

"Markus, in case you haven't noticed, this is a private party. Guess what? You weren't invited, and I see that you've got guests, so why not hold a party of your own?"

Markus sniffed as if something particularly vile had expired and the garbage-men had forgotten to take it away. He brushed his tailor-made suit to get rid of any traces of someone else's hand. "I suppose that could be arranged. In fact, I've already arranged it."

A curious smile flashed across his face. It seemed as though he was hiding something, but then again, Markus had always been a secretive kind of guy. Mortals had a saying — the man with the plan.

Markus had a different saying — a devil with the details. He left nothing to chance. Ed had worked with him a few times before his appointment to New York, and the older demon was always in control, calm, and collected — the epitome of a professional.

However, Markus was also a vainglorious, hedonistic, self-centered, supreme egotist. Still, he was smart enough to know when he wasn't wanted. With a courteous bow to everyone, he said, "TTFN" and vanished, along with his consorts.

Ed turned to his guests, somewhat embarrassed. "Sorry about that. I didn't know he'd show up."

Frank's anger had faded. He finished off his fifteenth bottle of beer and carefully wiped his mouth with his napkin. "That jerk would have to ruin things."

He reached out to take his girlfriend's hand. "Anyway, we'll have to make it a short night. I hate to eat and run, but Mariko's sort of tired."

As if on cue, she yawned, and if that wasn't a signal that private time had to be observed, Ed didn't know what was. He wasn't offended, though.

Clearly, Frank cared for her, as he behaved like a complete gentleman, putting her jacket on for her and even carrying her bag. Some might have seen it as being old-fashioned, but Frank didn't seem embarrassed in the least.

Ever the generous host, Ed bobbed his head, grateful for their understanding. "No problem, Frank. Thanks for coming by. Happy Next Year to you."

"It was nice to meet you," Mariko said sweetly, bowing as a sign of respect. "Please visit us when you have the time."

Ed returned the gesture. "I'll see what happens."

With that, they vanished, and Ed set about cleaning up. Small party or not, he suddenly felt deflated and alone. Everyone had someone. He didn't, but as he reflected further, a lot of it had been his choice, and a person — or demon — had to live with the choices they'd made.

A snap of his fingers got rid of the dishes, and soon the apartment was sparkling. Another snap got the television going, and he took the bottle of champagne over to the couch to sit and sip while the news played.

"Atmospheric disturbances continue across the world. Meteorologists and scientists are exploring the phenomena, but they have assured us that this is not dangerous. We repeat, not dangerous."

Ed only half-listened to the broadcast. He closed his eyes, only to have a vision flash in his mind's eye. A wooden room . . . a warehouse, the bang of something exploding, and then . . . darkness. He'd had those visions before and could never figure out what they meant.

With a sudden gasp, he sat up, breathing hard. "Humph."

Nerves jangling, heart thudding in his chest, he wiped sweat from his face. In mortal form, he never sweated, but now? Something bad was coming . . . something even unholier than the hell he lived in.

Thirsty, he felt thirsty. He needed something to drink. Water wouldn't do. As luck or fate would have it, the bottle of champagne was still in his grasp.

Throat parched, he took a sip, but the bubbly had lost its appeal, and with a grunt of dismay as well as disappointment, he placed the bottle on the carpet and got up to walk over to the window. There, he stared into the quiet of the night.

Am I searching for something? Ed's throat wasn't dry anymore, and the champagne no longer held any fascination for him. He continued staring at the darkness, though, and he focused on a red streak that had appeared out of nowhere.

Nothing to worry about, the experts said. Ed knew something was wrong, although he couldn't figure out what, and he continued to gaze at the sky until the break of dawn.

Chapter Three: Here We Are

December thirtieth. Morning.

For most people, mornings were for coffee, toast, scratching various body parts, and then showering, not necessarily in that order.

Ed's routine took a different course. It always began with a check on his soul takings. The master required daily reports. Considering how many of his disciples lived and worked across the globe, the number of reports was astronomical. If a report came in late, then it was cause for extinction, and Ed wanted to precisely avoid that.

While preparing breakfast, the events of the party came back to him, which spoiled his mood for a grand total of four seconds, but then he dismissed it.

He also dismissed his dream from last night. It was probably the stress of his unwelcome guest's visit, as well as the other additional stresses of preparing for the party, as well as wondering who'd win the year's soul-taking contest.

At the thought of that last point — who'd win — Ed laughed. Markus was a jerk, plain and simple, and he couldn't break the record, he couldn't win the year's award for most souls taken, and he wouldn't ruin today or any other day.

With his good mood restored, Ed mentally sent the report downstairs and instantly received a reply from the accountant. *Got it. I'll need some details later.*

No problem.

After that, a secret smile flashed across Ed's face. Eighteen thousand even. It didn't seem like a lot vis-à-vis the population, but adding up all the demons plus the cities and countries worldwide, well, the numbers were staggering.

Ed then hiccupped out a laugh as he went through the possible haul for this year. Count 'em and cry. Projections for the following year were equally positive. If his results didn't assure him of a promotion, perhaps as head of the North American contingent, then nothing would. Let 'em eat crow.

Plenty of people existed here who'd sell their souls for advancement's sake, or love's sake, or the sake of something else. They were all fair game.

Being a demon was everything. Ed had been one ever since he could remember.

He couldn't recall his former existence, only fragments, and the fragments consisted of something about a factory, harsh words . . . and gunfire. That was it.

When he'd woken up in Hell, Frank, who'd become his friend and mentor, was there to give him the lowdown on what to do. He had a gravelly, angry voice that sounded a lot like a tractor on amphetamines, but he proved to be most helpful.

Frank had given Ed his initial orientation of the lower depths, guiding him around the pits that housed the worst offenders. Every single one of Hell's inmates wore plain gray robes that never tore. They wailed and cried and begged for mercy as they were whipped and beaten.

Yes, they bled profusely. Guards slashed them, broke their limbs, and abused and abased them in the worst manner possible. But they healed — Hell's gift to the eternally damned.

Pity wasn't a word used here. Neither was mercy. Ed saw it all, absorbed it, and then his superior showed him where the administrative buildings were.

Once the tour had ended, they sat on a rock. Frank leaned

back, listening to the moans of the wailing souls around him with an air of satisfaction.

Initially stunned at waking up in the bad place, Ed had quickly gotten used to the sounds and smells and the idea of being a demon, and his guide assured him that he was in the right place.

"Whoever you were, whatever you did in your past life, that means nothing now. You pledged your soul to Lucifer. That means you're going to do his will. He'll give you some free rein, but you'd better deliver."

Ed had taken those words to heart. He'd started out as a regular demon. In Hell, demons were the devil's foot soldiers. They went to Earth to collect souls, and they did their utmost to earn Lucifer's praise.

Getting praise from the overlord of evil was a coveted thing. Praise meant advancement—that being measured over the course of centuries. In turn, advancement meant power. Anyone who had a sense of drive and supreme determination could rise above their present station.

At first, Ed had gone out on missions with some of the more senior members, observed how they talked the gullible into giving up their most precious possession, and he'd witnessed graft and bribery and the most abhorrent behavior imaginable.

"You have to be smooth, soft-spoken but persuasive, and also friendly," Frank counseled. "Mortals are stubborn. You can't make them sign anything they don't want to.

"You also can't force them to do anything if they're drunk or drugged. The master won't allow that, and you have no idea of how many of our kind forget that one simple detail."

"What happened to them?" Ed asked.

Frank shuddered. "They got erased. It wasn't pretty."

Hell was a most unforgiving place, especially when it came to fulfilling Lucifer's law. And the law was explicit—take souls only from those who were willing, get the writing down in blood, and never, ever, give anything in return save what the recipient asked for.

Failure to comply? Erasure.

Ed watched what the veterans did and how they worked their marks, and he'd taken those gems of knowledge and used them to his own advantage.

When the time came, he'd gone solo and soared. It all came down to having a sense of style, persistence, and stubbornness, and never taking no for an answer. Demons were the ultimate door-to-door salespersons.

Eventually, through dint of hard work and talent, he'd risen in rank, and the day came when Lucifer named him as chief soul-taker.

It was a proud moment for Ed, and as a reward, he'd been given New York City as his domain. Call it a well-deserved present. It was a gift for someone who took his job seriously.

Truth be known, Ed took his job *very* seriously. He never took vacations, rarely slept with anyone—although he knew many demons who did—but for some reason, he'd shied away from any version of long-term romance.

On rare occasions, after a successful mission, he celebrated with a willing female, but that was only a one-night deal. He'd always been careful. He'd left them happy, and then he went back to doing what he did best.

Some demons preferred same-sex relationships with the mortals they marked. Ed didn't, but he never judged. He kept a low profile, he rarely drank, and he never smoked. It wasn't as if he couldn't.

Demons didn't have to worry about high cholesterol or coronary disease or cancer or anything other disease that mortals feared. They couldn't catch STDs.

They could give them, though, although he never did. He wasn't like the other demons. His only concern centered on making his monthly quota.

"What can I do today?" Ed asked himself after taking a shower. Asking himself what he could do always meant whose soul he could take. Not being able to hunt left him somewhat at a loss, but he figured he'd do some people-sight-seeing later, make notes on potentials, and then relax. Next year was next year.

Satisfied at his lead in the soul-taking sweepstakes, Ed wrapped a towel around his waist and walked over to the window to look down on the street.

"Huh."

Sandwich-board man was at it again. He was a homeless dude of indeterminate age with a long, scraggly beard. He wore filthy jeans and a threadbare shirt, even in the worst weather. A sandwich signboard encased his body. *The End Is Nigh* was stenciled on the board in bold black letters.

Walking around with a sign like that was guaranteed to bring the stares. Sure enough, they came, some of amusement and others of contempt.

No one ever spoke to him, although a few generous people gave him money every now and then. He walked the same beat, always on the corner opposite Ed's apartment, and he bothered no one.

When it came to eating, he existed on handouts from the local diners or used the donations he'd gotten to buy something from a convenience store.

"The end is nigh," Ed mumbled. "Maybe for you, buddy. Not for me."

That was what separated him from everyone else. He was a winner. While he'd never let his ego get out of hand—there was only one supreme egotist, and that was Lucifer—but Ed knew he was good at what he did. He knew it, and so did everyone else.

So, what would this winner do? "Have breakfast."

While eating, something made him glance at the sky. That streak of red was still there. It was odd, to be sure, but for him, it was a mere atmospheric disturbance. Things like that had happened before, and the Earth was still there. It always would be—and so would he.

After getting dressed, he teleported downstairs. Milton, the doorman, greeted him effusively, as always. "Mr. Anderson, how are you today, sir?"

"Just fine," Ed replied while giving him a sunny smile. If nothing else, he had to keep up appearances.

Other demons deigned to get into the true-friendliness thing with mortals. After all, why become best buds with marks? It didn't make sense, but in Ed's case, he thought it a good idea. It made his job easier in the end. "Thank you."

Milton opened the door for him, and Ed reached into his pocket. He'd withdrawn the money from his account the other day and waited for the right time to give it. Now was the time. Five thousand dollars. "Oh, I almost forgot about this."

He handed the packet to the doorman, who received it with great surprise. It was a custom among the apartment dwellers to present their doorman with a New Year's present, but Ed's contribution dwarfed everyone else's.

Milton's hand gently squeezed the packet. "I won't look inside, sir, but it seems rather thick. I'm . . . I'm touched."

Ed smiled. He wasn't after this man's soul, either. Maybe in a decade or so, but not now. "Not a problem, Milton. Have a good one, and please buy your wife and children and grandchildren something."

The older man smiled and doffed his cap. "I will. Thank you, sir!"

Ed acknowledged him with a wave of his hand and walked outside. Along the way, he met Foster Williams, a producer of socially conscious films. They were crap, in Ed's opinion, overly talky, pretentious, and poorly acted distortions of celluloid, but Williams made a lot of money from his efforts and let everyone know about it.

True to form, he asked, "Ed, have you seen my latest endeavor? Breaking box-office records."

A large, flabby man in his fifties with a pushy manner, he continued to extol the films' virtues, while Ed endured the stream of BS and listened politely, mentally telling himself that a blowhard like Williams could talk for only so long.

It turned out blowhards had a lot of wind. After ten minutes of non-stop self-congratulations, Williams excused himself. He had to attend a meeting, something about raising funds, pressing the flesh, blah, blah, and more blah. "Have a good day, Ed."

He waddled off, clucking about his film being nominated for a prestigious award. Ed watched him go, wondering if he should snatch the man's soul, and then he decided to think on it.

"Sky, man, look at the sky," one man said to his friend as they walked by. "Pretty weird."

Ed glanced up. Yes, the reddish hue that he'd seen earlier on was still suffusing the sky, a shade darker than before. As well, a faint whiff of sulfur drifted over, accompanied by another, deeper smell, one that he didn't recognize. Still, he didn't think it was anything to worry about.

Something else, though, and that came in the form of a newspaper he happened upon. Incidents of crime, violence, and other unsavory doings were way up.

It wasn't unusual during the Christmas-New Year's season, but the way the editorial had been written, things were far uglier than they had been in the past.

There was an uptick in random incidents of violence, bombings, and beatings. It was as if the world had gone crazy and us along with it.

World's gone crazy. Well, why not? That was what the demon-core was there for. Infernal, forever!

His feelings of elation faded when a voice, a presence, spoke to him. *You are needed.*

It was the master's voice. Ed quickly walked around the corner and into an empty alley, closed his eyes, and concentrated. "Your wish is my will."

In a second, he appeared at the wall of Dis, the Gates of Hell. As usual, everything was on fire. That was its nature, a place of eternal torment for those who'd transgressed God's will.

Ed ran his hand over the crumbling yet inhumanly super-strong stone, and then he made his way past the pits.

Ah, yes, the pits. From the top, a series of concentric rings led to the lower depths where those who'd sinned dwelt. Murderers, rapists, drug users, profiteers, lawyers, doctors, athletes, gays, straights, every color of the rainbow, they were all equal in the sight of the master.

A few of the demons on guard duty waved hello. "Hey, Ed, how's things topside?"

"Same as always," he replied.

Another demon asked, "Ed, you never come down here in demon form. Why?"

For a moment, Ed didn't know how to answer. For some reason, he'd never liked it, although no one had ever complained. What could he say? "I have to go back soon. Shifting's a pain, you know?"

The other demon, who had a damned soul wriggling on his pitchfork, nodded. "I hear ya. I'd rather go au natural."

Whatever floats your boat, Ed thought, and then another mental call bade him go to the records center. He'd seen it during his orientation. A large building, one of stone, rectangular, with only one entrance and exit, it was a simple structure, and it was usually occupied by only one demon, the chief accountant of Hell.

Frank, Ed's mentor, met him at the entrance. "Hey, thanks for the party the other day," he said. "Mariko thinks you're the greatest."

A compliment. He'd take it. "More than welcome. What's going on?"

Frank's mug split into a wide grin. "This is something special," he said. "It's here!"

"What is?"

"The Colossus Five. It's been here for a week already, but today's the first day everyone's getting the chance to see it!"

He grasped Ed's upper arm and towed him over to where a group of demons had gathered around a short, skinnier version of themselves who sat in front of a laptop. "Irving," Frank called out. "Ed's here. He wants to see this!"

A computer? Was this supposed to be impressive? Ed waved his hand in Irving's direction. "This is it? I've used computers before. So has everyone else."

En-masse, everyone turned to him, wearing expressions of disbelief. "As usual, you're too clued out."

That came from Markus, who had come in human form, as well. Of course, he had to get in a nasty remark. He was probably still butthurt from being kicked out of the party the other night. However, this wasn't the time for rivalry. It was a time for cooperation.

"Thanks for dropping by my party," Ed replied in an even tone. "How's New Hampshire?"

Burn! A few of the others in attendance chuckled, while Markus grimaced. Everyone knew that Markus hated being stationed there, and they laughed at their fellow demon's discomfiture.

Although he'd been given the state as a present for loyal service to Lucifer, the master had not seen his greatness — or what Markus perceived as his greatness.

In fact, Markus had protested when the announcement was made. Lucifer listened patiently — a rarity for him — but after Markus had stated his case, he held up his hand for silence.

"Markus, this is my ruling. While it's true that you've been here longer, you're not better. Ed has more souls tallied, and down here, it's all about the numbers."

Markus had glowered at the statement, but he'd nodded, anyway. "Your wish is my will."

With that, he'd vanished, and Lucifer imparted a little advice. "Markus is a little impetuous. You're my best soul-taker, and that's why I gave you New York. I know you won't mess up."

"No, sire, I won't," Ed replied, polite to the end.

That was then, though. This was now. Ed craned his neck to get a better looksee at the machine, and he still felt somewhat disappointed. "I'm not dissing you, Irving. But what's so special about this?"

Irving, the accountant, looked up, his narrow face sporting a mile-wide grin, and he announced in the manner of a television pitchman, "Gentlemen, meet the Colossus Five. It's the only one of its kind, it's the most efficient super-computer around, and it'll replace the old ledger system."

He pointed to an enormous book that was over seventy-billion pages and weighed in excess of a ton. Irving picked it up as though it weighed an ounce. "This is how we used to enter all the data . . . by hand. Name, place of acquisition, nationality, and so on. I suppose you think that our master could magically enter everything by will alone."

A few of those in attendance nodded, but Irv held up his hands for silence. "There are only so many things that our master can do. This is one responsibility that he's delegated to me and the other accountants. Watch and learn."

Speech over, Irving flicked on the machine, tapped a couple of buttons, and a small holographic screen emerged. "We've decided to go modern."

After opening the ledger, he positioned it in front of the screen. A blue ray came from the computer, played up and down the page, and a tiny flash went off.

Irving flipped to the next page, then he repeated the process a few more times, and a collective murmur of appreciation ran around the room.

Finally, Irving closed the ledger, replaced it, and he sat, still grinning as if he'd conceived the whole thing. "The Colossus Five has a memory that's off the charts. It inputs data faster than we can think. It can search for any name we think might join our cause."

Another murmur of appreciation rippled throughout the room. Devils had a hard enough job as it was to get souls. Getting one's take tallied was an arduous process. There were always delays, and complaints about the slowness of the procedure abounded.

Not anymore.

"This makes accounting a snap," Irving said, petting the machine as though it were a cat. "And it'll make your jobs easier. This computer will give you all the leads you need."

He declined to say just how such a search could be conducted and fell silent. With that, the demo was over. Ed wandered outside to get a breath of putrid air.

While Ed was observing the landscape and wondering about the implications of having a computer find possible marks, Frank joined him. He was in his default demon form, and he proceeded to prattle on about his girlfriend.

Ed feigned interest. For many decades, he'd listened patiently to Frank recount his days and nights in the Far East. He'd formerly worked in Thailand, Malaysia, and China, and his love for anyone of the female Asian persuasion was evident in the details of his past conquests.

"Of course, that was before I met Mariko. I've been faithful to her, you know."

More BS, Ed thought, but since he had time, and since they were friends, he politely listened. Once a lull in the conversation developed, he asked, "What else do you know about that new computer?"

"Hell's gone high-tech," Frank replied with a shrug, repeating the accountant's words. "I heard it was invented by a scientist named Scott Alperstein. Mathematical genius, computer programmer, and totally bat-shit crazy. Spent half his life in mental institutions, and while he was there, he dreamed up the Colossus."

He grinned, exposing nasty, sharp teeth. "One of our guys managed to get Alperstein on our side. He pledged his troth to us, and then he committed suicide."

Suicides. They belonged in the seventh circle of Hell, along with the violent, the tyrants, the blasphemers, the murderers, and other assorted sickos.

He tabled that information for another day, and then he said goodbye to Frank and willed himself back to Manhattan.

Instead of going back to his apartment, though, he wandered the streets for a time, savoring the sounds and rhythm of the city.

Clad in a smartly tailored dove-gray suit and expensive dress shoes, he cut quite the figure, while the native New Yorkers wore heavy overcoats, galoshes and boots, mufflers and gloves, and they continually cursed the foul weather.

It was fifteen degrees Fahrenheit, and people stared at him as he walked along as if he didn't have a care in the world. No snow fell on him, no slush ever splashed in his direction.

As he walked along, he thought once again about the Colossus. How could it predict who would go to the lower depths and those who would ascend? Those who were believers talked about the Rapture. Well, it wouldn't be coming any time soon. In fact, it would never come. Ed was sure of that.

"The end is nigh."

Ed halted in his tracks in front of the sandwich-board man. He wasn't in his usual place today. The man, filthy and bedraggled and with a stink that could rival the Great Downstairs, seemed unconcerned with the cold.

He stared straight ahead through hollow eyes, and for some reason, Ed felt as though the man's eyes were boring into his core. Only Lucifer could do that, so who was this guy, anyway?

Sandwich-board man then repeated his earlier warning. "Do you know that the end is near?"

"Is it?"

It wasn't the cleverest comeback, but Ed had to say something. This guy wasn't crazy, not really. He didn't seem stoned or loony, only sort of lost.

"Only a matter of time," the man said. "Get ready."

Ed had heard enough. Going home was the best option at that moment. He fished through his pocket for some spare change, but the man waved him off. "I don't need the money. It wouldn't do me any good, anyway. The end is coming."

Far from being lost or a total loser, this man, whoever he was, seemed to have some unearthly power, and he exuded a calm that spooked Ed. "All right, tell me. How?"

"You will know. The skies will boil, the ground will shake, and then all will be nothingness."

Biblical prophecy, that was what it sounded like. Before Ed could come up with a retort, the man turned around and walked away.

Taken aback, Ed returned to his apartment, turned on the kettle, and made himself a cup of herbal tea.

The end is nigh.

For some unfathomable reason, sandwich-board man's words came back to him, and he glanced outside. The sky had gotten redder. A movie he'd seen about Martians invading the Earth came back to him. Perhaps the little green men from elsewhere had decided to try their luck against the Earthlings.

That thought made him laugh.

A moment later, he sobered up. Perhaps it had something to do with a scientific snafu. Those things happened.

However, a search on the internet revealed nothing. The scientists had said it had something to do with dust from China or an atmospheric disturbance—or something.

While sipping his tea, another series of tremors confirmed his suspicions. Earthquake? Impossible, yet . . .

Ed.

It was Lucifer, and he sounded concerned.

Yes, master, what is it?

I need you down here. It is a meeting of the greatest urgency.

Your wish is my will.

It had only been a half-hour, and now the leader wanted him back. No time for tea. Orders were orders.

Ed broke off his thought and willed himself to the great below. The leader had called a meeting, and he did not want to be late.

CHAPTER FOUR: CRISIS!

"**N**on-existence!"

Lucifer's voice echoed throughout the boardroom. A great hall, the boardroom was limitless, with a stone table that ran from the entrance to infinity and beyond.

On each side of the table were stone chairs. A throne of solid gold sat at the head of the table. It was reserved for the overlord, and now he sat on his throne, glaring at everyone, and tapping his leg with a thick forefinger in a rhythmic manner.

He was most displeased.

Ed arrived just as his master was warming up. The overlord was in his default form—that of a devil, horns, tail, and all. Horrific though his appearance was, his persona exuded inhuman health and strength.

As for his tail, lengthy beyond measure and yet something he controlled from limitless to a stub, if need be, it whipped around, occasionally slapping the wall and sending up a reverberation that clashed with the noises of the damned outside.

Lucifer cast his gaze around the room, staring at each of his subordinates in turn. Ed felt his ruler's eyes go right to his essence, his soul, as it were—that is, if he had a soul. Right now, he didn't, and he was eternally grateful for it.

With a grunt, the overlord snapped his fingers, and a cigar appeared in his hand, already lit. He puffed on it for a few seconds before angrily grinding it out on the table.

Another grunt of psychic and perhaps physical pain came

from him, and the other demons-in-waiting did not move a muscle. They didn't dare.

"Non-existence," Lucifer repeated, and for emphasis, he rapped the arm of his throne. It sent out a sharp, ringing tone that ordinarily would have ruptured the eardrums of any mortal within a proximity of ten miles, but for the unclean and undead, it merely made them wince. "That is what we are facing. All of us, even those upstairs."

For emphasis, he pointed upward with a dagger-shaped fingernail. Everyone followed his gaze and then averted their eyes. It was forbidden to gaze upon the eternal afterlife of Heaven without express permission, and no devil worth their sulfur and brimstone would have done so without a good reason.

"I have just consulted with our accountant, and he has informed me that we are two souls over the limit," Lucifer said. "The Colossus is infallible in that regard."

At the utterance of those two sentences, a gasp of disbelief ran throughout the room as did murmurs of conspiracy, clumsiness, and sabotage.

Two souls over? Madness! Insanity! How could this have been allowed to happen? Those were Ed's immediate thoughts, along with the thought that sandwich-board man had been right, after all.

Lucifer picked up on those comments right away. A number of those in attendance started to blame the accountant, but the overlord held up his hand.

"Do not blame Irving for this. It was not his fault, nor was it the fault of anyone else in the accounting departments in the countries on Earth. What with all the souls slipping through here and perhaps up there, and what with the sheer numbers of souls available, it is quite possible such a thing —"

"I don't understand," George cut in.

A small, wizened man when in human form, he had a withered face and a sallow complexion along with limited intelligence and capability. In Hell, being capable was everything, so he'd been assigned to the province of Newfoundland in Canada.

Ed resisted the urge to do the obligatory facepalm, and so did everyone else. George usually said something idiotic, and that was why he had no allies in Hell or anywhere else, for that matter.

"George," he began in an attempt to be helpful. "Maybe you should stop and think this over?"

The little demon glared at him. "What for? This is important, you understand?"

He'd been given assignments in other cities in the past and had proved himself barely adequate. Lucifer had often mentioned that Newfoundland was the safest place to assign him to. George had been there for the past forty years. It was better for all demon-dom. He caused less damage that way.

Ed waved his hands at George to stop, but the other demon ignored him. He was on a roll and spread his arms wide, approaching the overlord and saying, "This is all about the apocalypse, right? Well, the way I see it, we were just doing our jobs, and—"

A bolt of blue lightning shot out of Lucifer's fingertips and reduced George to nothingness. Everyone stood stock still, afraid of the master's wrath and fearful that they would be next.

"You failed, failed miserably," Lucifer continued without missing a beat. "You also interrupted me and approached me without permission."

Silence ensued for a few milliseconds as everyone pseudo-mourned the loss of one of their own. The demonic horde knew that George wouldn't be missed, and, at the very least, Newfoundland would eventually get someone better.

Obligatory nano-moment of silence over, Willard spoke. Tall and cadaverous, like the stereotype of a ghoulish mortician, he ran the Las Vegas area, and even though he was a rival in terms of soul-taking, Ed had always gotten along with him.

"Sire, not to be a killjoy, but that's our job, isn't it? I mean, as, uh, George said, we're supposed to start the apocalypse, and that's what taking souls is all about. We didn't know."

Lucifer raised his hand again. Willard, along with the rest of the unholy faithful cringed, but fortunately for Mr. Viva Las Vegas, nothing happened. The overlord then relaxed and uttered a sigh of resignation. It seemed that offing his minions wouldn't help matters.

"Ordinarily, it would be so, but this year, the two-thousandth-twenty-fifth year of my existence, the balance has to be protected. It is as it must be, and it has been willed by those, er, more powerful than I am. The apocalypse, therefore, will be put off until next year if there *is* a next year.

"I have been informed by those above" — he cast his gaze upward briefly — "that if the balance is not preserved by midnight on the last day of this year, then all existence will be wiped out. It will be wiped out not with a bang but with a whimper, and only yours truly and my, uh, maker, will be left standing."

Another gasp of disbelief and fear rippled throughout the room. This couldn't be happening. It couldn't.

"It is," Lucifer replied, once more reading the thoughts of his minions. "Did you feel the tremors in the Earth not long ago?"

Everyone nodded, and he continued, "Have you not seen the sky?"

Once again, everyone nodded. "Those are the signs."

Signs. Sandwich-board man's words came back to Ed once more. With an internal quiver of his organs that could have triggered a massive gastrointestinal spasm, which in turn would have resulted in an unsightly stain upon his pants, he managed to hold it together.

All the same, Ed felt lost. Sandwich-board man must have had some special insight . . .

"Long story short, ladies and gentlemen, if the worst-case scenario occurs, that means we'll have to start all over again," Lucifer intoned and lashed his tail against the wall, causing a resounding echo.

"It will take a long time, and that is something I do not want. I do not want to have a hand in recreating that which might be taken away on the off chance that our kind might be limited or even phased out."

"I didn't know that," another demon said, averting her gaze. "That bites."

Lucifer glared in the general direction of the one who'd spoken, but he did nothing. He simply said in a most cutting tone, "Yes, Nora, that bites, indeed. I cannot simply will humanity to be as it was, and neither can my maker. Despite what the mortals think, we do have our limitations."

He paused to let the words sink in and then asked, "So, I am inviting proposals. Ladies, gentlemen?"

Silence ensued, with only the moans of the damned and the screams of their agony breaking through. All those in attendance glanced at each other, and then a demon spoke up. "Sire?"

"Yes?"

This demon had a pronounced Scottish accent, rolling his *Rs* and with a brogue that not even hellfire could cut. "Sire, couldn't we just, um, give those guys two of ours?"

Lucifer pursed his lips. "That is a fine idea, McTavish, but the rules state that those who are here cannot simply be sent to the other place. They willingly pledged their souls to me.

"I, myself, can't do anything, as I can't escape the oath that binds me to this realm. This has been willed where what is willed must be. I can send agents to foment chaos, but that's about it."

A few more of the fallen groaned. What could they do? A pall fell over the boardroom, and for a hellish moment, it seemed that they were out of options.

Ed had the feeling that everyone had given up, but he hadn't. Not yet. He hadn't become the best soul-taker in New York by lying down and letting humanity trample all over him. It was then that he had a blast of insight. "Sire, how about we help two people go?"

En-masse, everyone swiveled their heads in his direction. "Say again?" Lucifer enquired.

Everyone took a couple of steps back. They'd seen George get incinerated, and none of them wanted to be next on the blue-blitz-list.

Ed noticed their moves, and now that he was on the spot, he felt acutely uncomfortable and stammered out his answer.

"What I mean to say is, sire, if there are two people sort of, like, undecided about joining up with you or them, couldn't one of us, uh, persuade them to go to the other side?"

More silence, and Ed, his heart beating wildly, waited for the end. Would the overlord do it, wipe out his finest soul-taker in North America? It would certainly be an act of biting one's nose off to spite one's face, and nothing was beneath the lord of all evil.

However, the demons of Fate were on Ed's side, as Lucifer got off his throne with a genuine smile working, and in a flash, he was at his junior's side. "Ed, that's the greatest idea I've heard in a long time. In fact, since it was your idea, you're the only one for the job."

The other demons gave a polite round of applause that also included mental sighs of relief that they weren't chosen. The unspoken question on everyone's lips was how this feat could be achieved.

Apparently, Ed had the same question, and his confidence wavered. Never had the master tasked him with such an assignment. Never had anyone else been given such a monumental job to do.

Over the years, Ed had managed to take the entire presidential family of one American administration. In another coup that no one ever expected, at a G-7 meeting that had been held in Washington, he'd gotten five prime ministers, eight other heads of state, along with three cardinals and one candidate who'd been tapped to become the next pontiff of Rome.

He'd also managed to hook athletes and movie stars, and they were the easiest, mainly because they'd do anything to keep their skills, their appearances, and their popularity. "Sire, I only know about taking souls, not saving them. I—"

"Have no fear. You'll have help. If there is one group of people who know about that kind of thing, it's them." Lucifer pointed upward again.

Ed cast his gaze upward for a moment and then whispered the one word that no demon ever uttered aloud. "Halos?"

The master nodded, and his features betrayed nothing. Among the Hell-spawned, Halos were hated more than mortals, simply because of what they were.

In truth, Ed had never met one in all the time he'd been on Earth. He'd dealt with and reeled in murderers, drug addicts, robbers, philanderers, religious hypocrites—they were the worst—and more, but statistical possibilities and probabilities aside, he'd never met a Halo. He didn't want to now, but there was no choice in the matter.

"Er, is it okay with their, uh, leader?"

At the mention of the ruler of all that was pure and holy, Lucifer started to roll his eyes, but he stopped himself short. Perhaps it was a show of strength, or maybe it was something else. Ed wasn't sure. He really didn't want to go, but now, he had no choice in the matter.

"It is," Lucifer replied in a manner most grave. "In spite of our antipathy toward each other, we keep in contact through intermediaries and sometimes directly. He and I are in accord on this, as they have just as much to lose as we do."

This . . . was exceedingly heavy. Ed had never heard of such a thing. The overlord of all evil darkness meeting with the lord of all light and goodness — impossible, but then again, the concept of non-existence was a mind-bender in and of itself.

Lucifer then turned to address the attendees. "For the next seventy-two hours, you are all on vacation. No souls will be taken. Any contracts made with those on Earth will not be observed. You are to do nothing. Our counterparts above have indicated they will do the same."

A murmur ran around the room. Do nothing? Frank raised his hand hesitantly. "Uh, master, what if someone dies? It could happen, an accident or a chronic illness or something?"

Yes, accidents happened. There was no shortage of potentially lethal viruses around, mainly from Asia. In fact, the world had only recently recovered from a pandemic, and there was no shortage of rogue states that had biological weapons on tap, just in case the natural-born viruses didn't work.

Of course, that didn't include the terrorists, the sexual and social deviants, and the crazies. What made them dangerous was their unpredictability, and even for enhanced beings such as demons and angels, it was difficult to account for the actions of the unstable twenty-four-seven.

Lucifer nodded as if he'd been expecting that question all along. "It has been made clear to me that no one will die. Under normal circumstances, accidents happen, illnesses claim people who are aged or chronically ill, but this time, death will take a holiday."

He waved his hand. The meeting was over. A few members mentioned that they'd go to the nearest bar and tank up. Get drunk and have a blast before the final possible blast—why not?

As Ed pondered the possibilities, Markus wandered over, a coy smile on his face. What was his game? He'd never been especially friendly or cordial, and his appointment in New Hampshire had royally pissed him off. Everyone knew about it. Markus had never kept it secret, so why the friendliness and why now?

A moment later, Ed took back that thought. Maybe it was his rival's way of dealing with the possibility of fading into nothingness. Or being blasted into nothingness.

Even if the end came with a whimper, as the overlord had said, it was no less frightening than the prospect of ceasing to exist because of some cosmic blast and subsequent inferno.

And, considering the dire situation they were in, perhaps his rival had decided to let bygones be bygones, and that was a good thing. He clapped Ed on the shoulder in a gesture of supreme bro-ship. "I knew our master would choose you."

Ed practically recoiled at the other demon's touch. He didn't even like looking at him, and for that to happen, someone had to be on the far side of ultra-nasty.

Still, the fate of the world thing resonated with him. Markus was in the same situation as everyone else. Rivals or not, now was not the time for rancor and strife.

"Thanks for the support," Ed said in an effort at civility. "It means a lot to me."

No, it didn't, and once more, he wondered why he'd been chosen, and then it came back to him—his stupid idea on how to send two unbelievers upstairs to eternal bliss.

"Not a problem," Markus said. "I think I'll get back to my reading. Time is on our side, at least, for the moment."

"Reading?"

That was unusual. Considering his hedonistic lifestyle, going after any warm body, male or female, when the opportunity presented itself, that came as somewhat of a surprise.

"Yes, the library here has several hundred tomes that beg to be read. Our kind, we've always been too busy snatching souls, so why not take advantage of this opportunity and gain a little knowledge? Best of luck—friend."

With that, he vanished. Frank came over, sighing and muttering something about spending the final hours with Mariko. "Hey, she knows who and what I am, but I don't want to tell her the truth about this, you know? It, uh, it wouldn't be right."

Ed nodded. He wouldn't tell anyone the truth of impending non-existence either, not if he could help it. "She's pretty special to you, isn't she?"

A sound like a grunt mixed with genuine fondness came from the senior demon. "Yeah, she's a fine person. We enjoy our time together. She's even talking about marriage when she turns twenty-two, after she graduates from university."

Marriage between a Hell-spawn and a mortal. It had happened before. Rumors about Lucifer and some of his more powerful underlings came to mind, and he wondered what the offspring looked like . . .

"How about you," Frank was saying. "You got anyone?"

Call that a stumper. Relationships didn't seem to be in his future. "No. I'm still looking."

Frank grinned. "You always were a bit odd. Just too pure for me. Good luck." He gave him a friendly shot on the arm and vanished.

With nothing else to do, everyone else disappeared from the room, and soon, only Ed was there. Pressure closed in upon him like a vise, and he fought off a bout of nerves. This was it. Existence or extinction. There could be no failure. There was the mission and only that—and he had to do it with the cooperation of the opposition.

Lucifer then intoned, "Depart. Thou are sent!"

The world faded out, and when Ed emerged again, it was inside a coffee shop. His master had mentioned that someone from the upper realm would be coming soon.

Ed wondered if he should go in the guise of his persona in his apartment, but then he decided to go with a more youthful look and shifted his features accordingly. He didn't alter his clothes, though. He liked that classy look.

It was still early, so with a few ticks on the clock to spare, he bought a double latte and settled down to wait.

Chapter Five: Take One for the Team

The coffee shop, filled with plush chairs, elaborately engraved wooden tables, and highly attentive waiters and waitresses, was warm and comfortable, and Ed amused himself by checking out the inhabitants, guessing who a potential mark was and who wasn't.

A quick count netted seventeen patrons, twelve women and five men. The men wore heavy coats, boots, and mufflers. Inclement weather demanded that a person dress correctly. They had.

Ed had always had a penchant for fine wear. Perhaps it was due to being poor in his past life. He didn't know. Even if that was so, to him, wearing brand-name clothes was part of the equation. It lent legitimacy to his persona. Had he appeared in jeans and a hoodie as many teens did, who would have taken him seriously?

Of course, that question was rhetorical, and he answered himself—no one. Ergo, it was imperative that he looked like a young businessman with money to burn.

As he sat and drank in the atmosphere, he again took stock of the clientele. Off to his right, three young and attractive women in their mid-twenties chatted over chai, scones, and petite sandwiches.

Rotten weather or not, they'd shucked their heavy coats to reveal outfits that uttered slay at the top of their lungs. Short skirts, tight blouses, hair done up just so, and skillfully applied make-up made them stand out—that was what they wanted.

They were pretty, they knew it, and while they affected a haughty I-don't-care attitude, talking only among themselves and only looking up every now and then, they also knew that almost every young male's eye in the room was focused on them.

Ed glanced left. A fat man in his thirties, dressed in a heavy overcoat, muffler included, occupied the space of three seats, his butt practically splitting his already too-tight pants.

As he crunched his way through a stack of cookies, scarfing them down one after another, he gulped black coffee and grunted with immense satisfaction. And, yes, he shot an occasional look at the women.

A middle-aged couple, nicely dressed, prosperous-looking, sipped coffee and chatted about their upcoming second honeymoon. Did they know something everyone else didn't?

And even if they did, the other patrons who weren't eating or drinking were talking about the rotten weather outside, the previous tremor, and what they'd be doing for New Year's Eve.

Mortals had such a sense of positivity, it seemed. Even though danger had hit, even though they'd suffered from plagues and pandemics and horrible wars, mortals still had this ridiculous resiliency that defied the odds.

And now, they kept on feasting as though nothing else mattered. The trouble would blow over soon. Life would go on its merry way as it always had.

Fools, Ed thought, but a second later, he took back that negative idea. It wasn't their fault. They simply didn't know.

Had the situation not been so dire, every person there, including the staff, would have been possibles—possible acquisitions, that is. Possible, but not likely, especially now. The master had given the order that no one be taken.

A shame, really, but the truce between Heaven and Hell had to be observed. How anyone could have been so careless to have not noticed the oversight before didn't seem possible, but it had happened, all the same.

Ed turned his gaze to his right to take in another denizen of the shop, a tall and lean dude in his early twenties who sat at a table seven feet away and whose eyes roved over the three women from top to bottom. Ed recognized that look.

It was one of hunger. That man—a punk, really—wanted one or all three of those women. The look of lust on his face told the whole story. It would be an easy matter for Ed to arrange something that would be to his master's satisfaction.

Oh, wait, he couldn't, and once more, the unfairness of the situation rankled. By all rights, the master should have chosen Markus. After all, he had more experience, he knew New York as well as anyone, and he had talent. No denying it.

On the other hand, Markus was an egocentric maggot, and that was a bit much, even for a demon.

After that bit of back-and-forthing, Ed had a minor epiphany. He'd been chosen because no one else had the ability. The master had confidence in him. He had . . . faith.

Faith had always been considered a bad word for demons to use, yet it wasn't. Only those who believed in God were fit to use that term, or so the thinking went.

Faith meant believing in something or someone, and Ed most definitely believed in his master and his cause.

As well, in this situation, dire though it was, Ed believed in his own ability. While he still had to work with the opposition, he wouldn't let that deter him from his mission. He was the one in charge, the leader—in other words, winning.

While mentally pumping himself up, the air shimmered near the doorway, and a woman roughly his age stepped through a ghostly portal that hung a foot off the ground. The door didn't open—the air did. His contact, the Halo, had arrived.

No one noticed her entrance, but all eyes went to her instantly when she stepped down, and her feet touched the ground. A collective gasp ran around the room. The men salivated. The three women who'd been dressed to slay wilted, and it was easy to see why.

At a shade under six feet in height, slender and leggy, the visitor wore a simple white skirt and blouse with a pair of knee-high, high-heeled white boots.

A light matching white jacket hung jauntily on her frame. It gave her a retro look, a mix of nineteen-forty's chic and nineteen-sixty's mod.

Well, she had the figure, all right, and Ed had to admit that she was something in a physical sense. He'd been expecting someone far less glamorous.

His gaze then went to her features. Ash-blonde hair framed an angular, pretty face, and a pair of slightly slanted green eyes denoted possible Asian heritage.

The woman wasted no time in making her way over but was intercepted halfway by the young wolf who'd gotten up from his table to greet her. "Hey, girl," he said, using a very worn, sexist, and ill-advised phrase.

He followed said phrase by straightening the frayed collar of his coat. In another effort to appear suave, he flipped his dandruff-specked dark hair back with a dirty hand and showed her a full smile.

Said smile was full of tobacco-stained teeth, but a lack of hygiene didn't deter the man.

In fact, it hadn't deterred him ten minutes ago when he tried his luck with one of the waitresses. She was perhaps twenty-three, with long, dark hair and a plain, pretty face. She'd declined the man's offer most demurely, and that had set him off.

"Hey, I'm not good enough for you?"

The man continued to hurl abuse at her back until the manager, a fat man in his fifties with a mean face and large hands with knobby knuckles walked over to tell the punk to either behave or leave.

Said punk had apologized and sat quietly in his seat, but then this Halo showed up, and something—perhaps inbred stupidity—set him off.

Again.

The woman stopped in her tracks, eyes wide at first, and then they narrowed. "And what is it you want?"

"I just wanted to know if you were in for some fun."

It was a stale line, uttered by an equally stale individual, a line guaranteed to turn anyone off. The woman studied the man like a scientist observing a particularly nasty specimen of slime mold. "And what kind of fun were you thinking of?"

Her voice was low and husky, but the challenging tone in it was unmistakable. The man blinked. Undeterred, he said, "Anything you like. Name it. I'll do it."

He then leaned forward to whisper something in her ear. Message delivered, he stood back with his arms folded across his chest and a smirk working overtime.

For a moment, nothing happened, but then she lashed out with a right hook so fast that Ed could hardly track its movement. The punch itself connected with the scumbag's jaw, and a sickening bone-shattering sound followed.

A millisecond later, the impact hurled the lone wolf over the counter twenty feet away. He hit with a crash and didn't get up.

Everyone glanced at what had just gone down. A few laughs broke out, a couple of patrons yelled, "You go, girl," and, "Yaass, queen," and then everyone returned to their own worlds of coffee, donuts, and inane small talk.

Without wasting another word, the woman walked over to Ed's table. "I'm Nellie Wong," she said in a flat tone without the hint of an accent. "I was told to come here. My superiors gave me your description. You're my contact?"

Stunned by her display of power, Ed could only nod. "Uh, yeah. I'm Edvil. My friends . . . they call me Ed. Please, uh, sit down."

She did. They both looked around and spoke softly, shielding their words from the other patrons. Angels and devils had that ability, and right now, it came in handy.

To everyone else, it must have appeared that they were simply drinking coffee and gazing into each other's eyes, as two young lovers would.

Nothing could have been further from the truth, but the rest of the patrons didn't have to know that. "That was something," Ed said, still somewhat in awe. "You got a mean right hook."

"Sometimes you have to take the halo off," she answered, looking blasé, but then she focused her eyes on his. "Edvil. Unusual. You don't have a last name."

That came out as a statement and not a question. Somewhat taken aback at her directness, he shook his head. "Uh, no, I, uh, don't remember."

A feeling of shame—something he'd never experienced before—washed over him. No last name. No past, no history. It had never really bothered him, but now—here, being with her—for some reason, it did.

"Some of, uh, our kind, remember the basics, but most don't. That's what I heard, anyway."

Nellie gazed at him with a mixture of compassion and disgust, and her voice underlined the latter feeling. "You must have had some life before you went over. Taking souls, sending those you deem unworthy to the lower depths. How interesting."

If sarcasm could be measured, her reply would have come out to something akin to a freighter landing on a person's head. Her words lashed him as surely as a whip would have, and Ed's sense of being in control suddenly got up and left, along with his previous sense of shame. She'd just insulted all of demon-dom. Now, he had to take a stand.

"Hey, what's with the judging? We're supposed to work on this thing together. You don't have to love me. You just have to work with me."

Nellie's gaze never wavered. "Yes, we have to work together. Not that I want to, either, but here we are."

"And you'd rather be up there, floating among the clouds."

This was ridiculous. Two minutes, and already they were arguing. Jousting, even with a Halo, wasn't on the menu, and there were more important things to think about.

A waitress came over, and they stopped their mini spat long enough for Nellie to drop the shield surrounding them and say, "Coffee with milk, please."

She added after the waitress left, "It's not what you think. I have my own room, I have books, and I talk to my friends."

"Friends."

She chuckled. "Yes, friends. You know what the word means, I take it?"

More points for sarcasm, and now, he felt like he'd been put on the defensive—permanently. "Yes, I know what it means. Y'know, in my line of work, friends are a liability."

The waitress returned with the coffee. Nellie promptly took a sip, pronounced it good, and she daintily set her cup down. "All right, do you have a plan?"

In fact, the plan had been set in motion. Now, they had to actualize it. "Yes, I do. We're supposed to get two potentials who are swinging to my side of things over to your side. Yes?"

Nellie bobbed her head. "Yes."

His moment of triumph arrived. "So, we do the good."

"How's that?"

Ah-ha, he'd finally flummoxed her, as she gave him a

confused look. Now, Ed had to back up his statement. Do the good — where had that come from?

Confusion reigned, and then he got his head straight. "I mean, we show them how bad things are where I'm from, and then they'll be anxious to, er, you know, join up with your squad."

"My squad," Nellie echoed with the faintest trace of sarcasm. "Yes, the spirit squad, the eternal do-gooders, the angelic continuum — "

"I get the point."

Chastened, Ed blew out a deep breath. This was not working out at all. New York was his turf, and now he felt as though he was the outsider. He didn't like it, not one bit. "I'm sorry. I'm not used to dealing with Halos, er, angels. To be honest, this is my first time."

"What did you expect us to be?"

Words failed him. He'd never been the talkative type, not like Frank or his other acquaintances, but this was ridiculous. Everything he said, she seemed to turn it inside out and use it against him. "I don't know. Not like this — you."

"You mean my looks." Once again, that came out as a statement on Nellie's part.

Ed's defensiveness now segued into supreme embarrassment. Far from projecting an aura of confidence, he felt that he now projected the aura of supreme dorkiness. "Well, you *are* pretty."

Nellie suddenly smiled. "Thank you. It's been a long time since someone said that."

"Truth."

With that admission, he fell silent and sipped his latte. Heaven would have to send a pretty angel. He'd been warned by Frank and the others. Never trust a Halo. They were always up to no bad.

Still, he didn't get any negative vibes from her and pointed to his beverage. "This is good. You should try it."

Nellie gazed at him with uncertainty, and then she called the waitress over to order the same drink. The waitress soon returned with the order, and Nellie blew on her drink and took a sip. "Fine suggestion. Thank you."

Ed, who was now in awe of her self-assuredness and aware of her ability, bobbed his head somewhat sheepishly. "You're welcome."

Another lull in the conversation developed, and then Nellie cleared her throat. "How old are you?"

"Almost nineteen, I think," he replied. "I'm not sure of my true age, but this is my, uh, default appearance. You?"

"Same here. I was born in eighteen-forty-one in Shanghai, grew up there, and I merged with the infinite in eighteen-sixty."

Facts uttered, yes, and they'd been uttered in a most confident fashion, but underlying them was a note of sadness. "Shanghai," he mused. "I've never been there. Mostly North America, some places in Europe, but never Asia. My friend is there, though, in Japan. He runs the Tokyo contingent."

Nellie rested her elbow on the table. In turn, she rested her chin in her hand and gazed at him so directly he found himself fumbling around. "And, I suppose, you don't know where you were born. Or are you more interested in the Far East?"

The memory of his dream came back to him. A warehouse, the bang . . . and a place name whispered in his head. Like a puff of smoke, it came, and then it was gone. *Virginia . . . Roanoke.* "Uh, I was born in Roanoke. I . . . I guess I went to school there, and my parents . . ."

His voice trailed off as the memory faded.

"That's all you can remember?" In contrast to her earlier sarcasm, Nellie sounded sympathetic.

Ed nodded, aware of the change in her tone, and he

decided that getting angry wasn't worth it. "Yeah. But it's okay. I get by."

He gulped down the rest of his latte and got back to the business at hand. No more pity party. "Okay, so, we need two people, right?"

Nellie looked around the shop as if gauging each person's potential. "Yes, we do, but these people here, uh-uh."

She proceeded to close her eyes and began to nod. "Wait. I have something . . . yes . . . I can see them."

Astounded, Ed asked, "You can, er, sense people?"

"Up to a point."

Nellie's eyes were still closed. "I can't read minds, but I can read impressions, and I have to be near them, no more than two hundred feet. My powers aren't limitless. These two people are young, sort of dumb, and they're broke."

Ed picked up on it right away. "Broke means desperate. Desperate usually means they'll do anything to get money."

"Which is your cue to swoop in?" Nellie opened her eyes when she spoke, and it was sarcasm-mode all over again. A moment later, her expression turned contrite. "Sorry. I sometimes forget what I've been taught."

"Taught?"

She nodded. "You were told what to do when you first started out, right?"

"Yes."

"Me, too. But I'm . . . I'm sort of new to this."

Uh-oh, wait a second. Ed had the feeling he was dealing with an amateur. "Just how many missions have you been on?" he asked carefully.

"This is my third one."

Oh, wonderful, and his head began to pound. He sensed a headache coming on, which was impossible. Demons didn't get headaches. They never got sick, so what was happening?

It was bad enough that he had to work with a Halo, and

even worse that the fate of all existence hinged on them doing this job and doing it right.

But this? The powers above had sent a rookie. He massaged his temples, and that helped . . . a little.

His gesture wasn't lost on Nellie, as she said, "Don't give me that look. I'm here to help. My creator chose me above everyone else."

What look? One of angst? One of uncertainty? He didn't know, but he took her word for it, and even though it constituted another uh-huh reply, he stifled the urge.

"I wonder why. I mean, I understand you've got some experience, but what were you doing for the past one-hundred-and-sixty years?"

Now, her face turned crimson. Halos could get embarrassed, too, a fact that he filed away and which also gave him no small amount of satisfaction.

Nellie coughed into her hand and cleared her throat. "Our program is more rigorous than your training, I imagine. When we join with the infinite, at first, we go through a period of self-reflection on our past sins. We meditate. That takes about twenty Earth years."

It sounded like an eternity to Ed, but whatever. Nellie continued with her work history bio. "Then we observe how others of our kind do things. Finally, when our instructors think we're ready, we're sent out with senior workers."

Uh-huh. And Ed had trained with Frank and the others for about five months before he went out on his own. It sounded like Heaven's policy was more than a little overly cautious.

"And that took around two centuries?"

Her reddish hue deepened. "Yes. There were other candidates, you know. I was better suited for the library. I always loved books in my old life."

A trace of sadness laced those words, and he wondered why. Nellie didn't offer an explanation. "I served as a curator in our heavenly book depository for over a century, and then I went out on training missions."

"And . . . you're familiar with modern English?"

She shrugged. "Angels can pick up languages and figures of speech as quickly as your kind does."

To Ed's way of thinking, speaking modern English didn't an effective operator make, but this situation had arisen rather abruptly. He had to deal with it, and he needed her. With an effort, he kept his voice level and fought off the rising pain in his head. "All right, you speak modern English well. Fine."

Nellie's mouth twisted with resentment. "I knew it, I knew it! Right away, you start dumping on me."

"As you did on me," Ed replied in the coolest of tones, and then he dropped the sarcasm entirely. They were getting nowhere with this. He waved his hands as if to wipe the slate clean.

"You're here . . . now . . . and I've got a serious question for you. What makes you special to do this job?"

"Our kind has empathy," she answered promptly. "My superiors sent me here because I'm empathetic. I care. I can do this, but I need your help, too."

Ed inhaled and then blew out a deep breath. His skull had ceased pounding, and to make sure his headache didn't return, he breathed slowly and regularly. When one had no choice in the matter . . .

"Fine. We do the job together. What do you sense now?"

Nellie closed her eyes again, rotating her head like a weathervane. Then she opened her eyes wide as if surprised to have locked onto someone. "They're outside."

Ed looked through the window. A young man and woman in their mid-twenties stood outside the coffee shop, dressed in jeans, sneakers, and cheap jackets.

They shivered in the cold, and the woman, a brunette with a pinched and hardened face, probably caused by life's travails, pointed down the block.

Her partner, the man, shorter than she was by around two inches, chubby, with an unshaven face and dark hair, nodded. A moment later, they set off.

"Let's go," Nellie said as she got up. "I sense they're going to try something." She didn't wait around, merely ran for the door. "C'mon!"

"Do the good," Ed muttered as he got up and tossed some money on the table. Waitresses needed tips, too, and he wasn't about to disappoint anyone.

It had started to snow, but that wasn't the problem. It didn't bother Ed. What bothered him was the sky. It had gotten redder than before. Something bad was happening, and it would only get worse.

When he looked back at the street, he couldn't spot their marks. "Where'd they go?"

Nellie tapped him on the arm and pointed to the end of the block. "There they are."

"Pigeons," Ed mumbled to himself. The pigeons had flown the coop, and he had to do the right thing—something that grated.

"Not all people are pigeons," Nellie said softly. "And, yes, keep your thoughts to yourself."

Chastened by her words yet impressed by her aural abilities, Ed mumbled an apology. "All right, people are people. Let's go."

In a gesture of camaraderie as well as chivalry, he bowed. She returned the gesture, curtseying with a crooked smile that somehow made him feel better about himself. That feeling disappeared quickly as a shudder ran through him, and he reminded himself that he shouldn't get involved.

Nellie gestured at the young couple. "They're on the move. Let's follow them."

Your wish is my command, he thought. The hunt was on.

As they strode along the pavement, dodging the other pedestrians while keeping their targets in sight, Ed asked, "Do you have a nickname? Nothing wrong with Nellie. I'm just wondering."

"My friends upstairs call me Nell."

He couldn't resist. "Am I a friend?"

"I'll think about it."

Chapter Six: Do the Right Thing

As Ed and Nellie strode along with the wind and snow accompanying them, almost every passerby stared with a sense of awe and perhaps a tinge of jealousy, for they made a striking young couple. Ordinarily, it would have pleased Ed to receive some of the attention, but now, he had more important matters to attend to.

Neither he nor Nellie returned the stares. Her attention remained on their marks, and she moved ahead with long strides, chewing up the pavement as she went.

In contrast, Ed turned his gaze briefly to the sky. It should have been gray and overcast, but the distinct reddish hue had settled in more deeply than before. Not a good sign.

Forget about that, he told himself. Concentrate on your targets. This was all about focus and commitment. Those two words had to become their mantra, in addition to determination.

"Any information on them?" Ed asked. He couldn't read minds, although he was decent enough at reading facial expressions. However, that wouldn't help much, not here.

Nellie swept some snow from her shoulders, sniffed the air, and opined that a bad smell meant future trouble, although she declined to say in what form it would appear. "I just know something bad is coming."

Good intuition—he had the same feeling. "Okay, now how about our targets?"

"She's tired and hungry. Her companion, he's got a one-track mind."

"How's that?"

"He's, uh . . . interested in her."

"Define interested, please."

"Horny."

Oh. Well, so much for that problem, and then Ed stopped dead in his tracks. "What did you say?"

Nellie halted as well and turned around. "I said he's horny. And he is. Come on."

This was . . . different. "I, uh, didn't think angels spoke that way," he said carefully. "You know, you're supposed to use proper language and — "

"We're all sweetness and light?"

Her comeback, sharp and biting, caused him to clam up temporarily. Finally, he got out a strangled, "Yeah," answer.

"I wasn't always like this," she replied as she pointed ahead. "They're going into that place of business. I think they want to rob it."

Ed followed her finger and forgot about her somewhat vulgar reference. "I'm on it."

Concentrating hard, he teleported inside the shop, a discount electronics store. The proprietor was a middle-aged black man, and he'd gone to the washroom. Ed simply sent a blue bolt of lightning from his finger at the lock and sealed the door shut. This wouldn't take long.

He then shifted into the owner's form, went out front where their marks were in the process of casing the joint, and he got his first good look at them.

The man, around five-seven, with dirty brown hair, a narrow face in sharp contrast to his pudgy frame, pockmarked sallow skin, and a slightly vacant look in his eyes, picked up a toaster. "Hey, Susan, what do you think about this?"

It was such an obviously fake act that Ed almost laughed — but he didn't. Instead, he said, "It's a really good model, sir."

The man paid him no attention. "Susan?"

She turned around with an annoyed expression working. "Dirk, just get on with it."

A chastened look came over Dirk's face. He put the toaster down and produced a knife, which he proceeded to brandish in Ed's direction, growling, "Gimme the money in the register."

Ed forced out a smile. Oh, yes, this guy was a rank amateur, dumb beyond belief, no skill, no finesse. "You really don't want to do that."

Every fiber of his being ached to rip this dipstick's soul away, but he refrained from doing so. "Son, go on home and think about your future."

Susan hung back, wary. From the look in her eye, it was clear that she hadn't been expecting this at all. "Dirk, you know what to do."

"I'm on it," he answered without looking at her. His hand shook, and from the look in his eyes, he really didn't have the stones to go through with it. "Man, just gimme the money, or I'll give you the shaft."

"Go ahead," Ed replied. "But you didn't earn this money. Change your ways, my son."

Okay, that sounded beyond preachy, and he caught sight of Nellie, who stood near the doorway. She'd obviously heard, though, as she had a grin a mile wide on her face.

"I'll cut you," Dirk said as his hand shook more violently. "Don't push me. I'll do it!"

In the most serious of all voices, Ed intoned, "If you must, then you must."

If that wasn't a clue for Dirk to do his dirtiest, what else could it be? His arm and the rest of his body quivered something awful, almost to the point of dropping his knife, although he didn't. "You asked for it, man," he said and proceeded to slash Ed's face.

A drop of bluish-red blood dripped out, and then as if by

magic, it healed up instantly. "Try again," Ed said pleasantly, feeling no pain. "Go for the heart."

From the doorway, Susan screamed, "Jesus Christ! Dirk, we're gone!"

Mouth hanging open, Dirk dropped his knife. Nellie deftly moved aside as the pair of would-be crooks ran out of the store.

Ed went to the bathroom, unsealed the lock, and as he walked out to greet Nellie, he morphed into his default human form again. She couldn't keep the grin off her face, and it set him off — mildly. "Okay, what is it?"

"Change your ways, my son?"

"I couldn't think of anything else to say."

Nellie busted out laughing. "You stink at being pure."

Somewhat wounded by her mirth, he shot back with, "Yeah, well, it worked. Could you have done any better?"

She shrugged. "Maybe. I sense they're still not turned to the light, yet. Let's follow them."

The path of the two potentials went from downtown Manhattan to the Bowery. It took about twenty minutes on foot to get there. Although it had been rebuilt and was now a fashionable area, there were still some pockets of seediness.

They halted opposite a cheap hotel. Men in overalls, torn jeans, and cheap-looking jackets walked in and out of the entrance. Nellie observed the comings and goings with an air of compassion. "In my day, places like this were much shoddier. They used to be called lodging houses."

"Pits, you mean," Ed said, as he noted the area and its denizens, as well as their targets going inside.

Nellie received the comment without moving a muscle in her face. "Pretty much. They were for people who had no money back then. No one did. I didn't. I earned my money . . . a different way."

Ed only half-heard her. He was too busy checking the hotel

out. Nellie told him to wait, and she subsequently vanished, reappearing a few minutes later.

"I just had to check on which room they were in. Let's wait here. They might come out again, although I don't think they will. It's cold. They aren't dressed for winter."

"I got an idea."

Ed pointed to a coffee shop that sat across the street. "We can wait there for a few hours. If they come out, you'll be able to sense them, right?"

Nellie's eyes widened. "I suppose we're going to wait all night?"

What else did she expect? His eyes on their targets, he murmured, "If we have to."

"And where are we going to stay if they close the coffee shop?"

Oh. That caused Ed to whip his head around, only to find Nellie staring at him with a mini thundercloud on her face and her arms folded across her chest.

Call this a problem and then some, and Ed realized the implications of the situation. He ran over the options in his mind and quickly came up with what he thought was the best answer. "Well, my apartment is in Manhattan. I have a spare room. We can always teleport in, and —"

"No."

Her voice came out forcefully in a tone that brooked no argument. She might as well have said, *You think you're going to get me into bed? Forget it!*

All right, there went best option number one. Fine, no apartment. Ed decided that he'd made an error in his choice of words and apologized, adding, "I wasn't thinking of, you know . . . that. I mean, look, how about we get a room at that hotel and shadow them?"

It made sense. If the dynamic dummies rabbited, they could chase them down easily. Nellie gazed at him with suspicion, then at the hotel, and finally, she nodded. "Separate rooms, please."

Ed threw up his hands in defeat. "Done."

Inside the hotel, they stood at the beaten and chipped front desk in front of a middle-aged, ratty-looking man who more than likely saw them as rich kids who wanted a little fun.

"Help you?" he asked.

"Two rooms," Ed replied and tossed two hundred dollars on the counter.

The clerk gave them their keys as he snatched the money up. "You're on the third floor, room three-oh-one and three-oh-two. Elevator's out of order," he said and pointed to the stairs.

The rooms themselves were basic — a bed, small shower with one towel, a toilet that gurgled when Ed flushed it, and ratty, time-worn drapes.

A small television sat on the lone dresser. No mirror, although the bathroom had one. It would do, although he missed his apartment.

Clothes. He decided to change them from a suit to something more in line with the season — and then, to his shock and surprise, he found that he couldn't. No matter how hard he concentrated, he couldn't will anything to happen.

Teleporting came next on the list. Nothing. His heart began to race, and he began to breathe fast. With a supreme effort, he stopped himself from hyperventilating. What was going on here?

Perhaps it was his proximity to Nellie, good canceling out evil and all that. In frustration, he kicked the bed-post and yelled as his foot contacted the wood. "Damn it!"

Hopping up and down from the pain and swearing quietly, he limped around until the initial pain receded and then went across the hall to his partner's room. "Are you, uh, decent?" he asked after knocking.

"Come in."

Nellie sat on her bed, wearing a nightgown covered with a robe. The television was on, showing a bright scene in California, all sunshine and swimming pools and flashy cars. She eyed the goings-on with no certain amount of distaste. "Is this what people watch for entertainment?"

The program was something about teens in a cushy neighborhood. He watched it with her for a few minutes, and all he saw were young, attractive kids in their late teens hopping into bed with each other. Mindless entertainment for the masses. That was what the public wanted.

"I guess people like that kind of stuff," he said. "I'm not much of a television watcher. I'd rather relax and listen to music."

A spark appeared in her eyes, and she clicked off the television. "Music?"

"Yeah. I like the classical composers, pop, rock—it's all good."

Frank had often made fun of his eclectic tastes. *"You're into dead composers,"* he'd once said. *"Half of them are down here, you know?"*

No, Ed didn't know that, but it figured. Many of them had reputedly sold their souls for success, so it figured they'd be in Hell. Nellie then snapped her fingers, bringing him back to reality. "What?"

"How about you teleport to their rooms to check on our targets? They're on the fifth floor. You could also change your clothes while you're at it," she added, and not unkindly at that.

A tiny sense of shame burned in his core. "I can't."

Her eyes widened. "No?"

Ed grimaced, still feeling pain in his foot. It had now segued into a cramp, and he worked it out by grinding his toes on the carpet. "No. It happened just now. I can't manipulate matter, I can't teleport, and I don't know why. Maybe it's because I'm around you."

A quiet chuckle came from her. "Maybe it's because you're seeing things a different way."

That cut, but he let it go. "How about you try?"

"Fine."

She closed her eyes and vanished, reappearing a few seconds later. "They're still there, arguing over what happened. She says he was on drugs. He's not budging from his position. Oh, wait . . . now she says she believes him."

Nellie fell quiet and closed her eyes briefly. "I can see them. They're making up. Romantic stuff, so I won't bother with the details. They're going to stay the night. I'll check in on them from time to time. Don't worry."

Embarrassed that he had to rely on a Halo, Ed bobbed his head as a sign of gratitude. "Thanks. I, uh, I guess I'll go back to my room."

He turned to leave, but Nellie said, "Stay. We can talk for a while."

Stay. Ed felt uncomfortable around her, especially due to what she was wearing — or wasn't, in her case. However, since they had to work together, for the good of the realms and all that, he decided to stick around.

After taking a seat on the opposite side of the bed, casting his gaze to the floor, he said, "Um, can I ask you something?"

"What?"

Ed picked his head up. "Who were you before? You said you had your memories."

A shadow swept across her face. "You want the abridged version?"

"I guess."

Nellie crossed her legs and spoke quietly. "My full name's Nellie Wong Stevenson. I was born in a foreign enclave in Hong Kong in eighteen-forty-one. It wasn't much of a life, but I didn't live that long, either."

The product of an interracial union — her mother was

Chinese, and her father was an American sailor—their life was one of poverty. Her father was at sea most of the time, and he came home on leave only twice a year.

"I don't think they ever got married. I grew up hearing things about my mother and me, the blonde half-Chinese girl with green eyes. Unusual. That's the word they used after some other filthy names they called me."

Ed listened, and as her story continued, he started to feel worse and worse. As a half-Chinese girl in a very bigoted society, her path to prosperity was severely limited.

"We had no money. My father sent very little, and he didn't make that much to begin with. My mother worked. I did odd jobs around my neighborhood in addition to helping my mother keep house. When I was thirteen, she sold me to a brothel."

That came as a shock, but not really. People had done far worse in difficult times. "I looked older than I was," Nellie said. "I looked exotic." She practically spat out the word. "Exotic—everyone said that, and it was good enough for the owner."

It was also good enough for the customers, many of whom liked the combination of Asian and Western traits. The innocent Nellie Wong—she'd stopped using her father's name—lost her innocence at the hands of a wealthy businessman when she was fifteen.

"The man was big, fat, and he smelled of cheap rice wine and garlic. He took off his robe and stood there, and when I didn't know what to do, he tore my robe off me and threw me on the floor. He . . . he took me then."

Nellie stopped speaking for a moment to stare at the ceiling and then resumed her story. She spoke in a toneless manner, as if all emotion had been burned out of her by the memory. Her tale continued, and she told Ed of being used on a nightly basis by customers who favored the blonde girl with the jade-green eyes and Asian features.

Her owner, the local Madame, took half of what she made. Escape was impossible. People knew her face, and it was a given that they'd chase her down and beat her severely if she tried to run. Other girls had tried. They'd never succeeded.

Nellie soon gave up her ideas of freedom. She continued to work, and she gave most of the extra money to her mother. Over time, she came to realize something—men would pay to be with her. They would pay a lot.

"Men wanted me. They liked me for my looks. They liked the fact that I spoke Chinese and English fluently. My given name was Na."

"Na?"

She shrugged. "It doesn't have a meaning. My life had no meaning, so it fit. My father named me Nellie. He said it was his mother's name."

A moment later, her voice grew fierce. "No one cared what name I used. They wanted my body, not my mind or heart. And they paid me. I didn't like being with those men. Sex is fine if you care for someone enough. I didn't, but since they were using me, I used them.

"When I pleased them and asked for more money, they never got angry. They paid whatever I wanted. That's when I knew I had power."

Ed nodded. "Sounds like the kind of people we usually get downstairs."

Nellie's voice filled with self-loathing. "Yes, I figured as much. But I wasn't like that. I knew I'd never be accepted by either side, so I wanted to make as much as I could and then leave."

She charged highly for her services, and the Madame was so pleased, she allowed her to keep more than half of the money. Business was business, and the brothel was soon the envy of all the other houses of ill repute. Nellie kept working and kept saving.

During her downtime, she immersed herself in books. "I never went to school, but my mother knew someone who could get her schoolbooks in Chinese and English novels. I taught myself how to read and write in English as a little girl. I practiced English with any foreign sailors or businessmen who came in."

Nellie lifted her arms in a gesture denoting helplessness. "That was my life. I was trapped, but books set me free. They held knowledge, and I wanted to know. That knowledge would help me escape my life. At least, I thought so."

Her plans for fleeing the country were interrupted by the arrival of something she couldn't fight—illness, in the form of tuberculosis.

Now calmer, fierceness in her voice gone, Nellie related the information in a matter-of-fact tone that was devoid of any self-pity. "It was common back then. I don't know who I got it from. It doesn't matter. I got it, and I was dying. I was only nineteen, and I was dying."

Naturally, the brothel owner couldn't have anyone diseased on their premises, so she kicked Nellie out, and the former star of the night had to take to the streets . . .

Weak, ignored, and dying, her path took her to a small church on the outskirts of Kowloon, her home city. She'd never stepped inside a church in her short life.

But now, she went inside, as it was raining and she was cold and tired, eyeing the crosses with suspicion. Her mother had always said religion wasn't for her—any religion.

A kindly-looking priest in his sixties, short and stout, stepped over to her. "Are you looking for something, young lady?" he'd asked in halting Chinese.

"A place to rest," Nellie replied in English. "Just for a while.

I can pay for my lodgings."

The man, Father Anderson, refused to take her money. "This is the Lord's work we do. You may stay."

And so, she'd stayed. There were other hard-luck cases — derelicts who'd fallen into the bottle and had never climbed out of it, prostitutes, orphans, and more.

At first, Nellie didn't know what to do, and the misery of the lowest of the low almost overwhelmed her, but the kindly priest and the nuns had guided her on the everyday workings of the church.

"Don't think about what you can't do," one nun had counseled. "Think about what you can."

It became a matter of pride to do a good job. She'd helped each downtrodden individual unselfishly, using her funds to buy food, clothes, and medicine.

In the end, though, her disease came back to overwhelm her. The deep, dry cough that wouldn't stop no matter how much water she drank worsened, she lost weight, and she had no energy.

A doctor was then summoned, and after he'd examined her, he gave Father Anderson the bad news. In turn, the good father gave her a room sequestered from everyone else.

"Why are you helping me?" she'd asked as he brought in her daily meals. He was the only one who did it, and he was not afraid of getting sick. "You should leave me at a hospital."

"They will not take anyone who has your sickness," he'd answered. "It is God's work that I do. Don't worry."

Don't worry. There was a lot to worry over, and her disease progressed rapidly. As she lay dying, she'd insisted that Father Anderson take what was left of her savings. It amounted to around five hundred pounds, a princely sum back then.

"Please," she'd whispered, too weak to cry out from the pain. "I can't use this money. Do some good with it."

He'd taken the money and set it aside. "If you want me to

pray for you, my child, I will."

Nellie had never prayed in her life, but she nodded as she lay upon her simple bed. The older man chanted a prayer in Latin, a language that she was unfamiliar with but sounded soothing, all the same.

Three-quarters of the way through the prayer, she'd felt something break inside her body, and it became hard to breathe. She struggled for breath, found that it wasn't coming, and she'd accepted her fate.

This was it. In her waning moments of existence, she could still think. *Is this what it's like to die?*

"*Yes, Nellie Wong Stevenson,*" a voice answered. It was male and youthful sounding. "*You are dying. Do you wish to join us?*"

Confusion hit hard. "Who are you? How do you know my name?

"*We know many things. As for my name, it isn't important. But if you pledge your soul to us, there shall be a place for you among our own.*"

"I . . . I am nothing. If you know who I am, then you know what kind of life I've led."

"*It doesn't matter,*" the voice had said. "*What matters is your willingness to seek redemption. Will you come with us?*"

"Yes."

In the last act of her life, Nellie had raised her hand, and the ethereal figure took it. She'd then exhaled her final breath, witnessed her essence rising from her body, and she bade goodbye to the world of mortals . . .

"The rest, you already know," Nellie said, finishing off her story. "Life is short, nasty, and brutal, but that priest showed me there could be a better way. I found one."

Ed felt something stir inside him. He wasn't sure what it was at first, but then he realized it was pity, combined with compassion. He didn't know what to say, but it dawned on him that there were other options in life. Nellie had made her decision, and somewhere along the way, he'd made his.

"I'm sorry you had that kind of life," he said. Then he added, "I'm glad that you made the right choice for yourself."

Confused at his sudden admission as well as weary, he got up. "I'm going to go to my room. Good night."

With that, he walked out, and once inside his room and lying on his bed, he wondered if a better way was possible, and if a new life could be as someone different than what he'd been created to be.

CHAPTER SEVEN: INTERLUDE

Ed lay in his bed, shifting, twisting, and turning in an uncomfortable semi-sleep. When in human form, he usually slept well, without dreaming, but in that early hour — twelve-oh-one, December thirty-first — he could find no solace in sleep.

Perhaps demon form would be better. He rarely used it on Earth, but he figured now was the time to see if his powers had returned. Concentrating fiercely, he gave it his best shot, and ... nothing. Still out of hell juice, so he lay there, wondering what he'd done to deserve being turned mortal.

He assumed that because he was largely mortal now, he'd sleep like everyone else. He'd assumed wrongly. During the night, images had assailed him, and he'd never had them as sharply as this before. Demons didn't dream, or at least, they weren't supposed to.

At first indistinct, the images coalesced into a view of a farmhouse. As a visitor observing the action, he saw himself standing inside the structure. It was daytime, and the sun shone brightly through a dirty window. A large man was yelling at him in a southern accent. Ed didn't recognize the other person.

The scene then shifted to a warehouse. It was night, he stood in a filthy storage facility surrounded by crates and assorted machines, and he was scared.

Odd — Ed had never feared anyone, save his master, as the master had the power of life, resurrection, and extinction at his fingertips.

Even when Ed had first started training, checking out the pits where the damned ran and bled and screamed and begged for mercy, even when Frank had chastised him for not being aggressive enough in taking souls, and even when he'd seen George's unlife extinguished, fear had never been part of Ed's vocabulary.

But those images — they all seemed so real.

He heard a voice. "You're not one of them, anymore." It sounded familiar, but where had he heard it?

Another voice shouted, "You're worthless! Get out of my sight!"

That didn't sound familiar at all.

And then, there was another sound, that of a gun being fired and the awful pain in his chest, and him choking on his own blood, and . . .

"Uh!"

With a start, Ed awoke, bathed in sweat. His heart hammered against his chest wall, and for a moment, he wondered where he was.

Oh, yes, the hotel. He took in a deep breath and sat on the edge of the bed, trying to regulate his breathing. After a few minutes, things settled down. That dream had been too unsettling. Dreams were supposed to make sense after a fashion, but those images had come before, the same each time, and he still couldn't make heads or tails of them.

Clad only in his shorts, he walked over to the window to observe the night sky. Now a dull red, it was glowing as if an ancient evil, something even more evil than what Hell could spawn, had somehow come to life.

An old mortal saying came back to him. "Red sky in the morning, sailor take warning. Red sky at night, sailor's delight."

Those down below had a different saying. "Red sky in the day, the good shall make way. Red sky at night is the devil's delight."

Now, he understood what the latter saying meant,

although delight didn't figure into it. There was no way he could go back to sleep, although his partner, Nellie, was probably dreaming of sheep and other cutesy things angels more than likely did.

A moment of anger born of frustration swept through him. How could Lucifer toss him into this mess and not give any decent backup? He had to rely on a rookie Halo, and what good was that going to do him? And what was the rationale here?

"Someone want to help me?"

His pleas for aid fell on deaf and pointed ears. No matter how much he concentrated, he couldn't contact his master or any of his friends. Someone or something had eroded his powers, and it frustrated him no end.

Wake Nellie? No, wait. Let her sleep. Ed stripped off his trunks and went to take a shower. The water came out lukewarm, and someone had left only a sliver of soap, but it was enough to get clean with.

Pity he had to put on the same smelly clothes again, but that couldn't be helped. "When this is over, I'm going to wear designer clothes every single day of the week."

Call that a personal promise. Ed wasn't a fashion diva, but he liked wearing clean clothes. Everyone did, didn't they? It was a natural assumption, but first, he and Nellie had to solve the riddle of how to make people believe in something that he didn't believe in himself.

Do the good—how in the name of all that was bad and unholy had he come up with that line?

With a sigh, more of resignation than of fury, he slumped down in a chair near the window and looked out at the condemned building that sat next to the hotel. It was boarded up, but a few slits in the wood provided a view.

People moved around inside—squatters. With nowhere else to go, no money, and no hope, they went to the only place that could offer some measure of protection.

Condemned and soon-to-be torn down buildings, the sewers, and long-abandoned subway tunnels—they provided a haven for the homeless. They were warmer there, more than likely, but they were also cesspools, holders of filth beyond belief, and at that moment, Ed had no desire to go there.

Ordinarily, he would have, for what better place to obtain a soul than among the hopeless? Yet, now, his mission wasn't to take souls, but to send them on their way to a destination he'd only heard horror stories about and had no wish to gain any greater knowledge of.

His eyelids grew heavy, and his last thought before fading into unconsciousness was that doing the right thing was a hellish kind of existence . . .

"Hey, wake up. It's time. We have to go."

Ed opened his eyes and blinked. Nellie stood in front of him, wearing her spotless blouse and skirt. She looked fresh and lovely and exuded a kind of wholesomeness that other mortal women lacked.

While he didn't want to admit it, she was the kind of girl mortals often spoke of taking home to see their mothers, and what was he thinking, anyway?

Reality check—he was mortal now, a sweaty mess, and even though he'd taken a shower, he was quite aware of his growing body odor. Having no powers sucked in the direst of ways, and he wished that all the power of Hell would help him, but no one heard his cry.

"Uh, sorry, I took a shower before," he said, still in a semi-fog and stupid from lack of sleep. "I know I probably stink, and—"

Nellie didn't seem to mind, though, as she repeated, "We have to go. It's early, but Dirk and Susan are on the move."

Immediately, he became fully alert. "What time is it?"

"Just past seven. Sun's sort of out, but the sky is getting redder by the second."

That, he already knew. "All right, we'll worry about the atmosphere later. Where are they?"

"At the coffee shop. They're almost finished. Let's get going."

Frustration hit Ed hard. "You know I can't teleport."

"Hang onto me. I'll get us there."

He got up, somewhat ashamed of his appearance, but Nellie put her arm around his waist. "Here we go."

They vanished. It was seven AM, December thirty-first. The sky was now crimson and glowing yellowish purple here and there, and a cold, harsh wind blew. It carried the stink of hellfire and ungodliness and more.

It carried the smell of destruction.

Earth's last day.

CHAPTER EIGHT: TAXI!

Nellie's aim was true. She'd teleported them to within twenty feet of their targets. "Hey, good spotting," Ed remarked after they'd arrived. He'd always come in a tad farther away. "You're a lot more accurate than I am."

A fleeting smile came to her face. "Now, you're just being nice."

It had to be said. "Yeah, I am."

She giggled, the first time she'd done so since they'd met. "Okay, I wasn't expecting that. Hang on, I want to get a bit closer to them."

Her body tensed, ready for action, but a second later, she relaxed and turned to Ed, a confused expression spreading across her features. Her look of confusion soon gave way to one of angst. "I wasn't expecting that, either."

"What?"

In another shift, the angst gave way to something deeper, confused, sadder, and more personal. "I'm the same as you now. I can't teleport. And it's cold, too."

Nellie sought out a nearby bench and sat, hugging herself as if to shut out the cold. "I don't know what's going on."

She lifted her gaze to the sky and put up her arms in supplication. "Father, have I done something wrong?"

Ed stifled a laugh. Her appeal for help verged on the comical, but then he realized that he'd done the same thing, so he changed his mind and tried to empathize. "I'm sorry. It's . . . well, it sucks. That's all I can say. We'll just have to deal with it."

Nellie's look of confusion vanished, replaced by one of determination. "Right, we do it the old-fashioned way. We walk."

It sounded better than it worked out. The crowds had grown. Holiday season, bad weather or not, brought out the shoppers. People moved around each other in a herky-jerky, irritable fashion, and occasionally, the shout of, "Watch where you're going, idiot," filtered over to them.

Nellie observed the goings-on with a sense of wonder. "Is that how mortals act?"

Her comment was an honest one, but it came across as being naïve. "You've been up there far too long," Ed replied with his gaze straight ahead and fixed on their quarry. He also felt cold but decided not to complain. "When was the last time you came here?"

"About seventy-five years ago, just after World War Two, but I was stationed in Colorado at the time. Things were easier, then. People were . . . nicer."

Ed wondered how, but then again, Halos were a different breed altogether. They worked differently, too, he imagined. "Er, not to get personal, but you said you've had only three missions."

"Yes."

"Were you successful?"

She blew out a deep breath that formed a cloud of fine mist. "On the first one, no. Numbers two and three went fine."

Not a bad batting average, he thought. "Well, I guess things have changed since your day," he said, keeping his voice level and trying to introduce a note of encouragement.

"I'm here twenty-four-seven, and I see how they act. New Yorkers have always been sort of aggressive. They're all after the same thing—money, advancement, getting noticed . . . that kind of deal."

A humph came from her. "Aren't you after the same thing?"

That stopped him cold, and he ran his hand through his

hair as a kind of admission. "Yeah, I am. Just like you and your kind are. But I don't lie about it. I do what I do, and I'm good at it."

A gust of wind hit him, and he shivered. "Now, I'm sort of handicapped. And I need your help."

Nellie turned to him with a look of sympathy in her eyes. "You're really lost, aren't you?"

Perhaps it was the way she said it, or perhaps it was something else. Whatever it was, it cut him to the core, and maybe she wasn't wrong, after all.

"I'm not lost," he said with defiance. "I'm not, but . . ."

Still, he was out of his depth, although he wasn't willing to concede weakness or defeat. However, nothing said that he couldn't ask for help along the way. "I can't do this alone."

Nellie pointed in the direction of their targets. They were in the process of hailing a taxi. One pulled up with a bumper sticker that proclaimed, *Deeks' Motors. You Dent It — We Fix It,* in bright gold letters against a brilliant red background.

They got in, and off they went.

"You won't be alone," Nellie said. "C'mon, take a ride with me."

She whistled sharply, and a cab pulled up to the curb, driven by an elderly gentleman with a long white beard and turban. "Where you go?" he called out in a thick accent.

Ed and Nellie piled in. "Follow that cab," she instructed. "The one with the red bumper sticker."

The driver bobbed his head. "Yes, of course."

As they weaved in and out of traffic, Ed glanced at the man's ID. Iqbal Simbal — perhaps it was an East Indian or Pakistani name. And considering the man had a turban and a beard, he must have come from that area, or his parents had. A Sikh — he had to be a Sikh.

Yet, when he spoke, his accent sounded strange, more Eastern European than anything else. Perhaps he'd been born in another country or moved there. "Mr. Simbal, where are you from, if I can ask?"

Nellie jabbed him with her elbow as a sign that he'd been rude, but Ed ignored it. Something screwy was going on.

"From Mumbai," the driver answered as he sped up and came perilously close to clipping two other cars and a delivery guy on a moped. "You know Mumbai? It's in east coast of my very populated country."

East . . . nope. Mumbai lay on the west coast of India, on an island. "Who are you, really?"

"Iqbal Simbal, from Mumbai," the driver answered, but this time, he spoke in a lilting Irish accent.

Irish? Alarmed and pissed by the deceit, Ed said, "Stop the car."

Their driver didn't. Instead, he stomped on the accelerator, and the cab shot forward, smashing into other cars along the way. As he drove faster and faster, a cackle came from him that soon segued into a bellow of deep-seated, evil laughter.

Behind them, the wail of police sirens sounded, but they were overridden by Nellie's yelps of fear.

"What in the hell is going on?" she shouted in a very un-angelic manner and beat her fists on the Plexiglas window that separated them from the driver.

"Speed race," Simbal intoned in a gleeful voice that stopped just short of maniacal. "Buckle up!"

If there had been any seatbelts — there weren't — they'd have used them. Ed's sense of fear grew. It was something new to him, but overriding that was the voice of the driver, and it seemed more familiar.

Joining Nellie, Ed smashed his fist against the divider. It shivered but didn't break, and he leaned back in his seat to kick it — hard.

Two kicks later, it caved in, and the driver yelled in a distinct New York accent, "Hey, what are you doing? Sit back and enjoy the ride, *yknowwhatI'msayin'*?"

Ed sat up and leaned over to grab the driver around the neck. The cab shifted left, hit another car, rebounded, and then it moved into the right lane with every car behind it honking madly.

"Stop this cab—now," Ed ordered. "Stop it, or I'll break your neck."

As the cab continued to swerve in and out of danger, Nellie screamed in fear for Ed to do something, and he yelled back, "What do you think I'm doing? I'm trying!"

The driver gurgled out, "If you kill me, what good will that do?"

"It'll get you to stop."

In a sudden shift, the driver shifted into Markus' form and said, "Fat chance. You really don't get it, do you, Ed?"

Simply hearing the voice of his rival, Ed inadvertently relaxed his grip. "Markus, what are you trying to do?"

"Having fun before it ends. Later!"

Markus vanished, and the taxi began to career out of control. "Hang on, Nellie!" Ed yelled as he leaned over to take the wheel in a vain attempt to steer the cab.

He was only partially successful, as they turned down a side street. It should have stopped, but an unknown force seemed to control it, and the cab sped on as if it had a mind of its own.

Ed let out a string of curses under his breath, finishing with, "Markus, you maggot, I'm going to end you."

Fortunately, there were no cars, but numerous pedestrians scattered like quail, screaming about idiotic drivers. "Straight ahead," Nellie warned. "Ed, watch out!"

"I see it!"

A sign up ahead read *Under Construction* and a tall scaffold with steel beams and wooden planks stood at least fifty feet high, blocking their way.

Time to panic. "Nellie, I can't stop this thing," Ed said, his fear growing exponentially. "You'd better bail."

"Not without you."

She grabbed him around the waist, opened her door, and with a fierce cry, she kicked out with her legs from the floor of the cab and launched them into the air. They fell onto the street, rolling over and over while the vehicle stayed on course and ended up bursting into flame when it smashed into the scaffold.

Ed felt his head hit the pavement, and it knocked him silly. He sat up, feeling pain in every single fiber of his body, his vision wavering in and out of focus. Being mortal hurt—a lot.

Still, he was alive. That had been close, and what was up with Markus playing tricks on them? Not unless he wanted to delay them, but why? Was he that nihilistic?

"Thanks," he gasped. "You, uh, you saved me."

Nellie was in the process of brushing her outfit off. Rips and tears in her jacket and skirt showed, and a few cuts on her face dripped blood, but she seemed more embarrassed than hurt. "Yeah, I did. How are you feeling?"

"Not great. I'm seeing double."

She put her hand on his shoulder. "Relax, breathe deeply."

He bent over, heaving in gasps of air and hoping that he wouldn't puke. Once he'd recovered somewhat, he lifted his head to ask, "Why'd you help me?"

"You're sort of a nice guy, so . . ."

She looked away, her face turning pink in the process. Ed didn't know what to make of that, but he knew something— they'd lost their quarry.

"You, what did you do?"

The voice, deep, harsh, and angry, came from behind them. Ed staggered to his feet, still half out of it. He swung around and came face to face with a group of no less than ten angry-looking individuals who seemed to have murder on their minds.

"We escaped from an out-of-control taxi," he replied, feeling his breath hitch in his lungs. His head throbbed with pain, and when he put his hand up to the main sore spot, it came away smeared with blood. Wonderful. "What did you do, watch the whole thing?"

"You murdered a taxi driver," one of the mini-mob members growled. The man, tall, balding, and in his thirties, wearing a cheap bomber jacket and a pair of ripped jeans along with a dirty t-shirt that had *Have A Nice Day* written on it, took a step toward them, fists bunched.

"Killed him in cold blood," he bellowed for the world to hear. "How about we take it out on you?"

En-masse, the group moved in robot-mode—stiffly, mechanically—eyes glazed and reading kill. They were being controlled, all right. Markus was very thorough. First the taxi, and now this. Glorious.

"Let's say you don't," Nellie suggested. "Stop and think about what you're doing."

Reason wasn't about to work on them. Ed realized that in an instant and curled his hands into fists, tensing his body for combat. "Nellie, these guys don't want to play nice."

In response to his statement, she took off her left boot. The heel was three inches high and looked sharp enough to cause major damage.

"Can you fight?" she asked.

There didn't seem to be much choice, and he geared himself mentally for the upcoming battle. "I think so."

"Good, because I'm about to swing for the fences."

Ed's eyebrows arched in surprise. "You're taking off the halo?"

She laughed, but there was no humor in it. "Taking it off and stomping on it. That's what."

Good enough for him. One man came at him, and Ed laid

him out with a right hook, but there were many more, and being mortal now, he knew that he couldn't take them all.

Spotting a plank of wood, he picked it up and got ready to disable and maim, if necessary, while Nellie yelled a fierce battle cry and waded into the group, smashing people left, right, and center.

She fought fiercely, using savate-type kicks along with elbows to the face and throat, and gradually, she cut a swath through the mob. Ed joined her, whacking out the bigger participants by going for their knees and semi-crippling them in the process.

A wail of a police siren caused the mini-mob to break off their attack. They simply stood there, bloody faces and all, and Nellie grabbed Ed's hand. "Run!"

Good idea, and they took off to find shelter in a nearby building. Once they were safely inside—fortunately, the building was deserted—Ed dropped his weapon, peeked outside a grimy window, and grunted quietly with approval.

The police had arrived, but by now, the crowd had resumed its normal mental process and things went back to the everyday pushiness and aggressiveness that was part and parcel of New York life, but without the violence.

"How's the action out there?" Nellie asked as she slipped on her boot. Her cuts and scrapes, like his, remained. Powers could be given or taken away. He was learning that in a big way.

"All quiet—for now."

He turned from the window. "You're really something, you know?"

She shrugged. "In my old life, the kids used to pick on me. I learned how to fight."

"Yeah," he breathed, still in awe.

Nellie didn't seem to be into heroine worship. "Let's go," she ordered, and they moved out of their shelter and into the world again.

While things were quiet, Ed, body aching but feeling better mentally, took stock of the situation. "All right, we've got no powers, we've lost our quarry, and I'm going to kick Markus' butt when I see him."

"You're sure it was him?"

It annoyed Ed that she couldn't see the obvious. "Well, it wasn't one of yours. Markus is out to delay us. He's always been jealous of me, but this is a new low, even for him."

A sense of frustration hit. Now, they had two fronts to fight against, Markus — who had his reasons for acting like a jerk — and getting their job done. "You see our targets?"

Nellie swiveled her head left and right, and then she pointed, saying excitedly, "There they are!"

Luck was on their side, after all. The wail of another police siren along with the be-boop of an ambulance came from behind them. Let the law handle this. They had another goal in mind.

Nellie took the lead, and when he fell behind, she grabbed his hand with a surprising amount of power and towed him along.

Soon, they found their quarry arguing over something at a hot dog stand. They'd obviously scored some cash from a sympathetic soul, and they were wolfing down their meals with reckless abandon.

Reckless abandon wasn't the wisest plan around. Dirk choked on his meal, and his face turned rapidly purple as he sank to his knees. He pounded on his chest, but nothing seemed to work.

Naturally, the onlookers looked away, and the hot dog owner said in a plaintive tone, "Man, I can't get involved. Lawsuit, you got me on this?"

"Man's goodwill to other men," Nellie muttered. "C'mon. That's our cue."

They ran forward, and Ed, attempting to do the right thing, whacked Dirk hard between the shoulder blades. A chunk of hot dog and bun shot out of his mouth like a missile, and then the rest of his meal came out even faster.

"Thanks," Susan said as she bent over to rub her boy-friend's back. "I didn't know what to do."

Point of fact—she hadn't done anything, merely watched. However, Ed didn't see the use in telling her. "Is he a good guy?" Nellie asked her.

Ed groaned inwardly at her attempt—it came off as lame beyond lame. He'd cornered souls with better lines than that. Why would anyone believe that claptrap?

From Susan's response—an annoyed sneer—clearly, she didn't believe one word. "What kind of question is that? He's someone I'm with."

Her expression then changed to one of concern, and she bent over to resume rubbing her boyfriend's back. Dirk was still coughing and massaging his chest, but his color had gone back to normal. Susan's annoyed expression hadn't changed. "We've been together six months, traveling around. And who the hell are you, anyway?"

Without waiting for an answer, Susan threw up the talk-to-the-hand sign and turned to Ed. Her attitude was neutral, but not unfriendly. "Thanks, mister. Appreciate it."

Before he could say anything, she kneeled to help her boy-friend up, tossed Nellie a glare that could have cracked ce-ment, and then they walked away, not deigning to look be-hind them.

"Guess I didn't make a very good impression," Nellie said, plainly disappointed. "You'd think they'd have a little grati-tude."

Ed tried to suppress a chuckle and only got halfway there. It came out as a burp-hiccup. "Welcome to New York. You know, if we're going to get through this, then you have to realize something. You're always looking for the good in peo-ple. I don't, and I've learned something along the way."

"Which is?"

He kept the lecturing tone in his voice down to the bare minimum. "People only have gratitude when you do some-thing for them, something big. Things like this, they say thanks if they feel like it, but they don't mean it. I know that sounds negative to you, but that's the truth, at least how I see it."

Nellie started to go after them. "We still have to try, don't we?"

Ed bit his lip and nodded, although he wondered if there weren't some other fools to go after. It didn't seem as though they were getting anywhere with these two. "Yeah, there's not much else we can do."

As they trailed after the pair, his only thought was how to get those two to change their minds. He did have another question, though, about his partner's past. "Did you hate peo-ple?"

Nellie glanced at him, her mouth twisting into a frown. "You mean, when I was alive?"

"Yeah. I don't mean to sound insensitive, but—"

"That's okay. I get it."

Up ahead, their quarry had stopped at a traffic light. Ed pulled Nellie into an alley and poked his head out. Dirk and Susan shivered in the cold while sharing a cigarette, and the other people around them waved the smoke away with a dis-gusted air.

"I learned to hate people when I was alive. They treated me foully," Nellie replied in a soft voice, although that softness couldn't disguise the hurt, even if it was over a hundred-fifty years ago.

"Learning how to fight was just a byproduct of my envi-ronment. Deep down, I hated them for being white. I hated them for looking at me like a thing, not a woman, not an American subject or a Chinese subject, but as some sort of thing.

"And I hated my parents for creating me, knowing how hard a life I'd have, and . . . I hated myself, too, for being what I was."

Ed listened, and he started to feel badly for her. This was empathy all over again, and he didn't know how to deal with it except to say, "I'm sorry. I, uh, I don't think of you as one thing or another."

"Oh?" Nellie arched her eyebrows so high they almost met her hairline. "How do you think of me, then?"

"As a nice person—and as a pretty woman."

Yes, it sounded sexist, but he had to be honest, and he also knew that feeding her a line of BS wouldn't work.

After a moment's hesitation, she reached out to touch his hand. She'd held his hand before, but that was under different circumstances.

Now, her touch, light and soft, sent his heart racing. "Thank you for that."

Ed felt the heat rise not only in his face but also in his body. Stomach quivering, pulse racing—he couldn't ever remember that happening with any woman. He turned away, mumbling, "You're welcome."

Nellie pushed past him. "The light's changing. They're on the move again. C'mon!"

Well, there went that tender moment, Ed thought as he followed her. While they trailed after their quarry, it occurred to him that this was a hell of a way to make a living. He only hoped that he'd be around tomorrow to pick up where he left off.

CHAPTER NINE: RED HERRING

Their targets had taken off down the block, grabbed some takeout coffee from the local coffee shop, and then they'd jumped on the subway to go uptown.

Ed and Nellie tailed them discreetly, always keeping them in their sights, but never getting close enough so that their marks might get spooked.

Susan had made her position clear vis-à-vis Nellie, but not once did she or her boyfriend look around. Whatever they were looking for, they remained focused on it.

The sky had grown redder, and an occasional rumble from underground startled the pedestrians who jumped when a mini temblor hit.

Ed thought it odd that they'd seen no stray animals around. New Yorkers took their dogs out in the most inclement weather, and on any other day, it wasn't unusual for people to be walking their pets and doting on them.

However, today was no ordinary day. Very few people were walking dogs or carrying cat cages around. Even the strays—dogs, cats, the ubiquitous rats that skulked in the alleyways—they'd all decided to seek shelter elsewhere. It was as if they knew what was going on and had taken cover.

Too bad that people didn't have that luxury. "They don't know it's the end of the world," Ed said as he searched for signs of animal life and found none.

He swung his arms around to get the blood flowing, hating the cold and this situation but also knowing that he had to fulfill his mission. There was no other way.

"I imagine you're happy about that," Nellie replied without looking around. "You and your kind are into that kind of thing."

Oh, here we go again, Ed thought. *Just when we're beginning to forge an alliance, she brings this up.* "Look, can we stop with the dump-on-me routine? I'm trying to help. Really, I am. Yes, my, er, leader wants the apocalypse to happen, but not like this."

For her part, Nellie grumbled but then said grudgingly, "All right, you have a point. We did it before. We can do it again."

They'd have to. Ed's powers were still on the blink, and while he tried sending out a mental command to his Lord and Master, nothing went through. The infernal internet had short-circuited, somehow, and no connection was possible.

"You really can't contact your superiors?"

Nellie stopped in her tracks. "What did you say?"

Ed joined her. "Before, you said that you couldn't contact your superiors," he repeated in a patient tone. "You know, for advice and all that? I can't do a damn thing in this condition."

Her expression reminded him of a dyspeptic water buffalo. He'd once seen that, and the image had never left him.

"And why would I do that?" she asked, crossing her arms over her chest and standing tall. Her response came out harshly, too harshly, he thought, and her vehemence surprised him.

"Because we need help, and I'm not being helpful to you right now. Your body language tells me so."

"And how do I look?"

He did an impression of her, standing like he was severely constipated and unable to do anything about it. "You look like an angry pretzel. You're all twisted up, like you're guarding yourself, and you won't let anyone in."

"Wait a moment—"

"Hey, I told you all I know about myself. I know you don't like me. I get it. But we're stuck with each other, and we have to make this work . . . and I need your help."

Nellie stared at him, and then she slowly lowered her arms, her stance becoming more relaxed. "And I told you about me, too. It's not that I dislike you. Your personality's nice enough."

Call her answer no answer at all. "So, what is it?"

"It's just that I don't like what you are, and there's a difference. We're total opposites, and if this end-of-the-world thing wasn't happening, I'd —"

"Yeah, we'd probably try to kill each other."

For the first time in his unlife, Ed spoke passionately, as he wanted to continue his existence. While taking souls was where it was at, first, he needed people to take them from, and that was where Ms. Halo came in. "But it is happening, right here and right now, and I . . . I need you. It's, well . . ."

A blast of cold wind interrupted him, and he fell silent. People swirled around them, most of them muttering about two morons arguing over something in the middle of the sidewalk, and it's cold out, and could you move your asses to the other side or take it somewhere private?

Nellie's mouth moved, but no sounds emerged from her throat. Finally, she got things working again. "You need me?"

Ed heaved in a deep breath and blew it out. "Yes, I do. I said so before, and now . . ."

He cursed himself for acting weak, but at the same time, he realized that being honest didn't denote weakness.

She tapped him on the hand and spoke in a voice that stopped short of testiness. "What?"

"I like you."

There, he'd said it, and his innards shriveled. They shriveled even more when his partner gaped at him with what he took as supreme disbelief. Her body became statue-like, rigid and unbending, and her voice stopped short of anger.

"You . . . like me? Why?"

Now, a measure of anguish seeped into Ed, and from where it came, he didn't know, but it was there, all the same. "Because you're everything I'm not. You're decent. I'm not. You save souls. I take them.

"And I respect you because you're a fighter. I saw what you did with that mob earlier on. You're different than what I expected, and that's fine. But me, I have to do this be-nice thing, and I'm, well, I'm lost without you."

Silence ensued, with only the sounds of the taxis honking and the pedestrians cursing the weather interfering. After only a few seconds but what seemed like an eternity, Nellie's posture relaxed from its formerly rigid, defensive manner, and she extended her right arm. "Truce?"

Ed breathed a sigh of relief and briefly clasped her hand. "Truce."

Their moment of détente was interrupted when Nellie tapped him on the arm and started to run. "They're on the move. Let's go."

Ed took off with her, his breath hitching in his lungs after he'd gone no more than three minutes at a fast clip. In contrast, Nellie seemed fresh, but then she pulled up short as they reached a large edifice.

"What's . . . what's going on?" Ed puffed out he pulled up and bent over, trying to get his breath back and wiping sweat from his face.

In the past, he'd gone out jogging from time to time and often broke into a run for the sheer fun of it. It wasn't uncommon for him to run five miles at an incredibly fast pace. He'd never sweated or gotten out of breath, but now, both of those qualities had gone with the wind.

"They went in there." Nellie waved her hand at the main entrance.

It was a Catholic church, St. Agnes. "Okay, powers or no,

that's out of bounds for me," Ed said as the door closed behind their targets. "Not my thing."

Nellie observed him with a wry smile. "I didn't think it would be. Hang tight. I'll be out soon."

High heels and all, she sprinted up the steps and into the church. He observed the tall spires, the massive stone carving of Christ on the cross, and the various cherubs placed at various points along the edifice.

It isn't totally ugly, he thought, and then his concepts on what constituted beauty were interrupted by the sound of an ambulance approaching. With a screech, it pulled up to the curb, the driver cut the siren, and two paramedics got out of the back, one of them pulling a gurney with him.

"Let's go," he said to his partner.

They moved up the steps and into the church. Nellie came out, a frown permeating her features, and Ed picked up on it. Something had happened, and it didn't bode well for their mission. That was the vibe he got. "What's wrong?"

"Trouble," she said. "Dirk's out."

"Out? I don't get it."

Nellie folded her arms across her chest. "Our orders are to stop two people from doing something bad and get them to see the good, yes?"

"Yeah, so?"

She jerked her thumb behind her. "I think we have to get someone else. Those two haven't done anything good or bad, not really. I couldn't read their minds, so I didn't know what they were thinking."

"Uh-huh." Ed sensed more bad news was coming, and his partner obliged.

"Dirk must have had a heart attack."

Ed tried to keep a level head, but he couldn't keep from exclaiming, "What?"

Nellie waved her hand at the ambulance. "You saw the

paramedics, didn't you?"

He nodded, and she sat on the steps, hugging her knees. "Dirk and Susan were sitting in one of the pews, and then he grabbed his chest. The priest, Father Nolan, called nine-one-one, and, well, you saw what happened."

For a few moments, moments where Ed's blood pressure zoomed into the stratosphere and he thought he'd explode from frustration, everything in the world ceased to revolve. People didn't breathe, cars froze while in motion, and no sounds were heard.

Things began moving again when he erupted with, "So, where are we going to find two morons to send upstairs?"

It wasn't the smartest thing to say, as a few people stopped to stare and mutter something about young people drinking too early in the day.

Nellie pulled him aside and over to an alley. "Ed, screaming about morons doesn't help our situation."

She would have to state the obvious. Ed rubbed his temples furiously and cogitated over what to do. Nothing in the bad-guy manual had prepared him for a situation like this.

Then, the proverbial light bulb went off, and he smacked the side of his head in relief. "I got it! Try thinking like a crook. If you wanted to steal something, especially now, where would you go?"

His partner shrugged. "I have no idea."

"I suppose they don't go over scenarios like this up there." Ed spoke entirely without irony, and to her credit, Nellie didn't take offense.

"We don't. We usually worry about what will happen after they do something bad."

Marvelous, this was just marvelous. "Lucky for you that you have slime like me around to help you out. I have a plan. Follow me."

He led her to a section where several pawn shops and small

businesses ruled. Nellie swept her gaze around the area. "Here?"

From the tone in her voice, she simply didn't get it. Now, it was Ed's turn to feel put out, and while he didn't want to get defensive, he couldn't help it.

"Yeah, why not? People come here, there are a lot of small businesses, and they get knocked over every single day. We just have to wait and watch."

Nellie's expression remained skeptical, but she hissed out a shallow breath. "Fine, we'll try it your way for . . ."

She suddenly stopped speaking and pointed to a couple of guys eyeing a discount jewelry shop. "Hey, look over there. Those guys."

He followed her finger. Two men in their thirties stood shifting their feet outside the store, gazing around the area. Dark-haired, stocky, and with ratty-looking, unshaven faces, they looked like prime candidates to do something extremely bad.

In addition, they wore long overcoats, which provided ample cover for either a handgun or a shotgun. Thieves like that were the worst, mainly because they were too unpredictable in what they'd say or do.

Nellie seemed to share his thoughts. "Get in closer. See what you can learn."

Who, me? Ed wondered why he had to be the one to take the initiative, but he dutifully nodded and strolled in as unconcerned a manner as possible toward the men. As he approached the men, he pretended to look at the cheap jewelry in the window, most of which was fake.

"Rick, we can't go in," the man on the left said as he glanced at the shop's door. "It's not open. You know I want to get the ring, but it's a bit, well, out of my range, you know?"

His partner glanced at him furtively and then around the area as if checking for additional security. There wasn't a policeman in sight, and the store didn't have a security camera. If these two wanted to bust in, they could, Ed thought.

"All right," Rick said. "Lane, you promised, you know that?"

"I know."

The two men started bickering like an old married couple, and then Ed stopped in his tracks at the realization that they *were* a couple.

In an abrupt U-Turn, he returned to where Nellie was. She waited with her arms spread wide and a what-good-news-do-you-have-for-me expression working. "Well?"

"They're looking for a ring."

Nellie shook her head. "I don't understand. For their girl-friends?"

"For each other."

Nellie's jaw sagged. "Oh."

Oh. It seemed that either his partner didn't understand what certain types of relationships could entail, or she'd been up among the clouds too long.

"I take it you don't approve," he said while keeping a straight face and speaking in the coolest tone imaginable with only a hint of sarcasm for flavoring.

Nellie continued to gape, and then, with a visible effort, she shut it. "Well, no, it's sort of sweet, really."

"What, gay couples are a twenty-first-century invention?" Now, Ed let the sarcasm flow. Mean or not, he considered it a small measure of payback for her earlier putdowns.

Nellie stammered out her response. "It's not like that, just that . . . when I was growing up and, in my teens, I never saw . . . that type of thing. I mean, it was probably around, but I never saw it."

Uh-huh. "You said you last came here in the nineteen-forty's. I'm reasonably sure it was around then, too, and now, it's pretty open."

"Well . . ."

"So, now that you've seen it, how do you feel?"

Her face turned crimson, and her voice came out in a whisper. "Surprised, but, yes, it's okay with me. I suppose you're going to tell me Hell has every combination around?"

This was one area where he had her beat and then some. "It does," he stated, and not without undue pride. "We're an equal opportunity, soul-taking organization. Any color, any race, any ethnicity, any orientation — we're all equal in the eyes of our master."

Nellie uttered a sound that sounded like a mix of disapproval and anger. Ed, though, wasn't about to let this go. "What, they don't have gay people in your neck of the woods?"

Oh, yes, the sarcasm was flowing, but still, he decided to stem it. This really wasn't the time. Nellie turned away. "We do . . . but it's . . . complicated."

"Uh-huh."

If Heaven has a special section for those who are LGBTQIA that's something for better minds than his to philosophize over, Ed thought. He then heaved a sigh of dismay.

"Just because you live up there doesn't mean you're above me. I mean, you're literally above me, but judging me — yeah, okay. We'll talk about it later. Let's talk about the here and now. In your opinion, are they going to rob the joint?"

Nellie didn't respond with anger to his barbs. Instead, she studied the men, as if reading their body language or their facial expressions, or both. They were still glancing around nervously, but they weren't giving any clues away. "I'm not sure."

A moment later, Lane answered their unspoken question as he threw up his hands in disgust and exclaimed, "Oh, fine, I'll buy you the ring. Come on."

Rick looked as though he was about to cry with happiness, and the two men hugged. The door to the shop opened, the proprietor removed the *Closed* sign—crisis, averted. Rick and Lane would have their happiness, assuming the world continued to exist.

From the looks of things, the situation still hadn't improved. The sky continued to redden, a bloody hue that seemed to drip on every building under the skyline.

The noxious smell that had been in the air before returned twofold, and the crackle of thunder resounded overhead, causing everyone to look up, including Ed.

Nellie waved her hand for attention. "Ed?"

"What is it?"

"Since I'm mortal now—more or less—I have to use the ladies' room. You could do with some cleaning up, too."

That made sense. Finding targets out of ten million people was proving to be impossible. Ed scanned the area, and he settled on the nearest structure. "There," he said and pointed.

It was a fast-food place. Truthfully, it looked like a flea trap, but beggars couldn't be choosers. Inside, the place was empty, smelled of grease and stale food and body odor, and Nellie wrinkled her nose. "You would have to choose a place like this."

He stifled a laugh. "I thought all Halos were pledged to help those of every station in life."

Once again, he went for the sarcasm bone, and once again, sarcasm—achieved. Nellie grunted out her answer. "We do, but they could use some soap, and this place could use a fumigator's services."

She headed to the bathroom while Ed went to the counter to scan the menu. Standard fast-food fare—burgers, meat pockets, soft drinks, and so on—but nothing appealed to him.

"Two cups of coffee, please," he said to the kid who popped up from behind the counter.

"You want food?" the pimply-faced server asked in a whiny tone. "We got burgers, fries, hot dogs—and they all stink."

Honesty from someone who was making minimum wage and didn't care if he lost his job or not. Ed developed a sudden, if minute, amount of respect for him.

"No, thanks. Just the coffee, please."

"Yeah, right, whatever."

Ed took the coffee back to a table. He withdrew his hand as he touched the Formica — a thin film of grease was on the surface. "Ick," he muttered.

Coffee time, and he took off the lid to take a sip. Not bad. It was hot but not overly so, and it warmed his insides. He took another sip and felt somewhat more relaxed.

As he drank, he found that he was getting somewhat light-headed, and he took a sniff of the coffee. There was something else in there, something different . . .

His vision blurred, objects wavering in and out of focus. A figure swam into his field of view. Nellie? No . . . it was the guy from the counter. "How's the coffee, sir?"

Voice — that voice — it sounded like . . . "Markus."

The man in front of him grinned. "Yeah. You think you've got it figured out? You don't know the half of it."

Ed's only thought before the lights went out was how he'd been suckered yet again. Then he spiraled down into a well of darkness.

Chapter Ten: Détente

Truth always came in dreams, as some psychiatrists had stated with certainty.

In Ed's case, nothing was a certainty save the fact that he'd had the same dream time and again. Unlike the previous times, now, the voices and images were clearer than they'd ever been.

Somewhere in the depths of his unconscious, a voice called out in a distinctly southern accent, "Boy, get your worthless carcass out here!"

More swearing followed, followed by the sound of slaps upon someone's skin. Was it him? Was it for someone else? He had no idea, but the sounds came through more clearly than they ever had.

So did the images. This time, he clearly saw a warehouse. Outside, it was night. Stars twinkled in the sky, and a full moon shone down. It was also warm, so it had to be summer where he was.

A new sense filtered in — smell. Mustiness, sweat, and the odor of oil on what appeared to be rifles, a dull yet distinctive aroma, hit him right away.

Two men appeared in his field of view. One of them looked very familiar, but all he said was, "The shipment is here."

Ed had no idea of what the shipment was or if it meant something else. As for the rest of the dream, the bang of the gun, the flash of light, and the pain that accompanied the shot never changed . . .

"Uh."

Ed woke up, his head spinning. He glanced around, waves of pain knifing through his head and impeding his vision. Was this a hangover? He had no experience with it, former demon status or not. He could only go on what he'd read in books and something Lars had told him.

If anyone knew about drinking, it was Lars. His capacity for imbibing alcohol astounded even the demons he hung out with. It was said that he could drink a dozen distilleries dry and still be thirsty.

And yet, by his own admission, he'd only suffered a hangover once in his unlife. He'd tried explaining it to Ed when they'd first met in a bar in Los Angeles roughly thirty years ago. Lars was in the process of going through every bottle in the bar, draining each bottle of scotch, rye, and bourbon in a single gulp.

"It's like your body wants you non-existent. Your mind will be unclear, your limbs will be uncooperative, and your stomach will rebel."

From that description, it seemed like the best summation of the condition Ed had ever heard or read. He did, however, ask the obvious question. "Why get drunk in the first place?"

"It's fun."

Fun wasn't the operative word now. Nausea had decided to rear its ugly head, and that got his stomach roiling. Whatever Markus had slipped into his drink, it was strong, strong enough to knock him out.

Of course, Ed was effectively mortal now. Any kind of drug or alcoholic beverage would affect him, and where was he, anyway?

In a welcome turn of events, his head cleared, and his stomach settled down. Focus, focus . . .

He was in a hotel room, a rather nice one, at that, a far cry from the fleabag he'd stayed in the night before. His hand encountered something soft and silky. Satin sheets. Satin always cost a lot. Cheap hotels didn't offer that kind of bedding.

Ed scanned the room with its cream-colored wallpaper and plush furniture . . . this was some place. It was luxurious, and he was used to that kind of luxury. "Wow," he muttered.

"Hey, babe, how are you?"

What? He looked to his left. A figure lay next to him, a woman. She was young, perhaps twenty, if that, blonde and blue-eyed, with an elfin face.

Although she wore a negligee, it left little to the imagination. In a high-pitched, breathy voice, somewhat reminiscent of Marilyn Monroe, she asked, "Hey, you feeling okay?"

Ed grunted out his answer and rubbed his temples furiously in attempt to place her face—and he couldn't. "Yeah, I'm . . . who are you, again?"

She pouted. "Winnifred. My friends call me Winnie. You remember me, don't you? You're my friend, right?"

Of that, he wasn't sure. He didn't know her and positive that they'd never met, he said somewhat apologetically, "Uh, no offense, but I don't remember you or how I even got here."

Her pout deepened as she sat up, covering her body with the bedsheet. "Don't you remember? You were walking down the street, talking to yourself, something about meeting a girl named Nellie?"

"Nellie," he echoed.

Immediately, guilt hit, and he could only imagine what she was thinking of him now. In his life as a demon, he'd never experienced shame. Guilt, yes—once, but shame, no. Now, he was experiencing it, big-time.

Winnie nodded. "Yeah, and you were singing at the top of your lungs. Then you saw me and called me Nellie and said we could be together."

Ed gulped. Oh, he must have been totally out of it. "I did that. I called you Nellie?"

A sympathetic expression crossed her face. "Yeah. You said I looked just like her and wanted to be with me. A couple of guys started to harass you, and then I stepped in. I felt sorry for you, but I didn't feel like calling a policeman, so I took you here. You're sort of cute, so I figured you needed to sleep it off."

A compliment, and he'd take it, but there were other, more important things to get answers on. "Where exactly is here? Sorry, I just don't remember. I guess . . . I guess I drank something I shouldn't have."

Winnie giggled. "This is the Drakon Hotel, Thirty-Fifth and Lexington."

The Drakon? With a start, that name came back to him. He'd brought clients here before, but only to the lounge area. The Drakon was one of the ritziest hotels in the business. Only the crème de la crème stayed there, and now Ed was here and, oh, this was not good at all.

With an effort, he swung his legs over the bed, saw that his clothes had been draped over a nearby chair, and got up, somewhat unsteadily, to reach for them. Garments in hand, he began getting dressed — slowly. "How long have I been here?"

"A couple of hours."

A check on the bedside clock showed that it was ten-forty-one. He had to leave, but he had to know something first. As embarrassing as it was, he had to know. "Sorry, but . . . did we do anything?"

A faint chuckle came from Winnie, and she shook her head. "No, you were too out of it. I just thought you needed to lie down. After I got rid of those punks, you said that you didn't want to talk to the police, and you didn't want to go to a hospital. I didn't know what to do, you know?"

Ed didn't remember that at all, but he was curious. "So, what happened next?"

"A man came over to me and gave me some money, and said he had a room waiting for us. I told him no funny stuff, and he said not to worry about it."

A man. With a sudden blast of insight, Ed figured out who Mr. Unknown was. He walked to the door and opened it. "Let me guess. He was blond, good-looking, and he probably had a lot of cash on him."

A slow smile spread across her face. "Yeah, that's the guy. Real friendly. He a friend of yours?"

"We know each other."

Ed started to walk out, but she called him back. "Hey, I'm not a bad person, am I?"

How could he answer that? He'd gotten no bad vibes from her, and he doubted she was a shapeshifter or something equally rotten. "No, you're not."

Curious, he asked her what she did for a living. "Aspiring actress and model, like a lot of other girls my age," she said with a wry smile.

"Nothing wrong with that."

Winnie gazed at him, and while her face still held a smile, her eyes told a different story. "You think so? Try telling my parents that. They said I'd never make it. Try telling my friends that. They said I was selling my soul."

Her last statement almost made him laugh, but this situation was so bizarre he didn't dare. Besides, he was interested in her bio. "Uh, so, you got into acting?"

In an absent-minded gesture, she reached behind her head to scratch the back of her neck. "Yeah, school wasn't for me. Look, I'm almost twenty-two. I finished high school, and higher learning didn't cut it. Someone said I had talent and that I was pretty, so I thought, get into modeling and acting. I also tend bar to make ends meet."

She hugged the sheet over her body, and then she tossed it away and reached for her dress that lay across another chair.

In a deft move, she slipped it on and reached behind her back to zip herself up.

"I was coming out of my acting class when I saw you. I scored a couple of bit parts on television, but I need to improve, so I keep up with my classes. Even though it's New Year's Eve, we scheduled a class. End the year on a high note, right?"

"Right," he repeated, not knowing what else to say.

Winnie ran her fingers through her hair, doing a quick styling job. "It was an early morning thing, and we had to improvise a rescue scene, so . . . when you came along, I thought, why not act it? But it wasn't acting, you know. You needed help."

In a situation like this, Ed felt that a healthy dose of skepticism was needed. "Uh-huh. But you took that blond guy's money."

Winnie stopped styling, and her attitude grew defensive. "It's not what you think. Yeah, I took the money. He told me to use the money for rent and acting classes. But I've never sold myself doing . . . you know."

She meant prostitution. "I never said you did."

In a sudden shift, a genuine smile came to her face. "You know, since I got into this business, you're the first guy who's ever said that. People think that because you go on casting calls and pose for pictures in lingerie, you're that kind of person. I'm not, but it's hard to make a living, you know?"

"I know."

In his unlife, Ed had learned that some people would do anything for money or fame or advancement, or all three, but despite the situation and despite what she'd done, he couldn't hold it against her. Nothing had happened. Besides, there were bigger problems to take care of.

"I'll go downstairs with you," Winnie said with a hopeful expression. "If that's okay."

"Sure."

They took the elevator to the bottom. When the door opened, Winnie leaned up and kissed him on the cheek. "Thanks, guy."

She looked out the lobby window. "Weather's bad. Maybe I should go home?"

Good idea. "Yeah, do that. It's safer. Trust me."

Winnie touched him on the hand. "You're a good one. Happy New Year."

With that, she bounced off, and Ed, now feeling somewhat better physically, as well as in a more positive frame of mind, started to go to the lounge but pulled up short.

Nellie stood five feet away, her arms crossed over her chest and a thundercloud on her face. His positive mood instantly melted away. This . . . would not end well.

"Hey, hi, thanks for coming," Ed said in a lame attempt at good humor. He was surprised that she'd come here, and yet, from the expression on her face, he knew that anything he'd say would be held against him in the eternal court of law, either the one upstairs or the one downstairs.

In an effort to calm things down and get their mission back on track, he added, "Uh, how'd you find me?"

Her stony visage would have caused Medusa to freeze for all eternity. "After you disappeared from that fast-food place, I went looking for you, asking everyone if they'd seen you.

"Then a policeman said he spotted someone who fit your description going into the hotel with a blonde. I just saw you walk out with her. Is she one of your conquests?"

Ordinarily, that wouldn't have bothered him, but now, it did, and he felt a flush of shame spread through his body. "It's not what you think," he muttered as he ducked his head.

"Oh?"

Clearly, she didn't believe him. "That coffee . . . it had something in it. I'm mortal now, like you. Drugs hit me."

He looked up, only to find a block of stone facing him. "I'm sorry. I didn't know what was going on."

Mentally, he was messed up, tired, and still somewhat hung over. All he wanted to do was to leave this place, and he did. Once outside, he heaved in great gulps of air, and it did wonders to clear his head.

"Hey."

He turned around. Nellie stood there with a somewhat less severe expression at work. "Are you telling me the truth?"

"Well, yeah."

"You weren't seeing anyone?"

He stammered out, "No. I'm . . . I'm with you."

Time stood still, and then Nellie exhaled loudly, her lips moved, but no words came out. Finally, she threw up her hands as if admitting defeat. "All right, it's done. Where to, now?"

In all honesty, he didn't have a clue. A glance at the sky told him all that he needed to know, and everyone else on the street was doing the same thing. It had gotten redder from the top of the horizon to the bottom, and even the sun shone a faint crimson.

A few people started to talk excitedly, and one man yelled, "This is Judgment Day! This is what the Bible said would happen, it's—"

"Shaddup!"

Another man punched him in the jaw, and some people started pushing and then fighting with each other. Ed took that opportunity to back off. "Nellie, we have to find Markus and make him tell what he's . . ."

His voice trailed off when he dropped his head and found that Nellie had disappeared. Maybe her powers had come back or maybe her master had called her home. "Hey, Nellie, you go to the bathroom or something?"

By now, the mini melee had died down. A few pedestrians

glanced at him with curiosity, but then they went on their way. It was too cold to worry about someone else's troubles.

"Nellie!"

Ed ran in and out of every store on the block, asking if they'd seen a woman fitting Nellie's description. "Nope, no one here like that."

He then ran across the street. No one knew anything, no one had seen or heard anything. After searching every store and alleyway, he stood in the center of the street, the cars streaming around him, honking at him and telling him to take his dumb ass out of there.

Bereft, he walked to the side of the street and sat down. Nellie was gone.

Chapter Eleven: Earthly Law

Without a partner or a plan, Ed walked disconsolately over to a nearby bench and sat, oblivious to the cold. People swirled around him, yelling at the condition of the world in general.

Being abandoned was one thing but losing someone he cared for—and he was honest enough to admit it to himself and damn the consequences—was more than he could take.

For the first time since this whole fiasco had started, he paid attention to the New York populace. He'd moved among them, worked them for his business, but he'd never really gotten to know anyone outside of superficial relationships with people like the doorman at his apartment house.

In a city that never slept, where business and fun and everything in between jockeyed for the top position, a certain amount of aggression was normal. New York was famous for its blatant I'm-walking-here attitude.

What wasn't normal was how much anger was in the air. He'd heard about it on the news. He'd been in it when Nellie had pulled him out of the taxi, and they'd fought an angry mob, and now, it seemed to be spreading.

A middle-aged woman wore her jacket open. People yelled at her to close it. She did so with a hurt look, and then she exploded at them, responding with a series of expletives that made them back off.

A man walking his dog got jumped by two other dog-walkers. Previously, Ed hadn't seen anyone with an animal on a leash or in a cage. Now, the pet lovers were out in force, inclement weather or not.

The other dog owners yelled something about the man's pooch having a too-long leash. Dogs and owners joined in the melee, yelling and growling and barking and biting until a couple of policemen arrived to break it up.

This being Last-Day, only a few had actually voiced the truth. The last person who'd done that received a punch in the mouth for his troubles.

Even more so than the anger in the air was the smell. Before, it had been a whiff of something bad, something evil, but now it had grown worse, an odor of sulfur and rottenness that was almost alien in nature.

Everyone else smelled it, too, with one couple gagging on the stink. It lay upon the air like a heavy blanket, and people rubbed their eyes and held their noses in disgust. A middle-aged couple covered their faces, and the woman said, "Let's go home. This stink is enough to drive you crazy."

Slowly, inexorably, everyone had gone from complaining about the weather to realizing that the world was going to hell in a handcart. Conversely, it also seemed as though no one cared anymore.

Did it matter? Did anything, really?

His thoughts were interrupted by the crash of glass. A short, fat man wearing jeans and a cheap jacket had thrown a trashcan through the window of a nearby electronics shop. He turned to a group of slack-jawed onlookers to announce, "News report. I wanna watch the news!"

Clearly, he'd lost it, but at the same time, he sounded curiously sane, and no one stole what was in the window. They merely waited, focusing on the news report. Soon, a few others joined him.

Ed pushed his way to the front, earning a few shoves from the other bystanders, but he paid them no attention. He had to see this.

"And the civil disturbances that have occurred all across the nation in days past have continued to grow in scope and intensity. Riots are breaking out all over the city — indeed, across the nation and around the globe," the announcer intoned. He was a middle-aged sort dressed in a seedy-looking sports jacket with an ill-fitting hairpiece. He reached up to adjust it — badly. It looked like a mop twisted sideways.

"Miraculously, even though no deaths have been reported by any country, law enforcement services are being stretched to the breaking point."

The picture changed to a montage of police forces in Paris, Monaco, Berlin, Montreal, and London, all in the process of attempting to keep order in the growing unrest within their nations.

"Law enforcement officials have urged all citizens to stay indoors, lock their doors, and not take the law into their own hands . . ."

Someone reached over to change the channel. A man in a white lab coat spoke, his expression grave. The closed captioning said his name was Horace Schmidt, a scientist.

"We are worried about the atmosphere, the same as everyone else, and the US Meteorological Agency is currently consulting with its foreign counterparts. This change in the planet's air composition is worldwide, and meteorologists are worried about static discharges of electricity . . ."

A rock, thrown by another bystander, shattered the television. Immediately, the crowd turned on the person who'd thrown it, a man in his forties who was wearing a pair of overalls and nothing else.

His hair was disheveled, and his eyes spun like tops. To say he looked mad was an understatement. Compounding the negative image was the fact that he was barefoot and had a three-day growth of stubble on his face.

"You idiot," a young woman called out. "This was

important, and you just had to ruin it!"

"Screw you," he responded. To make matters worse, he flipped her off.

There was always a right time and a wrong time to respond in such a rude manner. He'd picked the wrong time, as the crowd morphed into a mob and swarmed him.

"Get off me, get off me," he shrieked, and then only the sound of fists and thuds to his body could be heard. A couple of snaps and sharp cracks indicated bones being broken, and his shrieks of agony grew higher.

A few seconds later, though, his cries for help died away. Ed watched partially in horror and partially in fascination as the members of the crowd had gone from upright citizens with blank expressions to those who resembled demons, all twisted on the inside and out.

As a group of police arrived to break it up, the mob backed off, leaving the man a bloody mess. He was still alive, though, as his body twitched, and then he groaned as he turned over.

Lucifer's words echoed in Ed's head. *No one will die today.* Even so, people could be injured or crippled or maimed. Ed moved away, wary and scared at the sudden surge of hate and rage that flowed through everyone. End-of-the-world madness or spell?

Spell? Markus . . .

Maybe, but how? No one, save his master and the one above, was that powerful, and the one above wouldn't do this to his believers or even the non-believers. Still, whoever was doing this, Ed didn't want to hang around and become another victim.

His legs took him in the direction of uptown. Right now, he wanted nothing more than to get to his apartment, take a shower, crawl into bed, and hope this would all blow over.

Reality intruded. It wouldn't blow over, and he had to do something. As he walked, more and more anger seemed to flow in from the ether, and more and more people started to brawl for the tiniest of reasons or for no reason at all.

Madness had grabbed hold of the citizenry, and it was shaking them by their collective necks. "You!"

Ed jerked his head around. A gang of twenty men in business suits, coiffed hairstyles askew, stood on the opposite side of the street. They'd targeted another group of businessmen, those ones much older. Juniors getting back at seniors. Why not?

Bottles, rocks, planks of wood, and other kinds of refuse flew through the air. Heedless of the weather, the cold, and the possibility of getting run over, the younger men charged across the street and piled into the group of older men.

Fists flew and connected, the thud of punches and kicks made a dull sound when they met flesh, and cries of pain echoed through the air. No one tried to break it up.

In fact, they joined in, and when the police finally arrived — they'd come out in force — they also joined in, clubs hitting anyone within range.

"I have to get out of here," Ed muttered as he hailed a taxi. Fortunately, one stopped, and he gave the man his address in Manhattan.

"There, you're going there?"

The taxi driver seemed incredulous, and Ed wondered what the fuss was all about. "Something wrong?"

The cabbie shrugged. "Nope. Long hike. It'll cost you. You got the cash?"

Ed tossed two hundred dollars through the small window in the plastic partition. The driver snatched it up and said, "Sit back and keep your head down. People goin' crazy today."

"You got that right."

The cabbie took off at a high speed, and Ed sat back as a sudden lassitude filled him. He closed his eyes, promising himself he'd wake up soon. Instead, more images, similar to the one's he'd been getting, assailed his vision.

Farmhouse . . . an old farmhouse. It wasn't something he'd seen over the years. Flannel shirts . . . fields of cabbage and other vegetables. Maybe it was in the south, but he couldn't be sure. Maybe it was his home in Roanoke.

A moment later, the image faded, and he searched his memory for some other incidents. He'd always thought he'd been around for at least three hundred years.

Markus was older, yes, and so was Frank. They'd been in Hell longer, so it stood to reason they'd pledged their troth to Lucifer centuries ago.

But Ed couldn't recall any incidents beyond a hundred years or so. He remembered taking souls from gangsters in the nineteen-twenties. Zoot suits, machine guns, fedoras, speakeasies—those images flashed across his mind, along with expressions like the bee's knees, the great Yankees lineup known as Murderers Row, the Great Depression, and more.

Of course, Mugs Muldoon stood out among all the people he'd known. Big, fat, and incredibly mean, someone who enjoyed kicking puppies and kittens, he was a top-ranked assassin for one of the chief gangsters in New York.

Goals? Mugs had one singular purpose in life. He wanted to become the top dog in all of gangster-land. Ed had promised him that he'd do what was necessary. They'd signed the deal, and Mugs had become number one.

Public Enemy Number One. He'd been gunned down in a hail of bullets against the police after a bank robbery a week later.

Then there were the Hulton brothers, also notorious assassin-types. Their method of killing? Ice picks through the base of the skull. Sharp and lethal, they sliced through the brain, and the victims never had time to cry out.

Festus and Fenton Hulton killed without a qualm, without remorse. They, too, wanted to become leaders in the underworld.

Ed had given them their wish. Four weeks after signing their souls over, they'd become victims of their underlings, killed in the same fashion as they'd murdered their targets.

In Hell, Ed had met them in the pit of traitors. Muldoon and the brothers hadn't bothered looking at him. They were too busy running for their horrible unlives from the various demons assigned to torture them.

More memories surfaced, but they were recent ones, and why couldn't he recall anything outside of Nellie disappearing, and . . .

"Hey, we're here."

Ed started out of his reveries, wiped his face, and he stared out the window. The driver had pulled up to the Royal Heights apartment complex. Ah, it was great to be home, even in these times.

Plan one—take a shower, don clean clothes, and a good meal would help. After that, he'd think about what to do.

At the entrance, Milton, the doorman, waited. He'd been there for what seemed like forever, an aged yet dignified individual, tall, with a grave workmanlike attitude, quiet and unflappable in the face of danger.

As Ed approached, he held up his hand. "Where do you think you're going?"

"Inside," Ed answered, confused. "I live here."

Milton planted his feet and stood with his hands on his hips, much like a gunslinger ready for the final showdown. "You're a kid. You don't look old enough to vote. Now get going."

Hold on a second, what was going on here? "Milton, I'm Edward, remember? I'm in apartment three-sixteen. I've been here for a long time . . ."

His voice trailed off as he remembered his spell of disguise was no longer in use. Previously, his shape-shifting and facial altering ability guaranteed the appearance of a man in his early thirties. Now, he looked no older than eighteen and there was no convincing the doorman otherwise.

Milton remained unconvinced. "Son, you have three seconds to leave. If you don't, I'll call the police. A lot of very important people live here, and there's enough trouble on the streets as it is."

He'd already taken out his smartphone. Ed had heard enough. "Fine, I'm going."

In a huff, he pivoted around and banged into Mr. Williams, the producer. "Sorry, sir."

"Watch where you're going, you little jerk," Williams replied while brushing off his coat in the manner of someone who'd been accosted by vermin. "This isn't the place for vagrants."

Vagrants? Ed's temper peaked, although it shouldn't have. While this situation called for keeping a cool head, all the same, his resentment boiled over, and he let loose.

"Who are you calling a vagrant, you fat slob? I live here, and if this situation weren't so bad, I'd make sure you never made another movie again."

Williams took a swing at him, Ed ducked, and he let the fat man have it in the gut. One shot was all it took, and Williams crumpled to the ground, writhing in pain. Ed stood over him, and then fell over him as something hard hit his head.

"Ow!" Stars and bright lights flashed, darkness settled in for a nanosecond, and then he looked up to find Milton holding a pair of brass knuckles.

Another shot came, and this time, Ed's consciousness took a brief vacation.

When he came to his senses again, he found himself staring at a large policeman who wore a harried look. "Son, what are you doing troubling these nice people at a time like this?"

Nothing was going right. The world still whirled, but in an attempt to make amends, Ed said, "Officer, I live here. Look, I can prove it. I've got ID . . ."

He searched his pockets and came out with the key, but his ID had mysteriously vanished, although his wallet was still there. "Uh, maybe I left it upstairs?"

"I'll bet."

Ed started to say something, but then he cut himself short. Mr. Policeman wasn't about to listen or even keep an open mind.

"I'm the owner, officer," Ed replied, striving for calm. "If you just let me into my apartment for five minutes. I can show you the documents, if you want—"

"You can shut your mouth."

The officer—his badge read Johnston—had his gun out, and Ed knew deep down that since he wasn't bulletproof anymore, this confrontation would not end in his favor. If he got shot, he might not die, but it would prevent him from fulfilling his mission.

Mr. Policeman stared at him. "This is a really bad time to start breaking and entering. You understand me?"

Cowed by the man's response, Ed nodded and remained mute. Johnston continued speaking, his gun leveled in the direction of Ed's chest.

"If you want to show anyone anything, show the judge. You're going downtown to join the rest of the scum. We've got a lot in custody, so at least you'll have someone to talk to."

Heaving a sigh that meant his New Year's was about to be ruined, he took off his cap to reveal a thatch of thinning blond hair, and then he replaced it and motioned to the police cruiser.

"All right, I'm not going to cuff you, but make one false move, and I'll shoot you in the knee. You understand?"

Totally demoralized by now, Ed bobbed his head. "Yes, sir."

"Good. Get in."

After Ed got into the back seat, the officer slammed the door, and then he drove off through the crowd of people and police officers fighting it out on the streets.

Chapter Twelve: A Message from Below

Jail sucked. Ed stood inside a cell with twenty other men. There were three cells, and all of them were full, holding the worst assortment of humanity that could be found. Skinheads, vagrants, people raving and screaming incoherently—every single bad person in existence seemed to be there.

In contrast, Ed's cell held those that could in no way be considered scum of the earth, although some private citizens who were business investors might have taken issue with that opinion.

All of them had short hair, looked to be in their forties or fifties, and as a group, they stared at the ground, probably wondering why they'd been locked up and how this would look on their work records.

Their suits were torn, and everyone had scratches and bruises on their faces. Stockbrokers and lawyers gone mad. "What are you in here for?" one of them asked Ed, pitching his voice to get over the din in the other cells.

"Trespassing." It was the only answer he could come up with. "You?"

"I don't know," the man replied. He sported a black eye and a swollen lower lip. "I was going to work, like always. A man bumped into me on the street, and I just . . . snapped. Started a fight with him, and then a couple of the other guys here seemed to think, I don't know, that it was okay, and then they joined in, and now . . ."

He bowed his head and fell silent. Clearly, he was ashamed of what he'd done. Everyone else nodded in agreement. More than ever, all the signs pointed to Markus somehow carrying this off, but it raised the question of how the supreme overlord couldn't have known about it.

Ed remained by the bars, trying to inhale any fresh air available. Despite the winter season, the cell was hot and smelly, ripe with aromas from the overflowing toilet, pee on the ground, body odor, and worse. The stench from the adjacent cells didn't help matters much, either.

Noon rolled around, and he'd gotten no further, and where was Nellie? And where was Lucifer? And why had his powers disappeared? And why was this happening to him?

"What are you in here for?" one of the men asked him, bringing him back to reality. "You're wearing a suit, but you look like a high school kid."

Tell me something I haven't heard before. Fine, go with it. It doesn't matter. "I *am* a high school kid. I was looking for a job, put on my best suit, and I tried to score an interview. You know, get something going before the year ended. Then . . . something happened."

Sure, it was a lame excuse, but nothing creative came to mind. The man seemed to accept his excuse, though, as he nodded. Another man piped up. "Yeah, something happened, all right."

"Friggin' end of the world," a third man said. "Seen the sky lately? I'm not religious, but this is apocalypse-now stuff."

His statement drew a chorus of agreement. What could Ed say that would make any difference? This was the first time anyone had dared utter the obvious.

In the end, he nodded and bobbed his head, acknowledging the truth. "What can we do about it?" That came from a short, fat man who wore an ill-fitting suit at least twenty years out of style. He looked lost, just as the others did.

"I'm going to suggest we pray," the first man said, who

introduced himself as Herbert, a stockbroker. "It couldn't hurt."

Ah, the old standby—religion. That wasn't going to help, either, but Ed said nothing. The men grouped together, and he stood quietly outside their circle as they offered up a prayer for deliverance. Once finished, they intoned, "Amen," and the deal was done.

Just in time, too, as the door opened and a police officer came in and called out, "Anderson, Edward, I'm looking for an Anderson, Edward."

"That's me," Ed said, raising his arm and giving a wave. He'd never used a last name in his unlife outside of speaking to Milton at his apartment. He always went by Ed—that, and nothing more. Now, he was like everyone else.

The guard sized him up and then opened the door, gesturing for the other prisoners to form a line. "You made bail, son. So did the others."

Bail? "Uh, from whom?" Ed asked, plainly confused.

"Big guy. I didn't catch his name, but he bailed you out and posted bail for anyone who was with you. He's waiting outside. Get your stuff from the desk sergeant and get out."

He then motioned to the other men. "All of you, come with me. Single-file style, got it? You're out of here. We can't keep this going forever. There are bigger crimes happening."

As one, the men thanked the guard, Ed, and his mysterious benefactor, and they piled out. The other prisoners protested, but the officer yelled, "If you can't make bail, you're stuck here. Shut up and wait. You'll see the judge in the morning."

It remained to be seen whether the world would see another morning or not. Ed went to the main room. After collecting his wallet and personal belongings, he came face to face with a huge man, scars all over his mug, and a tiny grin working. "Hey, Ed," he said.

The gravelly voice was unmistakable. "Frank. I should

have known," Ed answered, feeling immense gratitude. "Thanks, but what are you doing here?"

Frank jerked his thumb at the door. "Outside. We have to talk."

It had gotten colder. A nearby clock read one-twenty-seven PM. The sky had turned a dull red, with rumbling sounds intermittently exploding into full-scale thunderclaps. Darkness was spreading rapidly across the city, and, indeed, the world.

People milled around like frightened children seeking the safety of their mother's embrace. Shouts of fear and anger combined to make the scene almost like the inmates in the pits below.

To their right, two blocks away, a loud bang sounded, much like an explosion. It wasn't the weather, though, as a thick cloud of smoke rose over a building, and the sound of an alarm went off faintly in the distance.

"Someone set off a bomb," Frank said. "This is what happens when everything goes to, well, you know."

Ed had no other choice but to agree. "You got that right."

Frank heaved a sigh of disgust. "Ordinarily, I'd be looking forward to something like this. Lucifer's been promising the apocalypse for a long time. I thought this was it. I was wrong. We all were."

"Mistakes happen," Ed replied, and then he immediately kicked himself mentally for uttering such a stupid statement.

Frank, though, didn't seem to think it was stupid. "We all make them, even our boss."."

He pointed to the sky. "And we *know* how screwed up they are up there. So, where have you been? Lucifer needs a report."

It was an honest question, and it deserved an honest answer, but Ed had another question first. "How'd you track me down?"

"The old-fashioned way," Frank replied while observing the chaotic scene dispassionately. "I asked around, asked all the police officers I could find if there was someone who fit your description. Remember, I know what you look like when you hang out with these mortals."

"I see."

Frank grunted out his response. "Pain in the ass, I'm telling you. But the big boss gave the order. I got lucky. I was walking around this precinct when you got brought in. I paid your bail and got some of the other guys you were locked up with out of there, too."

"Nice of you to do that," Ed said, brushing off his clothes.

Frank received the compliment without batting an eye, and his voice took on a new tone of urgency. "Fine, but that doesn't solve our problem. What's going on?"

"I've been busy."

That was the only excuse Ed could come up with, and he tried to keep the frustration from showing in his voice. He wasn't quite successful. "I can't teleport. I can't communicate with anyone. I have zero ability. Something's interfering with my powers. You have to find Markus."

His friend's face shone with confusion. "Markus? What's he got to do with it?"

No time to give every detail, so Ed gave him the basics. Frank's expression went from confused to incredulous and then back to confused again, and his jaw practically hit the ground. "Bud, talk sense. You were given your powers by Lucifer. What has been given can be taken away, but only by him."

"I know, but the fact remains that I can't do what you or anyone else does," Ed replied, feeling lower than low. "And I can't shift or hide my age, either. I'm . . . I'm like everyone else now."

A harsh chuckle came from his mentor. "Fate worse than non-existence, if you ask me."

A grimace made his friend's face look even uglier than it

was, and for a moment, Ed wondered what Frank had looked like in his former life. Probably the same, and then he decided that it didn't matter.

"All right, I'll pass on what you told me to the lower-downs," Frank replied, shaking his head in disbelief. "If we find Markus, then we'll lock him up." He turned to leave. "Later, if there is a later."

Ed called him back. "Tell the master that Nellie's gone, too."

Frank's eyebrows arched. "Nellie?"

"My, uh, upstairs helper. She's gone. I have to find her."

His friend shook his head. "Ed, don't get me wrong on this. I'm fond of mortals. You know, me and Mariko, right? She's cool, and she knows the score. But this—are you getting emotionally involved with a Halo?"

Was he? Ed realized that he liked Nellie, admired and respected her, but all the same, fraternization was a definite out.

"Yeah," he finally managed to get out. "Yeah, I guess I am."

Frank's eyes bulged. "Do you realize what kind of crap you're bringing on yourself?"

Ed knew. He was aware. He'd heard that Halos got sent to Hell, although that was only a rumor. In his case, he'd more than likely be erased from existence.

"I know, but I can't do this without her. I have to find her first, and then we can get the mission done. I know it. Just . . . just tell Lucifer that I'm on it. I'll get it done. I swear."

Frank's expression was grave, something Ed had never seen before. However, the way he figured it, if the world was going to end—nay, all existence—then why not be honest?

"You really like this Halo?" Frank asked with concern. "I mean, it's not like I'm for it or against it, not really, but still . . . it's kind of unusual."

"Yeah, I do."

A sigh came from the older demon. "I'll tell the master. He's put his trust in you, and so have I. Good luck."

They shook hands. Frank disappeared into the ether. And Ed was alone again in a world gone mad.

CHAPTER THIRTEEN: THE LOWER DEPTHS, PART ONE

Ed looked around, getting his bearings. People surrounded him, glancing up at the sky with fearful expressions. It was almost two PM, the sky was darker red than before, and streaks of lightning lit it up from time to time, causing a horrid ozone discharge.

A rumble from beneath the ground signaled greater seismic activity. To say that wasn't good had to be the understatement of the millennia, and Ed almost laughed at the concept.

His idea of laughter died away when yet another fight broke out between two men who looked to be in their thirties. They'd accidentally bumped into each other, and it quickly escalated from shouting to screaming epithets to a bloody brawl. More people joined in. Madness had taken hold of the populace.

"World's ending."

A voice startled him, and he turned around, only to find himself face to face with the sandwich-board man. What was he doing here?

Now, the police had arrived, and they were firing tear-gas into the crowd to try and stop the mini-riot. This . . . was not good.

Ed moved out of range, while sandwich-board man paid no attention to them. Ed felt the bum's gaze settle on him. "What are you doing here? I live uptown, and I always see you near my apartment."

With a wave of his hand that indicated something beyond extreme fatigue, the man replied, "I felt like walking. I've been doing this for fifteen years. I gave up my old life because I thought that I could do some good.

"But I'm tired. Tired of all this. Tired of the anger, the hate, the indifference, and you know something? Screw it. Everyone can take care of themselves for a change. I'm . . . I'm just tired."

With that, he shucked his board and leaned against a lamp post. He wore only filthy rags that barely covered his torso, and he looked at Ed, his eyes intense. It was almost as if his eyes had laser-vision, and Ed felt the man's stare bore deep inside him. "So, you're giving up?"

Sandwich-board man shook his head in a slow, ineffably weary gesture. "Yeah, I am, but it's not too late. Not too late for you."

A shot rang out. Almost as if time had decided to cut itself in half and give a slow-motion version of the events, something flew by Ed's shoulder and the sandwich-board guy's mouth opened like a fish that had been tossed onto dry land. He gasped, clapped his hands over his upper chest, and then he uttered a cry of pain.

Time and events slowed down even more as the shock spread throughout his body. His knees turned to jelly, and his muscles refused to function. He slid to the ground, staring at something and yet staring at nothing.

Nanoseconds later, time resumed its normal rhythm again. En-masse, the crowd stopped fighting, and they turned around, looks of shock abounding. One of their own had shot the least deserving person there, as if anyone deserved to get shot to begin with.

"Oh, hell," Ed muttered as he gently pried the man's fingers away from the damaged area. Blood leaked out of a gaping wound in his upper chest.

"Not too late," the man whispered as he slowly fell on his side and then onto his back. His eyes closed. His chest stopped moving.

Startled, Ed put his fingers to the man's neck. No pulse. He then grabbed the man's wrist. Not a beat. Sandwich-board man was dead. This was all wrong. People weren't supposed to die. Lucifer had promised. The one above had given his word, too.

"No, no, no!"

Ed began to work on the guy, doing CPR, breathing into the man's mouth, and alternating with pushing down on the guy's chest. "Please live, please live."

First-aid had never been his forte, but his frantic efforts paid off when the sandwich-board man coughed out some blood and groaned. His lips moved soundlessly, and then he whispered, "Thanks."

An ambulance's wail sounded, and Ed waited with the man until two paramedics hustled over with a gurney. "We'll take it from here," one of them said.

"Thank you," sandwich-board man repeated weakly. "Thank you."

Ed had to know. "What's your real name?"

"Hegbert Wallsnitch."

Sandwich-board man sounded better. The paramedics quickly wheeled him over to their vehicle, lifted him inside, and slammed the door. Then they took off, siren wailing.

"You're welcome, Hegbert," Ed muttered as he squatted down, wondering how much worse this day could get. Oh, wait, it could get infinitely worse.

Slowly, he rose to scan the crowd, wondering who'd fired the shot. He coughed as the tear gas hit and rubbed his eyes, squinting through the haze. A policeman had wrestled a young woman to the ground. A smoking pistol lay in front of her.

She screamed something incomprehensible and struggled as the officer attempted to cuff her. All Ed could think of was what a waste this had been . . .

"You shot him!"

Ed jerked his head around at the sound of the voice, only to find the mini-mob's eyes on him. What he saw in their eyes was insanity.

"Officer, that guy tried to kill that homeless man," one woman screeched, stabbing her finger in Ed's direction. "Get him!"

Uh-oh. It had to be another spell. Someone was controlling the crowd, directing them to think and move and act. To make matters worse, Ed had the sandwich-board guy's blood on his hands.

Time to leave, as things had gotten out of control, and Ed ran for his unlife-life. The crowd, now whipped into an irrational frenzy, gave chase along with the police.

Desperation fueling his flight in addition to adrenaline, Ed made it around the corner, first washing his hands in the snow to get rid of the blood and then hiding out in a shoe store as the mob passed him by. Five minutes passed, and he wiped sweat from his face with a shaky hand. "Hey, what are you doing in here?"

Ed whirled around. Facing him was a short, fat man with an Oliver Hardy mustache and a suit that threatened to burst open at its seams in the next few seconds.

He wore a scowl. Perhaps it was because the shop was empty, or perhaps the madness had infected him, as well. No way to know — yet.

"What are you doing in here?" he repeated. "Are you going to buy something? If you're not, leave. I'll probably get other customers, and I don't want to waste my time on someone who isn't serious."

Aggressive New Yorkers — this was known as the really

hard sale. Nowhere else would this attitude have flown, but New York was a different matter.

"Oh, uh . . . do you have something in a ten-double-E? Black. That's my color."

Sure, it was a lame-ass excuse, but Ed was wearing a suit, and despite the dirt on his face and the sting of his wounds, he still thought he looked presentable.

A glance in a nearby mirror showed he was barely above the level of a homeless person. Cuts dotted his face, which was, in turn, covered by the filth from the street. What caught him was the haunted look in his eyes, something he'd never expected to see.

Mr. Salesman sneered at him. "I'll have to check in the back. You're wearing *Regal Smart* shoes, aren't you?"

"Uh, yes, that's my brand."

"Wait a minute."

While the salesman went in the back to check out his stock, Ed glanced outside. Life seemed to have resumed its semi-normal beat, so he quietly left the store.

No one stopped him. He kept walking and turned down an alleyway, only to find two men leaning against the wall. They immediately straightened up as he passed by, but Ed realized he'd made a huge tactical mistake. There was no exit.

When he turned around and tried to leave, the men blocked the way. Neither of them said anything. They only stared at Ed as if rating him for possible danger and then dismissing it. "Uh, guys, would you mind letting me by? I'm sort of in a hurry."

"We're not," one of them said. "Stick around."

As if he had a choice? Ed didn't, and damn it all, this wasn't the time. From the expressions on their faces, cruel, almost feral, this was not going to end well. "Guys, you've seen the sky, right? Think about it."

"Red dust from China," one man said with a sneer. "We're

not responsible for that. Blame their Mr. Panda president."

Reasoning with them wasn't the way. Perhaps all they understood was violence. "Don't you think we can talk this out?"

If that didn't come as the stupidest question of the decade, Ed didn't know what was. The man closest to him, tall, bald, with flame tattoos covering his face and neck, walked over, hands in his pocket. "Talk is cheap. Money talks, bullshit walks. You've heard of that, right?"

Crap. Ed tried to back up, but he tripped over a crate and fell flat on his back. Before he could do anything, rough hands grabbed him and slammed him against the wall.

This was it, but Ed lashed out, catching flame-tattoo man in the jaw and staggering him. A moment later, his sense of triumph faded as the second man caught him with a right hook to the gut. That doubled him over, and then their attack began in earnest. Cover up, he thought, and curled into a ball.

It didn't help much, and he soon lost consciousness. Before he blacked out, though, he heard one man say, "Let's go find another victim. This one was too easy."

If the world ended, he wasn't going to miss those two.

CHAPTER FOURTEEN: THE LOWER DEPTHS, PART TWO

"Unh."

Minutes or hours later, Ed woke up, spat out a mouthful of blood, and then he tentatively felt himself all over. When he touched his face, his fingers came away smeared with blood. At least he could see, and he struggled to his feet.

His ribs hurt as did his arms and shoulders, the latter two groups having taken the brunt of the beating. Focusing proved to be a problem at first, but then his vision sharpened up as did his thought processes. "Crap, saving humanity sucks."

The words came out of him unbidden. Why wasn't he dead? Oh, wait, just like the case with Hegbert, death had taken a brief vacation, and no one would die. Demons couldn't die, as they were already dead. Same deal with angels.

Humans, though, they were a different story. Hegbert should have died from his injuries, and as Ed slowly breathed in and out and winced while doing so, he thought that his injuries would have been more severe, but no.

The rulers above and below thought they were doing humanity a favor by giving everyone an extension. What kind of favor, though, prolonging the inevitable?

In an oblique moment of self-reflection, he wondered if it was all worth it. Moreover, he wondered who was truly worthy to ascend. He'd been taking souls for a long time, and there'd never been anyone's soul that he'd taken whom he'd deemed worthy of staying on Earth.

For sure, a few people could have been considered on-the-fence cases, but in his line of work, there was no room for sentiment. His concern was taking souls, not winning friends.

"I need help."

Those three words summed up the situation, and he staggered out of the alley, only to halt suddenly as a sign the size of a school blackboard materialized out of thin air and hung a few feet above his head.

A neon sign—here—now—and what else could happen? He had no idea, so he simply stopped to get his wind back. Annoyed comments of, "Get going, buddy," and, "Move your ass," assailed him from both sides.

Obviously, they couldn't see the blood and the bruises on his face. They also couldn't see the sign. Something was preventing them from doing so, but it shone out, clear as day.

If you want to find your Halo pal, boogie on down to the Bronx. You'll find your way.

"Markus, you maggot."

Ed spat out the epithet, added a few more for good measure, and then he headed in the direction stated. He'd started from around midtown, so he estimated it would take twenty minutes or more on foot to get to his destination.

Take the subway? The nearest entrance to one had a mob fighting in front of it. Good luck in getting by them.

People stared at him as he walked along the street. In spite of the bad weather, many of them had decided to brave the elements and the upheavals in the earth.

"Nowhere is safe," he muttered.

A few people glanced in his direction, but then they looked away. Just another New York crazy. Time of the year and all that. Not their problem, and Ed was grateful for the anonymity.

He quickened his pace, and thirty minutes later, he ended

up near One-Twenty-Fifth and Shore, and another sign greeted him.

You made good time. You're getting warmer. This is mainly a Hispanic neighborhood, so go to the El Gato Bar and Grill, on Eugene Avenue. You'll get more information there.

"Markus, since you're listening, you're beyond jerkism."

This was getting tiresome, but Ed knew that he had no choice. He followed directions and eventually arrived in the heart of a Latino neighborhood.

Spanish signs over small, neatly kept bodegas and shops identified the area, and as he ventured along, pretty little houses, old, but neatly kept, supplanted the shops.

But the outward appearance belied inner turmoil, and it manifested itself by the nervous looks of everyone. A man, forty-ish, short, with close-cropped hair, who wore a skintight long-sleeved muscle shirt even though it was terribly cold, was in the process of berating a woman.

In a fury about something, he kept screaming at the woman who stood in front of him, tears running down his face. He looked up, his expression fierce. "You want something, punk? Get lost."

Whatever. Ed was a little pissed off, but fighting now would solve nothing. When he'd been invulnerable, he would have had no hesitation about ripping this man's head off.

Not now. Ed began stepping lively but soon crossed the street as a gang headed in his direction. Most of them were armed. In spite of the weather, they had their jackets open to reveal pistols tucked into their pants.

Getting shot wasn't part of the equation. He took off down an alleyway and hid behind a dumpster while observing the goings-on.

One man pulled out a pistol, showing it off to his friend and speaking with a grim purpose. "All I'm sayin' is, if someone messes with me, they get a popper in their head, y'got me on this? I took out Rodrigo before, so I ain't afraid of doin' what's gotta be done."

"Sure, Luis," his buddy replied hastily, as if unsure if he was next in line for a bullet. "I get it, but ain't no one robbing us, not today."

He looked nervously up at the sky, practically quivering in his boots. "I ain't religious, man, but it's like friggin' Judgment Day. You know what I'm saying?"

Luis glanced up and then tossed a sneer at his friend. "Don't be dumb, man. Just dust from China. That's what the news shows are sayin'. C'mon."

He and the rest of the gang faded out of sight, and Ed breathed a sigh of relief. Maybe Markus would show up, and they could settle it once and for all . . .

"It's the end of the world."

The voice came from behind him. Ed pivoted around and found a middle-aged priest sitting between two discarded crates. He had a bottle of scotch in his lap, and his brown eyes looked quite mad.

"What are you doing here?" Ed asked.

The priest held up the bottle. "Father Miguel Rodriguez, at your service. I used to be of service here in the St. Michael's Church, but why bother?"

Ed had no snappy comeback to that question, save, "Isn't it your job to, uh, help people?"

Father Rodriguez shook his head and repeated, "It's the end of the world. I haven't had a drink in twenty years, but now, why not? The gangs can't be controlled. The people are trying to kill each other or will try to kill each other, so have one on me."

He proffered the bottle. Ed, angry at this man's indifference, shoved it away. "No. What's wrong with you? You're supposed to help people because it's your job, and because those people out there need you."

A hoarse chuckle came his way, followed by a series of

non-sequiturs and a huge belch. "They don't need me," he rambled. "They need . . . need someone who can minister to them. That's not me."

The priest continued to mumble, and then he drained the bottle. "That was worth it!"

A flick of his wrist sent the bottle against the wall where it shattered. Rodriguez hiccupped and made the observation that getting wasted was probably the best way to go into the next life.

After that, he passed out. "Waste of space," Ed grumbled, but an idea popped into his head. Yeah, this would work.

Working quickly, he stripped off the priest's cassock. The man wasn't wearing much underneath, so Ed switched clothes with the priest, not forgetting to take his own wallet and cash with him. Fortunately, he and the priest shared similar builds, so the priestly garb fit him well enough.

Ed walked out of the alleyway and over to the man who was still shouting at the woman. The man turned on him, saying, "What you want, huh, padre? I got nuthin' for you."

"This isn't the time for strife and anger, sir," Ed replied after furiously searching for the proper words. What would a priest say in a situation like this? Then it came to him—speak the truth. "These days are dark, yes, but you must have . . . er, faith, to overcome. And you shouldn't abuse your wife."

The man stared at him. "You were just here before, wearing a suit. What is this crap?"

"I had to get changed. This is what I usually wear." Ed uttered those words as smoothly as possible and hoped they'd be convincing. Getting beaten up again wasn't part of the equation.

Mr. Tough Guy's eyes narrowed. "Job or not, you're pretty young to be a priest. You look like you just got out of high school detention. You also look like you went a few rounds with someone."

"I got caught by a gang, sir," Ed replied, thinking fast. "It's like they think nothing matters anymore. People everywhere, they have the same mindset. This is no time for negativity."

The man spat on the ground and rolled his shoulders as if he was aching for a fight to release the rage that roiled inside him. "Maybe it don't matter. And since it don't, why shouldn't I or one of my homies up ahead rip your head off?"

He took a step forward, fists bunched. Ed, more unnerved and heart beating fast but steadfast in his quest to find Nellie, stood his ground. "You could. I probably wouldn't stand a chance. But don't fight me. Fight what's inside you. You got hate. Let it go."

His semi-well-being hung in the balance as the man took another step toward him with murder in his eyes. "Call me an abuser," he growled. "Call me a scumbag, tell me what to do?"

One second later, he stopped, his lips moving but no sounds coming out, and he stared at his hands. An expression of remorse crossed his face as reason crept in. "You're right, padre. I'm sorry. I don't know . . . this cold, the sky . . . guess I'm just scared."

It was understandable. People always feared what they couldn't comprehend. "Don't take it out on your wife, sir. If these are the end times, take her home. Be with her."

Corny though those lines were, Ed didn't feel as embarrassed as he had earlier on when he'd stopped Dirk from robbing the electronics store. The man turned away, crying now, and he put his arms around his wife, whispering, "Forgive me."

Job done, Ed hustled over to the nearest alley to breathe deeply. At the end of the alley, though, another sign hung in the air. *Very clever! But you're not done yet. Manhole cover ahead. Take it off. You'll find out where to go from there.*

With no other course, Ed did as the sign instructed. He'd descended into the depths before, but that was as a demon, and those depths were far worse.

His mission was different now. At the manhole, he looked around. No one was in the immediate vicinity, as the area had been blocked off by orange cones and small metal fences. The workmen must have taken a break.

Ed tugged on the heavy cover and finally managed to get it off. A horrible smell came from below, one of feces, ammonia, and worse, and he descended the ladder quickly.

At the bottom, he found himself on a ledge. Another sign materialized, glowing a brilliant white. *Go straight ahead. You'll see a construction sign.* Abandoned 47th Street Subway Tunnel. *Follow it. That was a tunnel the city started in the nineteen-thirties. They stopped building it about sixty years ago.*

Angered by the BS, Ed set off, loosening his collar as the heat built. He walked on rusted subway tracks. A squeak off to his right made him look around. A beady-eyed rat stared at him with a baleful glare, its red eyes winking in the semi-darkness.

Ed kept going, careful to step only where he was supposed to, although a number of rats, mice, and roaches dotted the area, running this way and that, all in the search of a meal. They were in their milieu. He wasn't.

A few stray cats and dogs huddled together, trying to stay out of the way of the roaches. They spat and yelped as the roaches swarmed them, and then took off in the opposite direction, trying to shake their mini but numerous opponents from their fur.

As Ed walked along, he checked his surroundings carefully, especially the ledges, which were about six feet up. People lived there, he figured, and perhaps they wouldn't think twice about jumping off them onto some unlikely victim.

Yellow lights had been strung overhead about ten feet apart, sending out a sickly glow upon the ground. They also illuminated movement on the ledges overhead.

People—but the average citizen had another name for them—skells. Denizens of the underworld. Those who'd been marginalized and ignored and shunned. Those who had mental illnesses or physical infirmities. Those who'd given up on life.

"Nellie?"

While it wasn't wise to call out, he had no choice. Markus had kidnapped her, and maybe she'd yell for help. That would be his signal.

Sounds of shuffling feet. Smells of body odor, rotting food, piss, and shit, and more. Murmurs. Mutterings. The scrape of metal upon wood or concrete. The sounds of feet moving and the grunts that accompanied them. All those sounds and smells got louder and more redolent with every step he took.

"Welcome committee's forming," he muttered. "Might as well get ready."

Ed steeled himself and pressed on. As he ventured further along the tunnel, the lights grew fewer and fewer overhead. Three hundred feet ahead, he came to a junction. Another sign popped up. *Turn right. You're almost there.*

After making the obligatory right turn, another sign appeared that gave the direction to go down two more levels. Ed proceeded with caution, and once he reached his destination, he realized that he'd reached a pit of filth.

Filth didn't really describe it. Mounds of garbage were everywhere, piled high at the sides of the tunnel. The sheer amount of refuse staggered him. Worse, the smell of bodies and waste and more was incredible to the point of suffocation.

Finally, a blinking red, neon sign directed him to walk straight ahead in the gloom. A couple of light bulbs barely illuminated the area, and he stumbled twice before a voice called out, "Stop right there."

Ed halted. Three skells, tall men with gaunt faces obscured by months if not years of filth and grime, stared at him. They wore rags covered in equally torn-up overcoats and ripped-up work boots.

"What you doin' down here, Father?" one of them asked, squinting mightily. "Ain't no churches here, you know? And there ain't any worshippers here, that's for sure. Sure you're in the right place?"

"Looking for a woman."

Ed immediately cursed himself for not thinking things through. Phrasing his quest in that fashion hadn't been the brightest idea around. "I mean, I'm searching for a woman. She was wearing a white blouse and skirt, has blonde hair and green eyes. She's a member of . . . my flock."

The trio looked at each other, and the lead man spoke, his voice gruff and menacing. "Your flock? Father, I been down here a long time, but I never seen no priest your age around here—or any priest. In case you ain't noticed, this is the next rung down to Hell."

Foolish—this man was on the other side of foolish. He had no idea of what Hell really and truly was, but Ed didn't have time to explain the ins and outs of the true lower depths. It was time to post forth a little white lie.

"I'm, uh, I've recently joined the priesthood."

One of the men had moved off to his right. Another man sidled over to his left, while the third stayed to stare him down. Peace wasn't part of their mindset. Ed knew it, and he settled into a fighting stance, just in case things got ugly.

They soon did. Skell number two, totally bald and with dirt-brown eyes that matched his skin and clothes, leaned forward. "You got any money, Father? Seems that a man of the cloth might have some extra cash for us unfortunates. You all take a vow of poverty, don'tcha?"

His eyes shone, and Ed tensed, ready for action. "Son, don't make this harder for me. I don't want to fight you. I'm just trying to find my friend and leave here. That's all."

Apparently, it wasn't enough, as the three men rushed him from all sides. Then the beating began, kicks and punches and curses. "Give it up, padre," they mocked him as they threw every possible combo at him in the book.

"No," Ed replied. "I can't."

Every bone in his body hurt, every muscle fiber was on fire, and every nerve ending felt like it was about to be severed. Oh, wait, there'd be no death today. It was taking a holiday.

Even so, he felt like he was going to die. This beating was far worse than the kicking he'd taken up top. Rough hands tore his clothes, thick fingers probed his pockets, and the smell of their breath and bodies was truly vile.

Even though he'd managed to land a few shots of his own, it wasn't enough, and the trio of skells beat him into the ground. Ed lay there and took it, feeling each and every stomp, kick, and punch on every single part of his being and in every fiber.

Wasn't that what the son of God had taken, being beaten within an inch of his life, or so the legends said? Ed wasn't sure, but if that did happen, then he could relate to it, big-time.

Finally, one of the men said, "That's enough. We got his money and his watch. Let's go."

Laughter, long and loud, and yells of triumph erupted from them. Their footsteps faded into the distance. Ed groaned and tried to move. It hurt worse than the beating had.

Something lay ahead of him. It was his wallet. One of the skells must have dropped it. With an effort, Ed reached out, every nerve ending in agony, and he closed his hand around the wallet. It was the only thing he had right now that gave him a sense of who he was.

After that, he passed out.

Chapter Fifteen: Willie

M inutes or hours later, Ed woke in severe pain—again— groaned, and then he coughed and choked on the blood that flooded his mouth and nasal passages.

It astonished him to find out how much blood he had in him. Could the human body carry this much? Apparently so, and it was a miracle how much a person could lose and still live.

With an effort, he staggered to his feet, coughing and spitting out blood and mucus, breathing deeply, and trying not to vomit from the pain that racked his body.

Still, after an impromptu self-examination, he found no broken bones, but he felt like one large hematoma, and he didn't want to see what his face looked like.

"Yeah, I got it already. I can't die. Crap. Thanks, Lucifer."

After heaving in a few deep breaths and feeling his ribs protest, he set off down the passage. If he ever met Markus again, he'd make him pay for this.

The tunnel seemed never-ending. Ed kept trudging along, wincing with every step, but he did his best to keep his sounds of pain muffled and avoided the skells by hiding in the shadows whenever the sound of footsteps drew near.

When he'd been immortal, he'd also been immune to pain, sickness, dirt, and more. Now, he'd become like everyone else, subject to injury and disease. Being mortal sucked, and he hated it.

A moment later, he took back that thought. Hate was too strong a word. As he inched along, doing his best not to slip and fall face down—for if he did, he probably wouldn't be able to get up—he searched for a word that could adequately describe his feelings.

"Hate? No, too strong. Loathe? No, that won't work, either," he mumbled as he covered more ground.

Then the word dislike popped into his head. Yes, that was it. He disliked this situation intensely. That sounded better, relatively speaking.

"Aw, crap."

His shoes, three-hundred-dollar custom-made specials, flopped around—the heels had worn away. He felt dirt seep in, covering his feet and ruining the leather.

This was no life for a demon, yet, he'd been chosen, and he also had to find Nellie. Find her, get her back. He . . . he cared for her, he realized, and that spark of humanity carried him along.

His nose hairs wilted the deeper he went, and his eyes watered from the ammonia in the air. With a sense of wonder, he couldn't fathom how other mortals could put up with the squalor. Then he realized that many of them had been victims of circumstance, and they weren't down here by choice.

"Hey."

A voice interrupted his musings. He looked up to find a man of indeterminate age sitting on the ledge, wrapped in rags.

Incredibly fat—obese, in fact, a rarity here considering the lack of food—he had short, ratty-looking hair, a round face covered in grime with scabs on his cheeks, and a lost air about him. It was the attitude of someone who'd given up on life.

A distinct aroma of cheap wine and body odor emanated from him. He didn't move, though. In spite of his previous experience, Ed felt no fear from this person.

"What is it?"

"Spare some change?"

Ed dug into his pockets. The skells hadn't taken everything. He took his hand out, holding his last few dollars, and handed it over. The man gratefully accepted it with a sincere, "Thank you," as a comment.

"You're welcome. Uh, do you know where this passage goes?"

A fearful expression crossed the man's face. "It ends somewhere around Times Square. Don't go there. I wouldn't if I was you."

"Why not?"

The man picked at the scabs on his face. "Lots of bad people hang out. They're permanent undergrounders, you know?"

"I met them a while ago."

"Hmm." The skell looked more closely at him, peering through rheumy eyes. "Don't take this the wrong way, but you look like hell."

Ed stifled the urge to laugh. This man didn't know how close he was to the truth. "That bad, huh?"

"Yeah. Like a truck ran over you a few hundred times. That's what I meant 'bout not going near them. They been down here a long time. I don't go near them. I go up top sometimes, usually at night, get what I need from the dumpsters. Then I come back here again.

"The others . . . they do bad things, like . . . I hear they eat people, you know?"

Since Ed had already experienced the worst of humanity — so far — he didn't think people could go any lower.

But, according to this man, they could. Cannibalism — had North American society come to that? It should have horrified him, but he'd seen much worse. "I'll be careful, thanks. Er, how long have you been here?"

The skell ticked off the years on his fingers. Five — he'd been here for five years.

"Up top is too hard?"

"It's hell."

Uh-huh, tell me something I don't know. "Thanks."

As he tramped along, he thought about the man he'd met. A name whispered to him from the recesses of his mind — Willie. Willie Starling. It had been ten years since he'd taken that man's soul, and now the memory came back to him, live and in Technicolor . . .

Fat Willie — that was Ed's target, and he seemed the kind of person who was easy pickings. He sat in a bar, grousing and grumping about life. The bar picked up where his life left off after he finished his shifts on the docks of New York.

Greasy's Bar & Eatery — the establishment's name, and it got its name from the fact that it was owned by a man named Bob Grisanis and due to another unfortunate fact. It was incredibly filthy, with a thin film of grease on everything from the floor to the tables to the windows.

That didn't stop the patrons from entering. It happened to be right next to the loading docks where all the ships came in and went out of the harbor after unloading their cargo, and there were always those with a thirst for a quick drink or six.

It also served a variety of burgers, fries, hotdogs, and sweets, all guaranteed to clog up a person's arteries. Grisanis had been in business a long time, and Starling happened to be one of his best customers.

At five-thirty PM sharp, Ed found his target sitting at the counter, getting tanked. No one else had shown up, save Grisanis, the owner of the establishment. He was a wizened, older man in his sixties who walked with a limp, courtesy of a stroke five years earlier.

Despite his infirmity, he moved about in a quick, economical motion, serving Willie his drinks and then mumbling something about going to the can. He disappeared into a back room. That was when Ed made his move.

Starling was a short, obese man in his forties, with a thinning hairline and a torso that had seen better days two-hundred pounds ago. If he'd been thinner and had more hair, he would have been somewhat attractive to look at.

Not now. Apparently, Willie wasn't into self-care. With the food he had on a plate beside him—greasy fries smothered in ketchup along with three donuts, he was a heart attack waiting to happen.

He was also a heavy smoker and got drunk on a daily basis. Five empty shot glasses that had previously held whiskey proved that. Willie was primed and ready, but the rules were explicit. Anyone who offered their soul had to be of sound mind. Drinking impaired judgment, and the overlord was all for keeping the rules—and then breaking them, if necessary, once the contract was signed.

This wasn't one of those times. When Grisanis came back, Ed ordered two cups of black coffee and slid one Willie's way. "Drink up, friend."

Starling glanced at him through bleary eyes. "Friend? Who the hell are you?"

Grisanis echoed the question, and Ed stared hard at him. "Don't you have something to do?"

Immediately, the older man's eyes glazed over. "Yeah, I guess so."

"Go into your stock room and count the boxes."

Grisanis did as he was told. This wasn't a case of mind control, for demons didn't have that ability. It was more like how Ed intoned those words, and Grisanis wasn't the type to argue things.

Willie and Ed were alone. Ed had shifted into the guise of a man in his mid-thirties, dressed in a pair of jeans, rough work boots, and a flannel shirt. Who cared if it was mid-summer?

Willie eyed him curiously, half out of his drunken stupor. "Some trick you did."

"He's an annoyance, is all," Ed replied.

The fat man nodded. "Yeah, he's like that at times. So, who the hell are you, really?"

When asked a question about what he really did, Ed couldn't lie. He could, however, embellish the truth a little. "Let's just say that I'm a facilitator of sorts. Are your union dues paid up?"

Apparently, Starling believed the story, for he grunted out his answer with extreme displeasure. "Yeah. They take their cut. You here to ask for more?"

"Nope. I'm here to ask you what you want."

Willie's jaw dropped, and then he belched out a laugh. "What I want? What I want is to get promoted."

Call that the opening Ed had been looking for, and with a fair amount of élan, he laid out his idea for getting Willie what he desired most. The fat man's fondest wish was to become foreman. It offered a better salary, fewer hours, and the pension was to die for.

It was music to Ed's ears. Chances were that Willie would kick off in a year or so, but that could wait. The deal came first. While said target was drinking his coffee, Ed let it slip that everything could be arranged — for a price.

"And what's your cut?"

Willie's question was standard, and the rules said that they had to be answered honestly. "Your soul. In exchange, you get the foreman's job for as long as you want it, but there are conditions."

At first, when the subject of selling one's soul arose, potential customers always laughed. They thought they were dealing with a nutcase, although a very polite one. It was at that point where the mark would either say, *"Tell me more,"* or, *"Get lost."*

Willie chose the former response after laughing, and then

his beady eyes turned crafty. "All right, say you're on the level. I wanna know about the conditions."

Ed answered promptly. "Be on time, don't call in sick unless you're truly sick, and don't abuse your position of authority. Simple."

The fat man's eyes shifted. "What if there's a snowstorm or I have an accident, and I can't come in?"

At this point, Ed allowed himself to smile. He was oh-so-close to achieving another entry in his logbook. "The contract allows for that," he said smoothly. "You can't foresee catching the flu, and you can't control the weather, so we let that go."

Far from being reticent, Willie asked, "What do I have to do?"

"The old pricking thing."

Ed produced a handkerchief and his ballpoint pen. "Put your thumb out."

Hesitantly, Willie did so, but just before the sharp end went in, Ed asked, "You're sure?"

"Yeah."

Now, he had him, and his target was ready to be signed and sealed. In a quick movement, Ed jabbed the tip of the pen into Willie's thumb, and a bead of blood dropped onto the handkerchief. "Your initials will do. Here, please." He pointed at the spot.

Willie signed his John Hancock on the cloth, and the deal was concluded. He then sat back with a huff of disappointment. "I don't feel no different. What happens?"

"You go home," Ed said as he stowed the handkerchief away and then entered Willie's name in his logbook. "Tomorrow, you'll be the foreman. Guaranteed, but remember our deal."

Willie smiled, revealing rotten teeth. "Friend, you don't know how happy you've made me!"

"Likewise."

Ed excused himself, walked out of the bar, and then he teleported back to Manhattan. Job over, he treated himself to a gourmet meal at a local French café.

Everything went well at first. Ed checked in on Willie from time to time, and, surprisingly, in the first half-year, the fat man proved himself a most capable administrator. He played no favorites, he treated everyone with respect, and, sick or not, he came in and did his job. That earned him the respect of everyone who worked under him, as well as those who outranked him.

But mortals were flawed. Ed knew that. Moreover, he counted on that. Flaws made people what they were, and a major flaw in Willie's character was consistency.

Slowly, over time—mainly a period of nine months after the first half-year period had elapsed—Willie began drinking more, missing days, and acting like the slob that he had been.

Ed waited, giving him time to clean up his act, and while he felt that he should have stepped in earlier, deep down, he hoped that Willie would have lasted on the straight and narrow path a little longer.

He didn't, and after a week-long bender, Lucifer called Ed in for a little confab in the boardroom, just the two of them. The other disciples were busy doing what they did best.

Lucifer summoned up a cigar and spoke while puffing on it contentedly. "Ed, I've found out that one of your people, that reprobate, Willie Starling, is out of control. He's abrogated the agreement. You know that, and you know what you have to do."

"No more time?"

Lucifer tossed his cigar in the air. It disappeared, and he eyed Ed carefully. "Ed, if I didn't know any better, I'd say you were getting soft."

"I'm not!"

Ed's answer came out quickly, as well as defensively. He

realized it, and in the depths of his being, he knew his very existence was on the line. The master did not tolerate weakness.

"Sorry, sire. I'll deliver him at once."

Lucifer offered a fatherly smile. It came off as a grimace combined with a snarl, but it was a smile, nonetheless. "I'll be waiting for your report."

Before he left, he leaned over to whisper something in Ed's ear. Then he straightened up. "Depart. Thou art sent."

A moment later, Ed found himself outside Willie's house in Palumbo, New Jersey. It was a cool day, and the sky was overcast.

It was a lower-middle-class neighborhood, but even though there were potholes in the streets, the houses were neatly kept, with wrought-iron fences and tiny but abundantly flowered gardens.

All except one — Willie's place. Empty liquor bottles and beer cans littered the front lawn, and once Ed pushed the gate open — its hinges squeaked — he smelled something coming from the house.

The door was unlocked. Inclement weather or not, Ed walked in and found Willie sitting in a threadbare chair in the living room, chugging from a beer can. He wore only a pair of boxer shorts.

A horrid stink of body odor, stale beer, rotting food, and other unmentionables permeated the atmosphere. Ed cracked a window to air out the room and then closed it. It didn't matter anymore.

Ordinarily, seeing mortals at their worst wouldn't have bothered Ed at all. The smells down below could make even demons ill. All the same, though, for someone to let themselves go as this person had . . . it was a little too much to take in at first.

He turned to eye the hulk lounging in his chair. "Willie,

what's going on?"

The fat man gazed at him through half-closed, bloodshot eyes. At first, there was no recognition, and then he blinked. "Hey, it's my old bud . . . y'know, I never got your name."

"I never gave it. Willie . . . what happened?"

Starling sighed, a sad, lost, and lonely sound, one filled with self-pity. "I guess I couldn't take the pressure of being someone on top. I thought I wanted it. I was pretty good, you hear?"

Inebriated state or not, his voice grew impassioned, and he pounded his chest. "I was good, but it got to me, makin' decisions and bossing people around. Couldn't take it, so I went back to drinking."

He finished off the can, crumpled it up, and then he tossed it away. Despite his ruined condition, he focused his gaze on Ed and blinked as though he remembered who his visitor was and why he'd come. A look of fear flickered in his eyes, and then it transitioned into something akin to respect. "So, are you here to collect?"

Straight up and out with it—that was Willie—and the very directness of the question unnerved Ed. For the first time in his unlife, he experienced a sense of remorse, although initially, he wasn't sure if it was that or something else. It felt as if something had been taken from him, and he didn't know how to deal with it.

However, he reminded himself that if he didn't do what had to be done, someone else would, and they wouldn't be half as gentle. "I guess I am."

"I . . . I messed things up good, didn't I?"

"Are you going to ask for an extension, Willie? If you are, then you know the answer."

Willie shrugged. "No, guess not."

Ed bowed his head. He really didn't want to do what he'd been instructed to do, but he picked his head up to say, "I have to tell you, you managed to pull things off for a long time. That's something, more than a lot of others could do."

Willie gave him a faint nod. Unlike so many others who'd been forced to give up their souls, the fat man didn't bother asking for an extension. For that, Ed's respect for him went up a few notches.

With the others, respect had never figured into things. They'd pleaded, they'd wept, they'd gotten on their knees and begged for more time, but it was a fruitless effort on their part. They went to the afterlife anyway, still screaming and in horrible pain.

Pain was something they'd have experienced no matter what they did, but their behavior on Earth made it seem worse, somehow. Not Willie. Suddenly sober, he sat back, arms spread wide. "I just got one question. Is it gonna hurt?"

Ed wondered if he should tell him the truth. The way he'd heard it, if the prey was in pain, then a little more wouldn't matter. If they were dying, then the soul-taking would come as a cold shock.

On the other hand, if they fought to keep their souls, then, as Frank once put it, things got ugly. He was about as insensitive as a demon could get, but when he and Ed discussed it once, even Frank admitted to feeling uneasy.

"I had this man once, about eighty years ago. He wouldn't give up. I pulled his soul out of him, but he fought back. Mental battle, you understand? It came out of him, a gray essence, and then he managed to suck it inside him again. And all that time, he was screaming, "No, no, I won't go, I won't."

Frank's voice grew hushed. *"His skin turned black, and he started to rot. His teeth and hair fell out, and he kept screaming.*

"Finally, I gave a yank, and he was gone, a lifeless husk. I think he's in the river of blood. Haven't looked. Not interested."

Willie repeated the question, and Ed, knowing that he was compelled to tell the truth in this matter, softened his answer. "Yes, Willie, it'll hurt, but only if you struggle. Just relax, and

I'll make it quick. I promise."

The fat man extended his hand. "Gimme your word on that."

Shaking hands usually didn't happen in cases like this, but Ed did as his mark requested. It seemed the right thing to do. Willie sat back and closed his eyes. "Okay, I'm ready."

Not saying a word, Ed morphed his hand into an ethereal claw, reached into Willie's chest, and proceeded to pull out his soul. A faint gray color, it had no shape, and it pulsed ever so slightly. If Willie was going to go downstairs, then Ed would have put the soul into his pocket.

However, this time, just before he left for Earth, Lucifer had given him one last order. "I don't want that man's soul. He was a lazy bastard on Earth. I don't like slackers here."

Limbo. Willie certainly didn't deserve to go upstairs, but he also didn't merit going downstairs, either. In a rare case of apathy — or mercy, and Ed didn't know for sure, and he never asked — Lucifer had given another potential Hell-inductee a way out.

Ed blew on the soul, and it drifted away in the wind. It would enter the netherworld of Limbo, and it would remain there for all eternity unless the head guy from upstairs decided otherwise.

Willie's eyes had snapped open from the shock. In a final act of what could only be termed decency, Ed closed them. "Goodbye, Willie. Neither of us got what we wanted, but maybe you'll be better off."

With that, he teleported back to Hell, delivered his report, and then he went home and sat in his apartment and didn't take a soul for the next five days . . .

Now, as he made his way along the seemingly endless tunnel, Ed tried to figure out what Markus' endgame was. His opponent was incredibly clever. He'd kidnapped Nellie. It was a smart move, guaranteed to slow down Ed's mission.

A sense of something he couldn't identify filled Ed and made him rage, and he realized it was righteousness. It was a totally new feeling for him.

With that sense of his mission being a righteous one, Ed made one more promise to himself—he'd find Markus, and make him pay. But first, he had to track him down, and only the thought of getting Nellie, his only friend, back, made him trudge onwards.

It would only be a matter of time before he did find them both, but time was fast running out.

Chapter Sixteen: "Would You Die for Her?"

Ed followed the passage that wended its way in a gentle curve left and then right. It seemed to stretch on for an eternity. New York had an incredibly vast underground network, and he wondered how far down things went.

Then he reminded himself where he'd been existing on and off for the past . . . he didn't know how many decades. It was infinitely deeper than this subway system, though.

The stink was ever-present, and it seemed to grow stronger with each step he took. Rats and cockroaches, along with other insects he couldn't classify, scurried underfoot.

Along the way, he met two more skells who sat on the ledge, and they looked far worse than the man he'd run into previously.

"Hey, Father, what're you doing down here?" one of them asked. A man, perhaps in his forties—it was hard to tell—called out the question. Although this area was fairly warm, he shivered in a ratty old coat.

Rags covered his wraith-like body. Scabs on his face, a tangled gray beard, pale, filthy skin—they were all signs that indicated he'd given up on personal hygiene and life in general, long ago.

His partner was a woman. It was impossible to figure out how old she was, though. She might have been thirty or sixty. "Leave him alone, Don," she said in a raspy voice and stared at Ed through myopic blue eyes. "You're lookin' for someone, am I right?"

"Uh, yes, ma'am," he replied. "I'm Father . . . Rodriguez. I'm looking for a friend."

The woman leaned forward to get a better look. "What happened to your face? You look like someone stepped on it and then shoved it through a meat grinder."

She wasn't so far off the mark. "I, uh, had a little altercation," Ed decided to say. "A couple of punks, er, bad people up top, and a few of the people here decided to use me for target practice."

The woman chuckled. Her chuckle soon turned into a hoarse, wracking cough. She twisted away to spit out a lungful of mucus, wiped her mouth with a filthy hand, and muttered something about bad air and rotten lungs.

After she recovered her breath, she said, "You said you were looking for someone."

"Yes, ma'am," Ed replied. "A woman. She's young, pretty, she was wearing a white skirt and —"

"They went down that way," Don interrupted and pointed the way. "Yeah, I seen the lady. Real pretty, too. She was with another guy, havin' some make-out time."

The woman smacked him on the arm, and he winced. "Don, can't you see that this young man is trying to help her out? He's a priest. He's doin' God's work."

"Yeah, Sally, I see," he said peevishly. "I can see. I may be a loser, but I can see. Pretty young to be wearin' a priest's clothes, but whatever. Yeah."

Ed took a breath and coughed. The air down here was indeed, foul, and it surprised and saddened him that being mortal — or something close to it — made him vulnerable to just about everything humans could possibly suffer from.

"How long have you been down here?" he asked.

The woman stuck her finger in her mouth to fish around for something. Not finding her target, she withdrew her finger and smacked her lips. Only a few teeth hung crookedly in swollen gums. "Over six years for me. I was . . . working outside. Decided I didn't want to."

"Selling your booty, you mean," Don said, chuckling quietly.

His laughter stopped when she punched him in the throat. He gagged and fell on his side, coughing and sucking in wind through a bruised windpipe. "Sorry," he croaked.

Sally's eyes threw laser beams and daggers at him. "You watch your mouth! I live down here with you, but you don't got no right to talk to me that way. Understand me?"

Don nodded. "Sorry," he whispered. "Didn't mean nothing by it. Just tellin' the truth."

"Keep the truth to yourself."

For emphasis, she smacked him on the shoulder, and he shied away, repeating his apology.

Sally then turned to Ed, an apologetic look working. "Yeah, I sold my ass. Pardon the language, Father. I sold my butt. I ain't proud of it, but I did.

"Did it a lot, too, got into booze . . . ended up in this place. At least I'm clean here. Dirty as a pig, but I don't drink anymore, and no STDs, either."

It was an honest admission, and it made Ed feel sorry for her, although he had the feeling that she wasn't sorry for what she'd done.

Then he realized that if anyone had no right to judge, it was him. As someone who'd taken essences of life and, in a sense, immortality, from others, he had too many strikes against him. A tiny epiphany occurred—that being a person meant one had to accept others at face value and not rate them right or wrong due to what they'd done in the past.

In a world gone to pot long before this existence-ending scenario had come to pass, people had to survive, and selling one's flesh was only one way of many.

Considering how many times he'd gotten the souls of politicians who'd lied, raped, stolen, and used the law the cover up their dirty deeds, selling one's body ranked far down the list of evil things to do, and, really, it wasn't evil. For many, it was all about survival.

Nellie had done the same thing. Only in her case, illness claimed her before she could sink into disease and age and the ravages of being homeless.

Perhaps Sally would find it in herself to clean up her act — if someone else gave her a chance and there was still a world left tomorrow.

Don was still sucking wind. He sat up with a groan and squidged his butt a few feet away from his lady friend. "We don't always live here. Not like we own the place, right? We move around, go up top sometimes to get food. Dumpsters are usually full first thing in the morning. You want something to eat?"

He rooted around in the junk beside him and came away with a half-eaten sandwich. Ed declined, with thanks. "I, uh, really have to get going. Do you two need anything?"

Sally started laughing. "Do we need anything," she repeated, her laugh trailing away to a wracking cough. Once she regained her breath, she added, "Yeah, food, medicine, a job . . . oh, and protection from everyone else who wants to take what we got."

Another humorless laugh emanated from her skinny belly, and a note of true despair sounded in her next few words. "We're so low, we can't go no lower."

Oh, yes, there's always a place lower than this. Ed knew that for a fact, but he said nothing. His wind had come back. "I have to find my friend. Uh, take care."

Don waved goodbye. "Watch your backside, Father. That white-faced guy, he weren't so friendly."

No, he isn't, Ed thought. "I'll be careful."

He left them, then, and continued his journey. The passage got narrower, and then it opened suddenly to a larger space. This had once been a station, but it had been abandoned. Only one person was there — Nellie.

Ed started forward, but she spotted him and frantically waved her arms. "Ed, look out!"

"What?"

Too late, as something heavy crashed down on the side of his head, stunning him. The attacker hit him once again, and Ed saw the obligatory flashing lights before falling into a well of darkness.

"Wake up," a voice said.

Ed heard the voice, groaned, and then he opened his eyes. He tried to move but found he'd been tied up, hands behind him. He lay on his side, his head awash in pain and his vision, blurred.

"Wake up," the voice repeated. It was coming from two feet away, straight ahead.

Ed's vision sharpened up, and he focused on the figure in front of him. It was Markus. The senior demon stood with his arms crossed over his chest.

Behind him, Nellie sat, also bound and gagged for good measure. She struggled against her bonds, but she'd been bound tightly and wasn't going anywhere.

Markus snapped his fingers for attention. "I'm surprised you found us, Ed. You're a better tracker than I thought — even if you are wearing those ridiculous rags. Change them."

Ed's head was splitting with pain. "You know I can't."

A laugh greeted him. "Oh, yes, that's right. I'd tell you how I did it — a temporary spell that inhibits your powers as well as your lady friend's powers — but that's not very interesting. Still, you found me, even though you're mortal now."

"You left signs."

Markus chortled. "I thought it was a nice touch. Neon always stands out. I worked it so only you and your Halo girl could see it. Ordinary mortals — it's beyond them."

He squatted down to eye level with Ed and pulled on his collar to haul him up and prop him against a nearby pillar. "That's better."

What could anyone say in this situation? Ed went for the obvious. "All right, you got us. What do you want?"

Markus' expression was that of the cat that ate the canary — one of satisfaction. "I want . . . a lot of things," he said after a moment of deliberation. "Things that are best left unsaid for the moment. The question is, what do you want?"

Ed, now truly pissed off, yelled, "Cut the crap! You've got me and my friend tied up, so tell me."

With a half-smile, his foe stepped back and paced back and forth. This was a moment of control, and Markus had a smug look of certainty and knowledge written all over his face. He assumed the manner of a university professor imparting knowledge to a group of rapt first-year students.

"Our story begins over two thousand years ago, in a land of sand and scorpions and heat and misery. A man was born and grew up and became a shepherd, and then . . . then he found religion. For his beliefs, he was nailed to a cross. You know who I'm talking about, don't you?"

Naturally, Ed knew, but he said nothing. Pain consumed him, as well as worry for his partner.

Markus smiled. "I'm going to assume your silence means you understand. All right, so that man, the son of God, he said that he'd die for man's sins. Our sins."

His smile grew broader, and then it faded, replaced by a sober and serious expression. "Lots of people back then died for their sins, as well as their brother's and sister's sins, but they were never resurrected. They were either brought down below or sent up. Very few went to the middle ground, and only one person came back three days after his death—Mr. Cross.

"He died for the sins of mankind—all mankind—so I'm going to ask you the same question about this little lady here."

He stopped pacing long enough to raise his arms in the manner of a Shakespearean actor and intone, "Would you die for her?"

Ed had heard enough. "Markus, cut the bullshit already—"

"Would you die for her?" Markus's voice had gotten deeper, hoarser, and more intense. He was deadly serious. "You'd die for her?"

Would he? From the very moment they'd met, Ed was aware of the differences between them. From the very moment they'd met, they'd sparred.

And yet, he'd been attracted to her, even though he shouldn't have been. He nodded, but that wasn't good enough for Markus as he rushed forward to grab Ed's jaw and squeeze it hard.

"You little pissant, don't you nod your head," he bellowed. "Answer me, and do it now!"

Ed's response came quickly and sincerely. "Yes. I'd die for her. She's worth saving. I'm not, so . . . please, if you want to kill someone, take me. Not her. Don't take her."

A smile, tiny, and yet mocking, came to the other demon's face, and he released his grip. "How touching."

Ed tensed, waiting for the hammer to fall. Sure enough, it did. Lights flashed, a stab of pain . . . and then . . . nothing.

"Hey, man, you okay?"

The voice came from nearby. Ed woke up, groaned in pain, felt the cold on his face, and he found himself on the ground in an alleyway. With an effort, he turned over.

A tall, skinny black man wearing a threadbare overcoat stood three feet away. "You okay?" he repeated.

A cold wind whipped around Ed's face, bringing him back to reality. "Yeah. Where am I?"

"Manhattan. Times Square."

Manhattan. Times Square with its neon lights, its shops open twenty-four-seven and, since it was the last day of the year, it was also crowded. Oddly enough, no one was shopping or fighting. Something else had their attention.

Across the way, a crowd had gathered at the base of the Green Meadows building across the street, a skyscraper more than a thousand feet in height. Shouts and screams punctuated the air.

Ed struggled to his feet and noticed that his garments were different. He was wearing jeans and a long-sleeved shirt now. He was also barefoot.

A nearby clock struck four. A deeper shade of red suffused the sky, and the ground rumbled with barely contained seismic fury. The smell of horror was thicker than it had been an hour ago, but no one seemed interested, least of all the man beside him. He pointed to the Meadows. "Look at that!"

A woman was dangling from a rope thirty stories up. Ed didn't have to possess perfect vision to know who it was. "Nellie," he muttered. "Hang on."

He ran across the street, heedless of the honking horns, the pain in his skull, and the cold and hard concrete beneath his feet. Everyone was pointing to the sky. "Won't someone help that poor lady?" someone asked.

"She's around two hundred feet off the ground," another person answered. "Ain't no ladder can go that high, and it's too windy for a helicopter. Get ready for some roadkill."

Ed hung back from the crowd, trying to get a better look. He heard Markus's voice, although the demon had already shielded himself from mortal view.

"Hey, Ed, I know you're here. You said you'd die for her. Now's your chance. Save her if you can." He had a knife in his hand.

"No, don't do it!" Ed shouted.

Everyone looked at him and then turned their attention back to the only individual they could see up on high — Nellie. Markus shook his head. "I can, and I will. But I have to be going, so, good luck. Later!"

With a maniacal cackle, he slashed through the rope and disappeared. Nellie dropped like a rock, the crowd gasped and screamed, and Ed . . . heart thumping, sweat running down his body, spirit willing but flesh flagging, he begged for help, appealing to a power he'd never thought he'd appeal to.

No names were mentioned, nothing was uttered, but Ed's only thought consisted of three silent words.

Please.

Help.

Me.

And, lo and behold, the sound of flesh tearing greeted him. He knew it had come from him, although he didn't know why, but something had torn through the skin and his shirt, yet there was no pain. "What's going on?"

"Holy shit," someone whispered. "You got wings."

Ed looked over his shoulder and gasped. White, feathered, large, and powerful wings, had emerged from his back. No time to think. Wings were for flight, and like they'd been part of his being all along, Ed jumped into the sky and let his new appendages carry him aloft.

In a flash, they propelled him up and toward the woman he cared for. Nellie screamed in terror for someone to save her.

"Go, man, go," came the roar from the crowd, and Ed shot up like a missile, snatching Nellie from the jaws of death fifty feet above the ground.

"*Oh, yeah!*" The crowd bellowed its collective approval as Ed fought back the urge to grunt from the impact of his partner landing in his arms and almost popping his shoulder joints to infinity and beyond.

Still, it was the most beautiful pain he'd ever experienced, and he welcomed it. Nellie's eyes had been closed, but then they shot open, and she exclaimed, "Ed, you're . . . you've got wings!"

"Yeah."

Pithiness around her had never been his strong point, and right now, he couldn't think of anything else.

She clung to his neck, not even looking at the ground. "It's really you. I knew someone would save me, but you . . ."

With that, she passed out. Ed continued to flap his wings with strong and steady beats, flying over the landscape to the cheers of the crowd. Heroics were one thing, but now, he and Nellie had to talk. Soon, they left the cheering crowd behind.

CHAPTER SEVENTEEN: AFTERMATH

As Ed carried his precious cargo, the wind, cold and laden with that horrid stink, rushed by him, somehow carrying the stink of his smell from the sewers away. It was a cleansing of sorts, and he welcomed it.

In an epiphany, he also welcomed the fact that for the first time since the miracle had occurred—and what else could it be called but a miracle of redemption—he'd entered a new reality. He'd grown angel's wings.

Call that another major unlife-changer. Heavy though they were, they beat with an unearthly power. All right, he admitted to himself, they flapped with a heavenly power, and yet he was neither tired nor sore from the exertion.

In the past, he'd flown on occasion, but he'd never cared for it. He didn't know why, but it was something he'd never been comfortable doing.

His mode of transportation then had been leathery, hooked, and bat-like wings, as was the case with all the other demons. And for some reason, he'd always felt somewhat weak whenever he shifted his form from earthbound to sky bound.

Not now, though, and he didn't know what to make of his newfound ability, although he felt a sense of . . . elation. It seemed completely natural for him to sprout those wings and fly with them.

Nellie chose that moment to wake up, looking around and blinking in wonder, and then she said, "Ed, I'm cold. Do you think we can land?"

"Sure." The chill hit him, as well.

Their path took them in the direction of Central Park, and he landed near a bench and gently placed his cargo on it. His wings melted inside his back. As an experiment, he concentrated and willed his clothes to change.

It came as a distinct relief when they did. He now sported a new long-sleeved shirt and socks and shoes. His powers had returned, although from which side, he couldn't say. Perhaps it was both, but right now, he had other things to do.

Nellie slumped back against the rest, placing her arm on top of it. In turn, she rested her head on her arm. Her eyes were half-closed, but she didn't appear to be hurt, and he gently patted her cheek. "Hey, are you okay?"

She didn't answer him immediately, remaining half out of it, but her breathing was slow and regular. Shock, probably—getting dropped from two hundred feet up could do that to a person.

As she rested, Ed glanced up at the sky. It had turned a deeper shade of red, and clouds—or perhaps dirt in the shape of an interstellar sackcloth—obscured massive portions of it.

"End times," he muttered. "We've only got a few hours left, if the prophecy is true."

Naturally, he couldn't have known the science or the magic of it all, but the imbalance between Heaven and Hell seemed to be growing exponentially, and the incredible, unearthly, indeed—godly, as well as ungodly—powers that held the realms of above and below together, now threatened to explode, taking Earth with it.

And without getting two on-the-fence souls to go where they were supposed to go, whoever they were, it seemed as though there was no way of stopping things.

A few passersby glanced at them, but then they turned their attention to the sky, muttered something about the harshness of the weather and the bloody rotten atmosphere ruining New Year's, and then they went elsewhere.

Once they were alone again with only the snow and wind for comfort, Ed willed a hot towel and gently wiped the dirt, grime, and blood from Nellie's face. She didn't respond. Perhaps she was still in shock.

Not knowing what else to do, he wished away the towel and patted her face again. Nellie opened her eyes, blinked, and then said, "It was really you."

Somewhat abashed by her praise, he nodded. "Yeah."

"Why did you save me?"

"'Scuse me?"

Her eyes widened. "You saved me. Why?"

Ed was tongue-tied, not only by her beauty but also by the question itself. "Well, I, uh, you saved me once before, remember? In the taxi, you pulled me out, and . . ."

Nellie turned on her dazzling smile again. "Is that all?"

Oh, hang on a second. After all this, Nellie had suddenly decided to turn on the sex appeal. A trap, this was a trap, it had to be a trap, or was she simply being herself? "No. I did it because I need you."

A smile came from her, something simultaneously all-knowing, sweet, and yet, seductive. Yes, this was most definitely a trap. He was quite sure angels could seduce people — and it was happening right now . . .

Nellie flicked a lock of hair back in a casual move that came off as enticing. That, and the fact that her green eyes glowed made him think of a sacrificial lamb being led to the slaughter. If he'd uttered any sound now, it would have come off as a sheep's bleat.

"You know, Markus, he had me," she said. "He kept saying that he was going to drop me, and I'd go splat, even though I probably wouldn't die."

"Why not?"

Nellie slapped him gently on the shoulder. "I'm already dead, remember? You are, too. And there's that no-die law in effect. My maker said so."

Totally true on Ed's end as well. "But my maker, he might not have brought me back had that happened," she continued. "He might have sent someone else, someone he had in reserve."

A shiver ran through her. "It was so cold up there, and I felt all alone. I was helpless, and then I was falling. The ground rushed up to meet me, and I screamed and begged for help . . ."

Nellie's voice caught, and she leaned her head against his chest. "Then you were there."

"Uh, yeah."

A low rumble sounded in the distance. Not threatening, no, not yet, but she jerked her head up. "Who was that for?"

"Me," Ed replied, sniffing the air. He smelled sulfur—Hell's early warning system. He hoped that his master wouldn't be displeased over what he'd done. "Contact isn't in the contract, you know?"

"But you caught me," Nellie pointed out. "You came for me."

Ed felt uncomfortable at the attention, and his proximity to her made him feel even more uncomfortable. Her body was warm and supple and giving, yet with a hint of iron.

He'd met other pretty women before. Winnifred had been cute, but he'd never entertained the thought of being with her.

Now, though, things had changed. "Well, yeah," he finally managed to stammer out. "I remember that. I said I would."

She regarded him through soulful eyes. "Markus asked you if you'd die for me. He said that in the tunnel."

"Uh, yeah, I remember that, too."

Would you die for her? Markus' idea of mockery. His religion was chaos, but Ed had realized there was a deeper meaning in all this, and when he'd yelled out yes he most certainly meant it.

The religions of those above, be they Christian, Jewish, Muslim, or something else, they all had thought processes that he knew of but also that he'd never dared think about.

Even more dangerous for a demon was to have second thoughts about which side they belonged to. Yet, it had happened, and now, here he was with a beautiful young woman, and he couldn't help feeling what he felt . . .

Another rumble of thunder sounded, this one markedly closer. More sulfur layered the air, and Nellie wrinkled her nose. "That was also for me," he said. "Just so you know."

"Because of me?"

Her tone, as well as her expression, was innocent, but from her body language—she practically melted into him, and her fingers traced their way up his arm—he knew that she liked him, or was it more than like?

An uncomfortable thought occurred to him—she had to be teasing him. Yeah, that was it. She was playing with him. Nellie had to be doing that, and why would a Halo do such a despicable thing?

One moment later, his thought of her being a user faded as her hand came up to stroke his cheek, and it was the most intimate gesture she'd used since they first met, and . . .

Still another rumble sounded, this one the deepest and most ominous yet, and a bolt of lightning scorched a nearby tree. "That was definitely for you," Nellie said and abruptly giggled.

No sooner had she spoken than another bolt of lightning hit a water fountain twenty feet away. The fountain exploded, and brick and water flew around them, yet neither a drop nor a shard of stone touched their skin.

Nellie observed the happening with a rueful expression. "Uh, my bad," she said. "I'm also being watched."

Abruptly, he pulled away, clasping his hands in front of him. "This is all wrong."

"Wrong?"

Emotion overcame him, and he rocked back and forth. Ridiculous—he felt ridiculous. He was acting like a child or a dork—or both.

With an effort, he stopped his body's movement and bit the inside of his cheek to focus up. Conflict over contact—it wracked his mind and heart, and who and what was he, after all?

"Yes, wrong! I shouldn't feel this way about you. I mean, we're on opposite sides, and I've been trained not to, you know, be this way."

Nellie placed her hand on his shoulder. "Don't some of your people have relationships with mortals?"

Oh, there it was again—contact. Not in the contract, not in the contract. The very touch of her skin to his made him feel weak. Weak and powerless, not in a supernatural power kind of way, but in the emotional sense.

Fighting for a sense of self, a sense of being grounded, Ed stammered out, "Yeah, it happens, but . . . I mean, I've done it, but it . . . never made me happy."

Shame was a powerful thing, especially since he knew Nellie's backstory and that she was so . . . experienced. "Hey, you know something? When I was mortal, I had sex lots of times. It was difficult to talk about it back in my day. People then simply didn't. But some of the other women I spoke with in the brothel told me that it could be beautiful."

Ed bit his lip. "Um, was it beautiful for you?"

Nellie shook her head. "I never got any joy from it—never. Physically, yes, I could go through with it, but emotionally, no, not with anyone—ever."

He looked at her, mesmerized by her eyes. "Really?"

In turn, she looked back at him. "Yes. You know, it's okay to have feelings. We do, as angels. We're allowed, and we remember who we were in the past.

"I remember it all, the good times and the bad. Believe me, there were more bad than good. In fact, now is as good as it's gotten, if that makes any sense."

"It does, but I don't remember anything."

Her fingers tightened around his muscle, massaging it. It relaxed him, even though the rumbling of thunder continued. "Does it matter?" Her voice was very soft.

"No."

They locked gazes with each other, and he felt as though she was looking right through him. "You know, I said once before that my friends call me Nell. I think you're a friend."

She reached up to caress his face. "In fact, you're more than a friend."

He returned her gaze, and with a sudden movement, he kissed her, somewhat awkwardly, but then she melted into his arms. She kissed him back, and the thunder crashed around them, but no lightning bolts came their way.

Once they let go of each other, Nell leaned back to observe him with a somewhat breathless air. A smile began to form on her lips, but it stayed where it was, somewhere deep in her heart. Perhaps she wasn't sure, either. "There. Was that so bad?"

Ed didn't have a chance to respond. Without any warning, she disappeared in a puff of smoke. From beneath his feet, the ground began to shake, and he had the notion that the earth would part, and he'd be swallowed up.

Instead, a voice called out from the great beyond. *"Ed!"*

Uh-oh. It was Lucifer. And he was not pleased.

The world began to fade out, and Ed's only thought was that, at the very least, he'd done the right thing. If he was going to meet oblivion, then at least he'd meet it with a smile.

Chapter Eighteen: Back in the Boardroom

When he'd first arrived in Hell, Frank had impressed upon Ed the necessity of showing humility not only to superiors, but also to the superior of superiors. It was the only way to avoid being blasted into non-existence.

"Stand this way," the senior demon said, and he demonstrated the stance and facial gestures. *"Don't make eye contact. Wait until Lucifer speaks."*

"Does it always work?"

Frank shrugged. *"Usually."*

"What if it doesn't?"

"You're screwed." And at that point, the lesson ended.

Ed had kept his mentor's advice in mind. He stood in front of the throne, assuming the proper stance of remorse, head down and wearing a grave expression, his hands clasped in front of him.

Back straight as an arrow, Ed waited in front of Lucifer, who literally held his very existence in his elegantly manicured hand.

The master of all evil also sat in a semi-strict position, wearing a black, impeccably cut suit, but this time, his tail came out to lash the air around him in a whip-like manner.

Nothing in the way of conversation passed between them for a few milliseconds, and in that brief period of time, Ed's only thought was that he'd screwed up big-time, but that kiss — it had been worth it.

Finally, Lucifer spoke in a deceptively calm voice. "Ed,

would you kindly tell me what in the great depths you were thinking?"

He didn't appear to be outwardly angry, save for the tail. Outside of the mild tone of his voice, he displayed no tics, no twitches. It was a question, and nothing more, but Ed knew how powerful the overlord was, and he also knew that his master's mood could change in a nanosecond. Call this the calm before the eventual storm.

"You, uh, saw?"

Lucifer grunted. "Just the park. What happened before that, I have no idea."

For that, Ed was eternally grateful. Having wings — angel's wings — simply wouldn't work here. It was a given that Lucifer would never understand. Worse, it could mean extinction, something Ed didn't want at all.

The master of all evil continued. "As you know, my attention was on a number of other things, mainly keeping order here."

A sudden tremor ran through the room, causing the table to shake and the walls to quiver. Lucifer glanced around the room, shaking his head. "You felt that, didn't you?"

"Yes."

Lucifer grunted in dismay and ran his fingers through his perfectly groomed hair, a gesture he'd never done before, not to Ed's recollection. The master always seemed to be in control, but now?

"In case you haven't noticed, all existence on Earth is going to end, and Hell is beginning to break down. Those tremors will get worse, much worse. I haven't even thought about what's going on upstairs, and I've had no communication as yet with my counterpart."

"I see."

That wasn't the wisest response around, as Lucifer leaned forward, his gaze intense, and an unholy light gleamed in them, something laser-like and deadly.

Ed gulped as he remembered what had happened to George. He didn't want to suffer the same fate. He stood straighter than ever, his head down, but in a burst of courage he lifted his eyes to make contact with the master's, and what he saw in them was potential annihilation.

No, not potential annihilation, but total and absolute annihilation, the cessation of his unlife, his atoms scattered to the four winds of the underworld.

In other words, the master's eyes' message portended utter destruction. The very thought of being destroyed along with not seeing Nell again, frightened Ed, but despite that possibility, he still stood tall.

"You do," Lucifer said as he shoved his face forward to within an inch of Ed's. The master's lips quivered in barely controlled rage.

"Do you? It's bad enough that I can barely control what's happening down here. It's worse that I had to make a deal with my creator, and it's even worse that we have to employ a Halo as an assistant, but for you to consort with one of . . . them . . . where is your pride?"

He turned away with a huff of indignance. Had Ed possessed a soul, it would have shriveled with shame. As it was, he didn't feel overly happy.

However, he felt compelled to tell the truth, and when his overlord turned back, he locked gazes with him. "Sire, while it may have been wrong, she's, well—"

"Well . . . what?"

"I think she's hot."

"She's . . . *hot?*"

With that, Lucifer's tail smashed against the wall, sending up a sonic boom that quieted Hell for the grand total of three seconds. After that, it settled down to its usual din of pain. More tremors came their way, the last of them practically knocking Ed off his feet and Lucifer off his throne.

"Sorry, sire," Ed muttered, feeling mortally ashamed as he hung onto the table for balance.

His boss growled and turned his head away. "This is the very thing I hoped would not happen, and especially not to you."

"It's never happened before?"

Lucifer snorted and turned back. "Of course, it has. Don't be naïve. Relationships between our kind and mortals have been many and sundry in the past. You're a foot soldier in our war. Soldiers follow orders, and if that means sleeping with the enemy, then that's what we do. Sleeping with a Halo is no different.

"In your past life, you were a person. All my subordinates were people once. People have feelings and emotions. We play on those feelings and emotions. That's what we do, our kind and theirs."

He continued to grouse over the state of human affairs, and then he shrugged as if to say it couldn't be helped. "I suppose it would have happened sooner or later. The non-fraternization policy among our own kind is hard enough to enforce. Out there, it's even more difficult."

From that statement, Ed knew he wasn't about to meet oblivion, not yet, at any rate. After all, Frank and Mariko were together, and it was a given that Lucifer knew about their relationship. "Thank you for understanding."

The lord of all evil offered a brief grimace-slash-smile, a rarity. "I understand insofar as I am aware that there are other matters more important to consider."

He heaved a sigh. "As the old saying goes, to err is human, to forgive . . . you know the rest. You're the only hope we've got. I can't do anything more. I am bound by my promise not to interfere in Earth's realm, just as my creator is. We can send intermediaries, but not interfere directly. That's how things work."

Ed digested his master's comments. Feelings, emotions, he was feeling everything right now, and that raised another question. "Sire, who was I?"

His master's eyes grew round. "You mean, in your former life?"

"Yes. I have to know."

Lucifer pursed his lips, produced a cigar from the noxious ether by snapping his fingers, lit it, and he puffed away for a time before answering. "I suppose you deserve to know. Your name was Edward Harrow. You were almost nineteen when you joined our ranks."

Ed thought about it and tried to recall his earlier life. The dreams, the images, only bits and pieces remained, assuming they were true images and not implanted. The log cabin, the shouting . . . and the sound of a gun firing.

Finally, he shook his head helplessly. "I can't remember. I've had dreams, but they never meant anything. I couldn't make any connection."

"No, of course you couldn't."

The master spoke in a soothing, almost fatherly tone. "When those who've pledged their troth to me enter this realm, by and large, their memories are purged. Bits and pieces remain, of course, to keep a sense of self. That also explains your dreams, at least, in part.

"However, if you want to know who you truly were, I have it in my power to show you."

Ed steeled himself for the worst. "I have to know. Show me."

"As you wish."

Lucifer touched his finger to Ed's forehead, and in a blinding flash, it all came back . . .

Roanoke, Virginia.

"Worthless pissant, that's what I got for a son!"

Edward Harrow, age nearly nineteen, stood defiantly in the main room of his father's modest home, blood running from a cut lip. The year was eighteen-seventy-two, just a few years after the end of the Civil War.

His father, Judson Harrow, had ordered him to shoot any trespassers on their property, and Ed had refused. That earned him a hard slap across the mouth. The elder Harrow had a heavy hand.

"He wasn't doing anything, Pa."

It wasn't as if the trespasser could have stolen anything. His father raised cabbage, beets, and turnips, and they had a few milk cows to keep themselves going. Ed hunted and shot wild game when he had free time. He also tended the garden while his father conducted his business in the city.

Fifteen minutes earlier, a man—a black man—had wandered into their garden, his hands raised. "Sorry. I was looking for work. I was hopin' to find some."

Edward's father was still in bed, sleeping off a hangover. A heavy drinker with a violent temper and a strong streak of southern pride, he was not a man to argue with. Edward had seen him reach for his pistols more than once in the past when he'd had a disagreement with someone.

This man, though, didn't seem to be bad in any way. While Edward carried a rifle and knew how to shoot, and while his father's order rang in his mind, he also felt no fear of this stranger. "I'm sorry. We don't have any work here, but maybe they're hiring on some of the other farms or in the city."

The black man nodded. "Thank you. I'll be on my way, then."

Edward watched him go. The man carefully picked his way through the garden and disappeared over a low ridge. When Edward went inside the house again, he found his father waiting for him, a thundercloud flashing across his fat, unshaven face.

His father's sneer could have wilted a corn crop. "My son, the milquetoast. I was watching you speak to that . . . man."

"So?"

Ed had barely gotten the question out when a backhand to his face cut his lip. "So if you see someone like that on our property, you shoot him. You got a rifle — shoot."

The slap stung, and Ed put his hand to the side of his mouth. It came away smeared with blood. "He didn't do anything bad, Pa."

A note of pure rage sounded in his father's voice. "It don't matter what he did or didn't do. He ain't white! That's enough. Just because Lincoln freed the slaves don't mean I have to allow them on my property. And I don't, so, boy, when I give you the order to shoot, you shoot! Hear?"

"Yes, sir."

Edward didn't agree with that line of thinking, but in order not to get belted again, he played the part of a dutiful son.

His father, well over six feet with a large gut and a moon-shaped face in addition to a vicious temper, was a semi-successful cotton manufacturer originally from Texas who'd made a pretty penny supplying the Confederate troops with clothing during the war.

He'd also run arms obtained from France, run them through the blockades, and profited. When the Union had triumphed, he'd lost his estate and been forced to migrate up to Virginia, but he'd still kept his contacts and remained above water — financially speaking.

However, things only remained solvent insofar as his dealings continued. That was where Edward entered the picture. He'd been forced to help his father, and while he knew what he was doing was illegal, he'd kept silent. An only child, his mother had died a number of years back, and his father was all he had.

"Get your worthless carcass out of this house and go to the factory."

His father's harsh words interrupted Ed's reverie. "Yes, sir. Why?"

"I've got a shipment coming in from Germany, and I need someone to guard it. Can you do that, you poor excuse for an offspring?"

The words stung as much as the slap had, but Edward made an effort to sound positive. "Yes, sir."

His father gave him the details. The shipment would be delivered at midnight. All Edward had to do was let the men in, watch over the shipment until his father arrived, and then leave. That was it.

"I'll do it, sir."

The elder Harrow pulled a pistol from his pocket and handed it over, snatching the rifle back. "Use this if you have to. Damn Yankee spies are everywhere. Trust no one."

He then waved his son out. "Get going. Clean up the place while you're at it."

That night, all went as planned. Edward arrived at his father's factory just before seven PM. He set about wiping down the cotton gins, checked on and oiled some rifles ready for shipment to some ex-Confederate soldiers, inhaled the stuffy, dry odor of sawdust and subsequently sneezed it out, and once he finished his chores, he waited.

The delivery would be at twelve, so he walked around the silent machines, kicked a few rats out of the way, and wondered what his father was dealing now.

In the past, as the younger Harrow, he'd assisted in running arms. He'd also run alcohol, gold, and other assorted items that those with money wanted.

Not that he'd ever seen a cent. He wore threadbare pants, worn shoes that didn't fit, and an old but clean shirt. He'd finished the equivalent of grade ten—a fairly high level of education in those days and in his area—but then his father had put him to work in the factory, claiming that higher education was for those who were going somewhere.

"You aren't," his father had declared. "You're weak, worthless, and I'm glad your mother isn't alive to see how low you are."

Edward received those words, filed them away in an endlessly growing folder, and wondered why in the hell he'd put up with this mistreatment all those years. Oh, wait, he knew why. He had nowhere else to go.

He'd never given up his love for reading, though. He read whenever he could, learning about math and science and ancient Greece and Rome, and his imagination took him away from the reality of having no friends or future.

At times, despair nearly overcame him. It seemed that he was destined to spend the rest of his life in this city, despised by everyone, and . . .

A knock on the door jarred him. He glanced at his pocket watch, the only source of pride he'd ever had. It had been a gift from his grandfather, Jed, now passed.

Edward had kept it at his side for the past five years and faithfully kept it clean and in excellent working condition.

Checking it now, it was midnight. The delivery team was here. Edward opened up, and two men stood in the doorway. The first man was short and stocky with swarthy features that looked black under the lamplight.

The second man had the whitest skin that Edward had ever seen. Tall and lean, with the expressionless face of a ghost, he pointed to a large wooden crate that sat behind them and spoke in a quiet voice. "This is the delivery."

Silently, Edward ushered them through the doorway. They carried the crate in and stowed it behind one of the cotton gins. Not a word was spoken, and once they were finished, the stocky man asked, "Where's the money?"

Edward was confused. "I thought my father paid you."

"Yeah, he did. I was just testing you."

He then pulled out a gun and cocked it. Edward yelped in fear and dove behind some crates. He came up shooting, and his aim was true. It hit the stocky man in the head. He fell to the floor, but not before getting off a shot of his own.

The bullet hit Edward square in the chest, and its force hurled him a good five feet through the air. He landed on his side, and then rolled over on his back, the breath rushing from his lungs. "Oh, hell," he gurgled out.

A fiery pain filled his being, and he found it hard to breathe. Blood in the lungs. He was going to choke to death on his life's fluids and only in the most unpleasant way.

Mr. White Skin focused his gaze on Edward and took his time walking over. He squatted to address the dying teen.

"You're going to die very soon," he said in a matter-of-fact tone, one that indicated he'd seen this kind of occurrence all too often.

Ed could only get out one word. "Why?"

The other man ignored his question. "You have two choices. Accept your death and burn in Hell for your crimes, or join us and be spared burning. Choose. You've got about a minute left."

Edward's consciousness faded in and out. Ever since he was small, he'd been fed tales of Hell, pits, burning, torture, and more. Everyone in his area believed that Hell was real and eternal and terrible. Why would he join them?

Another concept hit his fast-failing mind, that of practicality. Spending eternal torment in a chamber of horror wasn't for him. Edward whispered, "I'll join."

White-Face had offered a ghostly smile. He held up Edwards' watch, crushed it, and then he muttered something in a foreign language.

A split-second later, Edward found himself standing in

front of a fearsome giant, a devil. The being stood immeasurably tall, with three faces, its two side mouths moving rhythmically, as if it were chewing on something. Whatever that food was, Edward didn't want to know.

"I am Lucifer," the devil announced in a voice deeper than the ocean depths and with a sonorous capacity that filled the immense space they were in and one that could also freeze anyone in their tracks. "Edward Harrow."

Frightened beyond the capacity to say anything coherent, Edward had simply nodded, trembling all the while.

The devil turned to him with the middle face, and he offered a smile of horribly stained, reddish-yellow teeth. "Edward Harrow, you've pledged your troth to me. Work as I say, do as I command, and the rewards shall be yours."

Edward bobbed his head once. "I will." He was too terrified to say no.

Lucifer then reached down to place a thick forefinger the size of a moon shuttle rocket on his forehead and said, "It is done. You are now Edvil, a minion of Hell."

With that, all of Edward's memories of his earthly life disappeared, leaving only traces, and his new life as a minion of the dark overlord began . . .

"Now, you know," Lucifer said as he withdrew his finger. "You know who you were. You know who you are now. Satisfied?"

Ed nodded, incapable of speech. Who he'd been, what he'd done . . . he'd shot someone in cold blood. Self-defense, yes, but he'd killed someone. And, due to eating the food that his father brought home, Ed had profited in a small way.

After thinking it over, he concluded that he'd deserved to die. But he'd never expected Markus to be the one to deliver him into eternal damnation. And that pestilent pissant had destroyed his watch, the only thing Ed had ever valued in his all-too-brief mortal life.

"I . . . I really didn't know."

"And had you known who those men were in your father's factory, had you known about me, would you still have made the decision you made?"

It was a good question. "I don't know."

Lucifer sighed and regarded Ed with a frank, knowing air. "In that split-second of time, many people make the choice to go upstairs. We have to get what we can. And you, Ed, you've always been my most faithful employee. I can count on you this time, can I not?"

"Yes, sir. Uh, there's one more thing, though."

"What?"

"Markus." Ed went through the dynamics of what had happened, and the overlord's face got darker and darker with each sentence.

"Frank mentioned that to me previously, but I didn't believe him. Now, I do."

Lucifer smashed his fist against the wall, causing it to vibrate madly. "Markus . . . that ungrateful Hell-spawn! After all I've done for him."

"That's okay," Ed said, ever aware of the time passing. "I'm back to normal. It was a brief spell. I can do this."

In a gesture of fatherly trust, Lucifer grasped him by the shoulders. "Well, then, I'm counting on you. All of existence is. Do the good, and do your job."

A sound of a bell rang. At the sound, Lucifer started and cocked his head in the direction the sound had come from. He released Ed. "That was a signal from my, er, maker. It's coming from Dis, the Gates of Hell. We'll meet there."

Curious about it all, Ed asked, "Do you meet, uh, Him, face to face?"

Lucifer paled. "Not now, no. Even I can't look upon my maker's face and not suffer extreme damage. No, I'm meeting

Peter. He's a lot easier to deal with. Excuse me. Thou art sent."

With that, he vanished.

Space and time wavered a moment, and Ed found himself inside his apartment, standing in front of his mini-bar. He felt filthy and wandered into the shower. While disrobing, he wondered what part of Hell his father was in, and then he decided not to think about it.

Instead, Ed's thoughts turned to who he'd been and what he might have become. It was too late for that, but it wasn't too late to rectify the current situation.

And that was what he'd do, the impending apocalypse notwithstanding.

Chapter Nineteen: Putting It All Together

The hot water washed away the caked-in soot, blood, and grime from Ed's body. While his powers were back, and while he could have simply willed the filth away, he still felt dirty. Some purists would have said it had something to do with an unclean soul.

Psychologists would have mentioned a guilty conscience. That thought made him laugh. A shrink would have a field day with him.

As for stains upon his soul, yes, they were there. It wasn't his soul, per se — it was his very essence. He'd once held a person's soul in his hands, and the memory shamed him.

While it was too late to help Willie, Ed knew that when all of this was over — if he could help it — he'd make amends, somehow.

He toweled himself dry and then went to his dresser. Fancy clothes could wait. Now was the time for action, and he needed to dress accordingly. He took out a pair of jeans, a shirt, a heavy jacket, and boots to don.

While getting dressed, he called out, "Alanna, television on, please."

"Yes, sir."

A newscast was on, showing the burning hulk of a truck in the downtown core. It had rammed a telephone pole and exploded, ostensibly incinerating everyone inside.

More than fifty people surrounded the truck, half of them

taking pictures, while the other half wore looks of horror and shock.

One of them, a man in his forties, with a harried, haunted look on a pasty face and a lumpy body, pointed at the truck and gave the news in a dead, emotionless voice.

"Norton Drexler, WNBN News. We're live at the corner of One East, One-Sixty-First Street, just outside Yankee Stadium. A truck carrying ten prisoners to another facility had lost control and slammed into a telephone pole. Two of them were killed instantly, along with the driver.

"The other prisoners escaped and are still at large. We warn the public that they are considered dangerous, having been incarcerated for murder and . . ."

Ed partially tuned out the report, but before he ordered Alanna to turn off the television, he caught sight of a familiar face on the screen.

Markus.

He held up a sign. *Top This! Your Death Count Is Up To Five!*

In a state of shock, Ed ordered the television off. Five more souls in Hell. The odds against succeeding had gotten even higher. How had Lucifer allowed this to happen? And how had the one upstairs forgotten?

Markus must have cast another spell. Either that, or the leaders of the Great Above and the Great Below had really messed up somewhere along the way.

None of that mattered now. There was only one person who could help him, and he knew of only one place where she might be.

Ed closed his eyes, concentrated, and in less than a second, he willed himself over to the park, the park where he and Nell had shared their first kiss. If her maker allowed her back on Earth again, he had the feeling that she'd be there.

It was empty and cold, although the bad weather no longer bothered him. A harsh wind blew, sending more foul smells his way, and the ground trembled intermittently. The sky, though, would have sent terror knifing through the bravest of the brave.

In a moment of pathetic fallacy, the night had truly become alive, and, like a living being, it had blood as its essence and its color. Streaks of yellow and blue lightning lit it up, exposing the wrath of Mother Nature, as well as the cosmic lords who'd kick-started the apocalypse, and in only the most unholy manner.

"Nell! Are you here? It's me, Ed. Where are you?"

He called her name again and again until he was hoarse. A nearby clock tower told him that it was almost ten-forty. Not much time left. "Nell!"

"Right here."

Ed whirled around. She stood before him, wearing the same white blouse and skirt combo, along with her jacket. Her cuts had healed, and her clothes were spotless. "Sorry I took so long," she said. "I had to give a report. It wasn't easy getting back here."

"But . . . you're here. That's enough."

Hesitantly, not wishing to incur the wrath of the one below or the one above, he extended his hand. She took it, and they walked through the snow, crunching the earth beneath them.

"My powers are back, not that they'll help us. There isn't much time left," Nell observed as she gazed around the park.

A streak of blue lightning split a tree open not twenty feet from where they stood, and the sharp smell of burnt ozone drifted over to their nostrils. The world was fast going to ruin, and Ed's only thought was *not if I can help it!*

"So, tell me about the plan," Nell said. "You got one?"

No, Ed did not, but he had an idea. "Forget the people we met. We got other problems."

"You mean the prisoners? We know about them. And they're not about to make the jump to our side."

Wonderful. This made their job all the harder. "They won't go for it," he muttered.

Nell gazed at him with curiosity. "What won't they go for?"

"Giving up their ideas. You know, like I do, that mortals are stubborn."

Simple, but true. From his long years of experience, Ed knew that mortals would never change their minds, no matter if they were faced with incontrovertible proof.

Even then, they wouldn't believe it. Flat-Earthers, genocide deniers, bigots — they all had entrenched thought patterns, and no amount of legitimate proof or public ridicule — or both — would make them see the light.

Nell swept her arm around the area, and she sounded on the verge of panic. "Ed, there's not enough time. Who are we going to get?"

"I don't know."

He searched every bit of gray matter he had and came up with nothing. Nell then snapped her fingers. "Mortals. They want things. Especially now, they want. The people we met wanted money."

"So?"

Her panicky disposition disappeared, replaced by a look of confidence. "So, if the prisoners who escaped are near here, then they want freedom *and* money. Right now, I'm guessing that they're thinking they have nothing left to lose."

As if the proverbial light bulb had lit, Ed turned to her, a grin on his face. That was it. That was the answer. By and large, outside of stubbornness, mortals also had a strong streak of greed in them. Now, it was simply a matter of getting five idiots who wanted more than what they had.

"Scan the area," he ordered. "I can't sense people like you can."

Nell closed her eyes, and then they suddenly shot open. "I see two people. Young — in their twenties. They've just gotten out of jail."

"What were they in for?"

"Robbery and assault."

Oh, this was a possible! "Where are they?"

She pointed to her right. "At the edge of the park. They're talking about scoring. Lots of drunk people out tonight. They're going to rob them."

Ed started in their direction, but Nell called him back. "Wait. I sense three more near the first two. They're very bad men . . . three of those prisoners who got out of that burning bus. They're talking about what they were in for."

Her lips moved soundlessly, and she vanished into the ether. A few seconds later, she returned. "Assault, murder, and rape. They're all scum."

Ed scratched the back of his neck, wondering what to do. He had his powers back, but there wasn't enough time to talk things out. "So, got a suggestion? It's not like they're going to walk into a trap."

"Why not?"

Nell's question caused Ed's hand to stop mid-scratch, yet it brought a smile to his face. "You mean, do the good?"

She chuckled. "No, I mean that you should do what you do best."

Oh, if that wasn't a signal, he didn't know what was. The park lay near a small power station, and the intense shaking had already caused a few of the transformers to burn out.

"Stay here," Ed told her. "I'll be back soon."

He started off, but Nell yelled, "Wait!"

"What is it?"

She didn't say anything, only kissed him. "That's for last time when we were interrupted. Now, go get them."

Good enough for him. The taste of her lips lingered on his as he shifted into the guise of another homeless person and ran over to where the five possible marks were. They had to be the ones. There was no time to find anyone else.

As Nell had said, two people, both in their late twenties, waited near the edge of the park. The man, tall and skinny with long, dark hair, and his companion, a short woman with equally long and dark hair, shuffled their feet nervously.

They wore jeans and cheap-looking bomber jackets and kept their hands in their pockets, but Ed had the feeling they were holding weapons, perhaps knives.

Off to their right were three more shadows. "Hey, cons," he called out.

They stepped forward. One of them asked, "You a cop?"

"Nope, I'm just like you."

That provoked a round of grim laughter. "Right, buddy," another man said. "If you're one of us, chuck us a few bucks. It'll help with our rehabilitation efforts."

Ed suppressed a smile—barely. "You want coin?"

As one, they turned on him. "We were hoping you had some extra," the woman said in a nasal voice. "How much coin you got?"

Ed willed a roll of greasy ten and twenty-dollar bills into existence. He pulled the wad out of his pocket, held it up in a fan shape, and waved it around. "This is for one of my bank accounts. Gotta buy New Year's presents for my family, you know?"

Immediately, their eyes lit up. Ed's hunch about greed being a powerful motivator proved correct when they took their hands out of their pockets. All of them held knives.

A sudden tremor nearly threw everyone off their feet, and the woman said nervously to her boyfriend, "Joey, we should get outta here. I don't like this place."

Joey, short and slight with a pockmarked complexion, grunted a wet, phlegmy sound. "Hey, Barbara, lighten up. We'll go, but not before getting his cash."

The other three prisoners joined up with Joey and his

squeeze. "Lots of money there," one of them said, the avarice practically oozing out of him. "Five-way split. How about it?"

As one, the other four members of the impromptu gang nodded and said they agreed with the idea of a split. Money, indeed, talked.

Ed turned to run, thinking that he could use some help. Wish granted, as Frank, Lars, Nebulazar, and a few others from below appeared in their true form, bracketing Joey and the woman.

Once Joey and his girlfriend beheld them, they screamed in horror. The hardened cons proved that they weren't so tough after all by joining the other two in shrieking like frightened four-year-old children. "What in the hell is this?" one man asked.

"Your future," Frank said. He then hissed, "See us. Join ussssssssss!"

Mr. Tough Con backed up, but another demon grabbed him and body-slammed him, like a pro wrestler slamming a jobber. "Oh, holy Jesus," the man gibbered as he swung his head back and forth to view the devil's minions. "Is this Hell?"

"Getting warmer," Lars said with a horrid grin, one filled with knives for teeth. "And we've got a nice place ready and waiting for you."

Everyone else tried to back up, but there was nowhere for them to go. Fear was fear, and Ed was ready to play on it. "Come on," he said. "You want to go somewhere safe?"

Joey slashed the air with his knife, looking around wildly and shrieking, "Get them away from us, man, get them away!"

He continued to swing his knife around, and as if by magic, several Halos appeared, standing by Joey's girlfriend. Ed recognized their glow, their aura, and he gave a silent thank you to the man upstairs for helping when it was most needed.

One of the Halos pointed to Ed and murmured to Joey and his girl, "I think you should go with that man."

That suggestion got through, as they looked to Ed for guidance. He took the cue and yelled as he took off, "Follow me!"

His newfound above-friends and his old below-friends stood together on opposite sides of the path, urging them on, much like football players emerging into a stadium and being cheered by an adoring crowd.

"Go, Ed, go," Frank called out. "Go!"

Fear, religion, and the promise of safety spurred the five slimebags on, and they almost caught up to Ed. He was still ahead of them by around ten yards, and as he ran by Nell, he said, "Move."

She stepped aside as another mighty shake from the ground caused the earth to heave and split open. This was it. The last chance had come. And it had come now.

Trees toppled over, steam erupted from under the ground, and the vibrations caused a power line to fall, sparking madly and lighting up the area.

Safely away from the electrical discharge, Ed pivoted around to watch. While he could have yelled out a warning—and Nell could have easily done the same thing, for that matter—neither of them did.

In a flash, the power line hit Joey, Barbara, and the three other men, frying them instantly. Before they expired, though, Ed distinctly heard them utter as one, "Lord, help us!"

It had been whispered through fried lungs with nearly shorted-out hearts and brains, but the thoughts were clear, and so was their intent.

A moment later, they expired, their burned corpses falling soundlessly on the snow. Nell went to Ed's side and grabbed his hand. "That's it!"

"What?"

She pointed upward. "Look!"

Five ghostly outlines in the shape of the ex-cons floated upward, all of them holding hands. Immediately, the ground stopped shaking, it quickly reformed, and the sky began to clear, although a residue of blood-red remained. The apocalypse was over.

"We won," Nell murmured, and then she kissed Ed on the lips. "We won!"

He returned the kiss full force, and then they broke their embrace to cast their gazes upward, saying simultaneously, "Yeah, we did."

"Yeah, you did," Frank said, suddenly appearing at his side in human form and clapping him on the back. "Nice job, Ed."

"You, too," he replied. "Thanks for stepping in."

He then turned to introduce his new girlfriend, or was she his girlfriend? A kiss had seemed to seal the deal, but who really knew? "Uh, guys, this is Nell. Nell, my friends from, uh, below."

Lars and the rest had also changed to human form. She bobbed her head at them, and Frank leaned over to whisper in his ear, "You got yourself a winner."

"Thanks," Ed murmured and nodded at the Halos.

A collective bow greeted him, followed by a salute. One of them said with admiration, "Nice job, Nell. Father will be pleased."

All the Halos subsequently vanished. Ed turned to Frank. "I appreciate the help. Say hi to Mariko for me, will you?"

"You got it."

Frank and crew also disappeared into the ether, and when Ed turned around again, he found that his new girlfriend had disappeared. "Nell? Where are you?"

Silence greeted him. Had she transgressed again? He thought that the one above would be more forgiving. He'd never be able to figure out Halos and their mindsets.

A moment later, the sound of police sirens came through, along with the sound of thunder overhead and a rumbling deep within the earth. What in the . . .

"This is supposed to be over," Ed shouted. "It's supposed to be over!"

It wasn't. The reddish hue returned to the sky, the lightning intensified in its strikes, bright flashes of energy and something unearthly lit up the night, and an unholy and foul-smelling mist blanketed the area like molasses.

Can someone tell me what I've done wrong? Ed yelled to the heavens, "What did I do wrong?"

For a moment, he thought that Heaven hadn't accepted the murderers and rapists. After all, many scumbags repented on their deathbeds and were granted absolution by priests and ministers. Sure, it was hypocritical, but that was how things worked.

Ed had no answer, but there was a place he could go to. Instantly, he thought about Hell and teleported himself there. The clock read eleven-oh-seven.

With a shock combined with dread, Ed realized that Lucifer and the one above had been wrong. Armageddon hadn't been averted, after all. In fact, it was just around the corner.

Chapter Twenty: Certain Facts

Ed gulped down a breath of air and then let it out slowly, trying not to panic. He had to find Nell, but he also knew that he wouldn't learn anything topside. Markus was too smart, too clever, and it was obvious that he'd been planning this for a long time.

No, if any answers were to be found, they'd be found at the source. That meant returning home. A moment of concentration, a quick disassociation of time and space, and Ed appeared at the walls of Dis.

Ordinarily, Hell had a solid, dull gray sky. Now, it was red, and bright blue streaks of lightning, much like those on Earth, lit up the ether. The damned stared at it with more terror than they showed the guards, and the guards stared at it with more fear than they showed the master.

It was both awesome and terrifying, guaranteed to frighten the most egregious offender into swearing fealty to the one above forever and ever.

As had been the case on Earth, Hell, too, shook, much more severely than on his previous visit. The walls of Dis trembled, and for a moment, he thought they'd crumble and fall, but they didn't. The infernal power of this realm somehow managed to keep everything intact, although how much more could it stand?

Ed was no physicist, much less an expert on the workings of Hell. He only knew the danger that confronted them all. At the seventh pit, he ran over to the guard on duty. "Hi," he said. "I know things are bad here, but I've got to see someone."

The demon, who was well over seven feet in height and

just about as wide as he was tall, stood at the edge of the pit, whip in his left hand and balancing himself with a pitchfork in his right.

He spoke in a gravelly voice, never letting his gaze wander from the damned souls below for an instant. It wasn't as if they were going anywhere.

Impending doom or not, they cowered against the sides of the pit, many of them lifting their arms in supplication to someone who hadn't deigned to recognize their predicament.

While the guards stuck to their posts, they were also spooked. The head demon on duty asked, "What is it? There's trouble up top, and things are bad down here."

Ed had to state the obvious. "I know. I'm the one Lucifer tasked to stop it. Like I said, I have to see someone. His name's Scott Alperstein."

The guard turned the name over on his forked tongue for a few moments before nodding. "Right. Recent acquisition. Go down three levels, make a left at the stunted trio of trees, and he's in the second cave on the left. The guy's non-responsive a lot of the time. Torturing him doesn't work, so we left him alone."

Call that a rarity, not being tortured. Perhaps Hell had a measure of mercy in it. He then turned around and grinned, revealing two rows of spiked teeth. "For now. We may have some fun, yet, when all this is over."

A moment later, a look of uncertainty—perhaps fear—crossed his face. "Can you do it?"

Truthfully, Ed wasn't sure he could pull this off, but this was no time for negativity. "I'll let you know. Take a break. You can have your fun when I'm done."

"Fun's what it's all about."

Ed forced out a grin and jumped into the pit. Over a hundred guards, all armed with whips and pitchforks, guarded the prisoners, but they didn't beat them.

As for the damned souls, they made no attempt to escape. Shocked beyond any measure of being able to absorb shock, they either sat or stared, and they spoke not a word. Even if they did get out, where could they go?

The seventh pit held the dregs of humanity, but Ed actually felt sorry for them — and not. On Earth, they'd been demigods. Here, they were pathetic wretches.

A large man wandered around, muttering something in an archaic language. Ed recognized it as ancient Mongolian. "Attila," he said.

Attila the Hun gazed at him through blank eyes, and then he turned away, still muttering to himself about demons and witchcraft and sorcery.

There were others down here, famous names from decades and centuries past. They also didn't speak to him or even to each other. Only one of them, a former president with a bloated body, orange hair, and a permanent spray tan, called out, "I didn't do it. I wasn't guilty."

Ed ignored him. That was what they all said.

The guard up top had said to turn left at a trio of trees. Ed found them, three stunted and twisted masses of charred wood and branch-limbs. They'd once been people. This was their fate for all eternity.

Around him, there was only eternity and damnation, decay, and horror. Ed shut those things out of his mind and began walking. Within a couple of minutes, he found a small cave and the scientist sitting in front of it.

Alperstein was a small man of spare build and indeterminate age. He wore the shapeless gray robe that all the inmates of Hell wore.

With a head of sparse gray hair and glasses that constantly slipped down his nose, he didn't seem the type to do anyone any harm. So why was he here?

Oh, wait, suicide. How a person died on Earth had a great

bearing on a person's future in the afterlife. Apparently, this man had chosen poorly.

"Mr. Alperstein?"

The man had been writing something in the dirt. Mathematical equations filled the space around him. Ed considered himself bright, but this was total gibberish to him.

Alperstein looked up, his eyes vacant, probably from all the misery around him, or maybe his mind had snapped as the guard had said. With a dirty forefinger, he pushed his glasses back into position. "Yes?"

"Hi, I'm Ed. I need to ask you some questions."

The vacant stare continued. "Questions? You're not here to torture or beat me?"

"No. I think you've had enough."

A faint smile tugged at the corner of the scientist's mouth. "They always beat me here. They beat me at the institution, too."

"The institution?"

Alperstein nodded. "Mental institution. I have problems. Problems with reality. My mind is far ahead of everyone else's. No one understands me. The doctors couldn't understand me."

He then went on a mini-rant about how no one could perceive the imperceptible, and Ed didn't have time for this. The man was a loon, yes, but he also held the key to understanding what exactly was happening. "Sir, I don't have time. None of us does. I need to know about the Colossus."

That triggered something, as Alperstein stopped raving. His eyes widened, and a spark of lucidity returned. He got down on his hands and knees, rubbing out one of the equations and then writing something new in the dirt with a trembling hand.

"No, that's not it."

With those words, he scratched out his new equation and

wrote something else. Then he got up, straightening his glasses as he did so.

His mouth worked in a dozen different directions, and he uttered a stream of gibberish before anything comprehensible came out. "I . . . I worked on the equations for fifteen years. Then another five on that computer. Molded it. Perfected it.

"Once I got out of the institution, I built it. Did all the equations there, used them when I got home. I built my computer, but the . . . the government wanted to take it away from me. Couldn't let them have it."

More gibberish followed. Then, he looked up at the gray sky, as if pleading for help. A thin stream of drool ran from the left corner of his sagging mouth. "I was afraid. I didn't know what to do. Then a man came to see me. A man."

"Who?"

"Blond hair. White like a ghost. Said he'd help me market it."

He'd just described Markus. It couldn't be anyone else. "What happened next?"

Alperstein wiped his mouth. "This man, he said he knew important people. He set up a meeting with some top men from the Pentagon."

His mood flip-flopped again, and he shook his fists at the sky. "But they betrayed me! They said that they'd take my creation away from me."

Ed knew who'd betrayed whom. Still, he let Alperstein rant. "It was mine," the scientist shouted. "Mine! I worked for it, I created it, and . . . and I couldn't . . . couldn't let them take it. Take my secrets. So, I did what I thought was right."

"You killed yourself."

Alperstein's expression switched to that of abject misery, and he dropped his arms to his side. "It was the only way, my confidante said. The blond man, he said so. If I died, then they'd never get the secret. It would die with me, and no one would ever be hurt by it. No one. It would be safe, then, safe for all mankind."

His manner, nervous and rambling, was incredibly distracting, but Ed told himself to be patient and to focus on the moment. "Mr. Alperstein, I've seen the Colossus Five. It's a beautiful machine, but what exactly does it do? I heard it holds a lot of data."

Alperstein took off his glasses and polished them against his filthy robe. His eyes cleared. "Oh, it does more than that. It's a data repository, yes, but I wanted the computer to do more than just input facts and figures."

"And?"

The mad scientist shrugged. "I wanted it to think, so I designed an algorithm that predicts which path people will choose."

Choose. "You mean, choose between good and evil?"

A nod. "Yes, that and more. It was designed to use their past decisions to formulate whether they'd choose ill or good in the future. Also to choose between political parties, toothpaste, which movie to see . . . everything. It was . . . it was ninety-nine-point-nine percent correct."

"That much?"

Another nod. "There's always the chance that people can or will change their minds at the last minute. That's part of human nature. I also programmed it with other knowledge."

What else could a person stuff into a machine? "Such as?"

"Such as learning in books," Alperstein replied in a suddenly airy, gay voice.

His mood turned positively euphoric, and he got up to walk around, expounding on his theories. "At the beginning of my programming, I thought only about the mathematics of it all.

"Then, later, I thought about a gift from the heavens. I searched for the books. Old is new. Ancient is modern. It was there. I found it. Escadron. Escadron!"

In a mad pirouette, he resembled a ballet dancer in the throes of some ecstatic trance. Call that weird and then some. "I told my blond confidante about the books," Alperstein continued. "He seemed interested. Most enlightening."

Just as quickly as he'd turned somewhat sane, he stopped in his tracks, and his eyes lost their lucidity. "It's hot. Can you get me out of here? Can you get them to return my machine?"

Sorry, that wasn't part of the equation. "I'll talk to the guards," Ed said, hating that he had to lie. "Sit tight. I'll see what I can do."

Alperstein returned to staring at the ground and his formula. He got on his knees to scratch the rest of it out and then began writing something new. Ed couldn't contain his curiosity. "What are you working on?"

The scientist gave him a half-mad grin. "This? It's a formula for peanut butter!"

A cackle followed, segueing into the high-pitched laugh of the truly insane. Nothing can help him, Ed thought, as he climbed out of the pit. The guard who'd allowed him entry greeted him at the top. "Basket case, right?"

Ed shrugged. "When you're right, you're right."

Despite the clamor and impending ruin around them, the guard grinned. "I told you. Do your best up top. I don't want to lose my job."

Ed gave him the thumbs up as he walked away. He had to focus up and ask those who knew. At the administrative center, he found Irving laboriously writing in his ledger. "Irving, I see you're back to doing things the old-fashioned way."

The accountant turned around, putting down the pen as he did so. The walls shook from a violent tremor, and a few of the books fell. Irving covered them up with the speed and care of a mother protecting her newborn child. "Ed, shouldn't you be upstairs?"

"I have to do some research first, Irving. I need your help."

The accountant's eyes glowed. "You need *my* help?"

"Seems so. Is the Colossus Five here?"

Irving shook his head in a slow, sad manner, the gesture of someone who craved some more free time and was denied just when said free time was in his grasp. "Nope. Gone. Someone took it, and now, I've got to fill things in, one at a time, just like I used to."

Ed observed the ledger. Facts of souls acquired, souls destroyed, crimes, pits in Hell, and more. This thing had a lot of detail. While he read, the accountant's voice came from over his shoulder. "What is it you need?"

Ed took his eyes off the ledger. "Do you still have the computer records when the Colossus Five was here?"

Now, Irving looked up, his gaze curious. "You're too late. Your friend took them."

His remark got Ed confused. "Who? What friend?"

"Blondy."

Blondy? "Markus," Ed growled. "When did he come here?"

Irving scratched the back of his head with a claw. "Two days ago. He wanted to run some numbers through the computer, and then he said he'd put the disc back. Hang on."

Irving rooted around in his massive desk and then shut the drawer. "It's not here. Damn it, I'll have to look for him."

He got up and went to the door, but before he left, Ed called out, "Did Markus go anywhere else after he looked at the computer?"

Irving paused at the doorway and turned around, furrowing his brow in concentration. Then he snapped his fingers. "Yeah, he mentioned something about going to the book depository."

The depository? Why would he . . .

Never mind. Ed suddenly knew what the game plan was. He didn't need to know the numbers on the disc. His interest lay in something older. He hastened over to his destination, running past startled guards who were escorting a batch of damned prisoners to a different section of the pits.

"Hey, where are you going?" one of the guards called out.

Ed didn't answer. He tore ahead and entered the structure, a one-story stone building that was practically as old as Hell itself.

He'd heard from Frank that one of the things Lucifer had done when he first fell into the pit was to construct the library. Knowledge was power. Power lay in books of the most unholy sort — and Alperstein had mentioned the same thing only a few minutes ago.

No one was around. His footsteps echoed on the rough stone floor, sending up puffs of dust. What was he looking for, and more specifically, what had Markus been looking for?

Ed searched the shelves. While the building looked small from the outside, like the boardroom, inside, it was much larger, virtually limitless. Hundreds, if not thousands, of ancient books lay before him. Escadron — Alperstein had uttered that name, almost in rapture, and . . .

Wait, two books that weren't covered in dust stuck out slightly from the shelves. Massive tomes, they were dust-free — The Journals of Escadron, and Spells of the Septinayad, the former dated around twelve-hundred A.D., and the latter dated in the mid-sixteen-hundreds.

With trembling hands, Ed pulled them out, carried them over to a table, and flipped them open. He noticed a few depressions on some pages, depressions made by fingertips.

Could this be it? While going through some passages, much of it didn't make sense. Markus had been searching for something, but what?

Oh, wait, some words leaped out at him from the book of spells. The ability to take the powers of the dark ones away and use them for one's own. These are the words . . .

So that was how Markus had done it. Never mind that now. Ed had more important things to worry about. He read the passages in the Escadron book, and while he couldn't understand everything, one word stuck in his mind. *Progenitorus.*

He turned the name over on his lips. Progenitorus. No . . . progenitor. That was what it had to be, and he gasped as the implications of it hit him between the eyes, harder than a lightning bolt could.

A millennia's sleep . . . power . . . control . . . there was too much information, much of it written in a mix of Old and Middle English, with many Latin and Greek phrases mixed in. It was almost like a code, and Ed wondered who could possibly comprehend it.

It didn't matter. He knew what the plan was. Markus had fooled everyone, right under their noses, and now, it was almost too late.

Still, he knew where his enemy was. Time was of the essence. He had to stop Markus, and now he knew just where to find him. If he found him, then he'd find Nell. She was all that counted.

That, and the fate of everything in the universe.

Chapter Twenty-One: Showdown

After some quick parlay with Lucifer, the overlord sent him back to Earth. The master wasn't in the mood to send anyone back, not at first, but Ed had brought the books to him and shown him the spells in the tomes.

"This is the evidence." They stood in the boardroom, the walls quivering and the shocks under their feet growing stronger. "This is what Markus was after."

Upon being given the facts, Lucifer practically erupted, lashing his tail and smashing a section of the meeting table to rubble. "That little weasel. He tricked me!"

"He tricked all of us," Ed replied, fully aware that time was quickly running out. "It was never about balancing accounts at year's end and the end of the world. It was all about this, but I can stop him. I know that I can."

Lucifer ground his teeth together. "I hope you know what you're doing."

Shaking with excitement and a sense of destiny, Ed said, "I do, sire. This is what we've been searching for. I'm asking you to trust me."

"So be it. Thou art sent."

A snap of his fingers, a temporary disassociation of time and space, and Ed found himself outside his apartment. He searched for his key, found it, and, his senses working overtime, he cautiously opened the door.

It was just as he'd left it—clean and untouched, although now, two individuals occupied its space, Markus and Nell. The latter sat on the couch, hands and feet bound, and she'd been gagged, as well.

Her eyes, though, spelled out all kinds of terror, and with good reason. Markus stood behind her, holding a gun at her head in one hand, and the Colossus in the other.

"Glad to see you," Markus said once Ed walked in. "I was beginning to think you'd chickened out."

"Not likely," Ed replied, seething.

There was nothing more he wanted than to erase this pasty-faced maggot from existence forever, but for now, he could do nothing. He knew his adversary would shoot. "Nell, are you okay?"

Her eyes bugged out, and she screamed out a muffled answer. Markus clocked her on the side of the head, which put her down and out. "Don't worry. She'll be spared the agony of watching the end of existence."

He then grinned, something that spoke of untold horrors that lay ahead. "You, on the other hand, will witness it up close and personal. Just don't move. This gun contains demon-killer bullets. You know what they are, don't you?"

Ed had heard about them. Something containing holy water, shavings from Christ's cross, and a super blessing from the Pope. "I know. I also know you were the one who brought me to Hell in the first place."

Markus favored him with a wicked grin. "Yes, I was the one. The warehouse, the shooting? Ah, sweet memory of a soul obtained. It seems like only yesterday."

With a magnificent effort of will, Ed controlled his baser impulses to maim and destroy and said, "Yeah, just like yesterday. Let's talk about now, though. How are you going to end all existence? You got a plan?"

He glanced outside. The sky had largely gone back to normal, although a dull red streak remained. A few tremors also hit, but the experts would probably chalk them up to aftershocks.

And, since it was the last day of the year — party time! — the shouting from the streets had died down to its usual dull roar of those who'd braved the cold weather to see in the New Year.

New Year's Eve was in full swing, and, just like every New Year before it, the revelers would ring it in with a lot of laughs, a boatload of drinks, more than likely the copious use of drugs in some cases, and probably even greater hangovers.

Maybe.

"I've always got a plan," Markus replied. "Would you like to hear it?"

Stall him, Ed thought. "I've got time. The balance problem — it's been fixed. We got those people to go where they were supposed to go."

While he felt good about completing his mission along with Nell, apparently, it served as a source of amusement for Markus, as he began to chuckle.

His chuckle then segued into laughter, and it was awesome and horrifying to see. Markus' face turned red, sweat coursed down his finely honed features, and his laughter went up another notch, verging into an insane cackle. It was then that Ed realized Markus had always been insane.

"Tell me what's funny," Ed demanded. "What's so funny?"

His nemesis shook his head and continued to shake with laughter, but a few seconds later, he stopped and patted his stomach. "That was quite a workout for my ab muscles. Thanks. It takes a lot to make me sweat, but you did it."

"What's. So. Funny?"

Markus wiped the perspiration from his forehead and smeared it on the couch, rubbing the spot as if to grind in the insult more deeply. "You. Your ideals, your antiquated sense of justice and honor. Silly. You talk about balance.

"Well, you did preserve the earthly balance. I was at the park, although you didn't see me. I saw how you, your girlfriend, and those other Halos and demons joined up to keep things level. Clever, I have to admit."

"Maybe you're not as smart as you think you are," Ed said with a sense of satisfaction.

Markus chuckled and shook his head, seemingly at the idea of someone else besting him. "Don't kid yourself. I'm still a step ahead of you and everyone else. You talk about balance? I'm going to talk about something even better."

He waved his gun at a chair, and Ed sat, body tensed, waiting for an opening. Markus leaned back, his smile still on full display. The bastard was really enjoying this.

"See, it's not about the balance of Heaven and Hell, old rival. It's about power, and power, as you know, is decidedly one-sided. Lucifer rules in Hell, the Lord, above. They hold the reins of absolute power."

That's how things are supposed to be, Ed thought. "It gives order to the world."

While that sounded somewhat lame, he meant it. Without order from a higher or lower power, anarchy reigned. It was the same on Earth. Granted, it wasn't perfect, but even in anarchy, someone always had to take charge.

Markus uttered a snort of derision. "I figured you'd say that. Order to the world—hah! You bought into Lucifer's mindset. You drank the *Kool-Aid*."

He shifted his position, but his eyes never wandered. "*Kool-Aid*," Ed echoed.

"Yeah, you drank it," Markus stated. "And you know what? It's total crap. For all your talk of order and balance, you still have two supreme beings who've been slugging it out for millennia, and what have they accomplished? Nothing."

Markus spat on the carpet, more bad manners in addition to megalomania and insanity. "We're ants to them. Foot soldiers. Pawns in an endless war that accomplishes nothing because it means nothing. *We* mean nothing to them, and it's only because they have power that they can keep this charade going."

"And you want that power," Ed said. "That's where the books come in."

In a sudden, smooth shift, Markus leaned forward, his gaze intense. "Ah, you went to the book repository. You're not as stupid as I thought. You also know about the spells?"

Spells. "You told me about them before, remember? You froze my powers with them. Nell's powers, too."

Markus chuckled. "Knowledge is power, baby! Knowledge is authority! Hey, I even put up a spell to blind Lucifer and everyone else to what I was up to and to block him and the others, especially the one above, from getting to me.

"It was short-term, only a few hours, but it gave me enough time to put my plan into motion. Nothing can touch me now. Nothing."

He spoke in a most self-assured manner. "You were talking about power?" Ed asked, hoping to get some more information. Not much time was left, and he felt the vibrations of the ground through the soles of his feet.

His nemesis smiled. "Yeah, it's all about the power. I intend to get it and wield it the way I see fit."

In a slow, careful motion, Markus got up and went to the bar, taking the Colossus with him. His gun hand never wavered. He carefully placed the computer on the bar and stroked it like someone petting a cat.

"You see, it's more than just souls taken and given. That's the game to you. That's all you know, and truthfully, that's all I knew as well, at least when I first started out five hundred years ago.

"In the beginning, I did what I was supposed to do. I played along because I truly believed in the powers of darkness. In a way, I still do."

A sigh, something akin to regret, came from him. "Still, I didn't see the bigger picture at the time. But after a couple of centuries, I finally got it. I realized that I could run after something more.

"So, I started reading ancient books on Earth, those concerned with black magic. It gave me a break from being with my boyfriends and girlfriends. Hedonism rules, but there is a time and a place for everything.

"Then I realized more knowledge lay at hand, and it was right in Hell where I could access it. Can I assume you understood everything in those books?"

Ed felt embarrassed to admit his ignorance, but he felt that he could play to his opponent's vanity. "You're the genius here. I only caught a few words. One of them was progenitor. What exactly is it?"

Markus chuckled. "It figures you wouldn't understand. See, all these years, I've been searching for a way around the power gap, but the technology wasn't there. The right people weren't there, not until Alperstein came along."

"Alperstein," Ed echoed.

"Yes. Him. He was the one, the person we'd—I'd—been waiting for. I first saw him on Earth, and oh, was he a hot mess! But he'd designed the Colossus, and he showed me everything ... just before I convinced him to kill himself. I saw the facts and figures the computer could input, and that was cool.

"I saw the algorithm that predicted what choices people would make in life, and that was cool, too. Then I saw how the computer predicted good and evil in possible soul-snatchings, and *that* was beyond cool. It made doing my job so much easier, giving me more free time to indulge in my lifestyle."

His eyes glowed with inhuman greed, something that would have unnerved Lucifer at his most lethal.

"But then I saw something more, something that really

piqued my interest, and it all had to do with the designer. I went down to the seventh pit and spoke to Alperstein. The guy is totally cracked, but he's also a genius. He didn't remember that I was the one who hinted at suicide, and he told me just what the Colossus could really do.

"More important, he told me where I could find what I wanted. He was the one who told me about the books. I'd never even heard of them. Me, a demon, in service to our master for almost five centuries, I never knew."

Markus gave a self-deprecating laugh. It was as if he was the only one in on the joke and didn't want to let anyone else share in the punchline.

"But Alperstein did," he continued while stroking the computer. "The guy is a bibliophile. I don't know where he found them or who he'd gotten them from, but he'd read those books on Earth, and I found them in Hell, in Lucifer's library. Alperstein understood them, and he used that knowledge as well as his own to construct the Colossus."

Ed had figured most everything out, but he decided to play dumb and find out what other information Markus could offer. He got up, slowly, waiting. "And the Colossus knows more?"

Markus obliged him by opening the lid and tapping a few keys. "The Colossus knows *everything*. That's where the true power was and is. The true power is the progenitor, something even Lucifer never understood."

Ed still didn't get it. "All right, so clue me in. I read the passages you marked, but I couldn't understand everything in them. What exactly is it?"

Markus carefully poured himself a drink, all the while keeping watch and keeping his gun level. "The mathematics are incredibly complicated, enough to drive anyone mad," he said with a touch of awe.

"That's what it did to Alperstein. He was always brilliant,

but after he'd read those books and used that knowledge to build his computer, well, he discovered something that was so mind-bending, it drove him over the edge."

"Uh-huh."

A curious smile came over Markus' face, something sly, crafty, and more than a little crazy. "You may very well say that.

"However, open your mind and cast your thoughts upon something we rarely think about down here—the heavens, the universe. That's what the writers of those books stated, although they didn't really know where the progenitor was at the time. It was only a supposition on their part, but still, they were onto something."

From the way he uttered those words, with total conviction, Ed knew something unholier than unholy was going on. But it wasn't the power of the underworld. It came from outside. "So, the progenitor really exists?"

Markus nodded, a grin indicating knowledge and unholy joy beginning to form on his face. "You bet it does. Imagine a door in our universe, a door that randomly travels the cosmos. It's just a door, that's all, something comprised of energy, but inside, there's a table, and on that table is the little gem I'm after."

Ed had never really been concerned about the universe. He enjoyed watching the stars, but as for visiting them, it had never really grabbed his interest—until now, when he saw the unholy glint in Markus' eye.

Then something else hit him like a punch between the eyes. The meaning of the word, the concept of what the Colossus could do. "It's a search engine, isn't it?" he asked. "It's a universal mapper."

Markus nodded, a broad smile on his half-mad mug. "Congratulations on figuring it out. Yes, you're right, and so were those writers of spells and incantations. They never

216

envisioned that science would create something like a search engine to find something they thought was Hell-given and unknowable.

"But in reality, the Colossus simply gave everything that was considered black magic four hundred years ago a modern, scientific grounding. Additionally, it gave everything a great measure of accuracy."

He caressed the computer with a loving hand after putting down his drink. "You're right in your definition. It *is* the ultimate search engine, not only on Earth but also among everything in the universe. The mathematics could nail down not only what the progenitor was, but also more importantly, where it was, something those ancient writers could never do."

Some of the explanation given, he picked up his drink and downed half of it in a mad gulp. Liquid dribbled down his chin, but he made no effort to wipe it away.

"So what is the progenitor? It's a spark, really, a building block of all creation. It's something the man upstairs discovered untold millennia ago. It existed before time began, and before even he and my master came into existence, believe it or not."

Ed gaped, and then he put his jaw back into position. "You mean before there was—"

"Yes, before there was God, before there was our master, the progenitor existed. And if you want to talk about hypocrisy, then let's talk about the greatest lie ever perpetrated against mankind by both our leader and theirs. He created people in His image?"

A sneer twisted his perfect features out of true. "Bull, I'm calling bull on that. But God is such an egotist—as is our master—that neither of them could ever admit something more powerful than they existed."

He cackled like a mean little kid with a secret that only he knew, a secret he couldn't wait to blurt out, but first, wanted to torture everyone else.

"And to think, mortals have been drip-fed the lie that God created the Earth in seven days and that Lucifer was cast out. It's true that Lucifer was an angel, but he *left*, just in case you didn't know. He left and decided to strike out on his own."

Markus quaffed his drink and poured himself another. "So, if the mortals really knew what—not who—created everything, you think they'd still believe in what their churches and synagogues and mosques preach? Nope, they'd go insane. Not everyone, no, certainly not the atheists, but a lot of people would. And the churches and synagogues and mosques would go bankrupt, so maybe that's a good thing."

Ed had to admit that Markus was right. The knowledge that something more ancient and powerful than his Master and the Lord of all hosts existed would render traditional religion obsolete.

It was a social order disruptor of the greatest magnitude. If the basis of everyone's belief disappeared, there was nothing left to support that belief system.

While he contemplated the what-ifs of no religion, Markus continued to expound on his future quest. "Now, as to what created the progenitor, well, that's the answer brighter minds than ours will have to figure out—if they can. It sort of puts an end to the chicken-or-egg theory—and not."

He chuckled. "Yeah, that's a real mind-bender. The progenitor created all that we know, all that created us. Wrap your gray matter around that if you can."

Ed couldn't. It was inconceivable, yet true. Markus continued, sliding his tongue over his teeth, really warming to the topic at hand.

"So, we have an all-powerful piece of energy, more powerful than anything ever in the entire existence of everything, everywhere, because it *is* the creator of everything, everywhere. I want that. And with it, I could —"

"Reshape the universe," Ed finished for him, now filled with horror at the possibilities.

Markus quaffed the rest of his beverage and tossed the glass at the wall. It shattered, and he offered a smirk as if to say a little more destruction wouldn't matter.

"Not just the universe, Ed. Once more, you're missing the big picture. I'm talking about reshaping all of creation in *my* image. And the best part is, I don't have to teleport anywhere. The computer already did the work for me. All I have to do is wait."

He mimed looking at a non-existent watch. "At the very least, I won't have to wait too long."

"How's that?"

Now, Markus looked bored. "You heard what our dear leader said. At midnight, the balance of good and evil will be totted up by those above and those below. Both of us know that the balance will hold. You and your Halo chick saw to that."

His demeanor abruptly shifted into something more manic, more intense, and he stabbed his forefinger at Ed like a game-show emcee announcing the grand prize.

"But there's more! Since you didn't get everything those books said, I'll tell you. It's fun, trust me.

"See, the progenitor, as powerful as it is, lies dormant every millennium until a certain year and hour. This is the year, and this is the hour. When the clock strikes twelve, the doorway will open, and the progenitor will come to life like a beautiful flower unfolding, fresh and new.

"That's how this whole plane of existence works. That's what those writers theorized, and that's what the Colossus told me as a scientific fact.

"Now, if the balance is off, then the progenitor destroys everything. If the balance is there, it goes back to sleep and waits another millennium. You getting all this?"

Ed nodded. "Like a bear hibernating?"

Markus chuckled. "It's more like a time bomb, but like all bombs, it's only activated under the right circumstances."

He transferred his gun to his other hand and offered a demented smile. "So before it hibernates, as you put it, it remains active for the most infinitesimal of seconds.

"In that incredibly tiny space of ticks between tocks, I will step in, grab it, and once I have it, well, existence is all mine. The Colossus and those books showed me how to join with it. Imagine that, if you will. I'll become a god. No, more than that, I'll become a legend!"

His eyes were mad. Ed saw that now. If his foe had been a bit unbalanced before, he was way over the edge now. "So, you arranged for the imbalance to appear before?"

Markus got up and began to pace, keeping his gun out front. He let his jaw sag in an obscene parody of someone explaining the obvious to a mentally challenged person.

"Duh, yes. I had to do something to keep both sides occupied. Kick-starting a false apocalypse was it. I simply took a couple more souls than necessary, and when Irving and his heavenly counterpart added everything up, they saw the imbalance."

And to cover his plans, he'd used a spell to blind even Lucifer as well as Heaven's ruler. Markus was far more dangerous than anyone had ever suspected.

His nemesis continued to expound on his discovery. "Call it mad, if you wish, call it foolish, or call it obvious, the plan worked.

"You, your girlfriend, Lucifer, the one above, and everyone else, you were so concerned about the world ending, you never entertained the concept of something else being just as, if not more, important."

If Ed possessed a gun, he'd have fought it out with Markus, and consequences be damned. But he was unarmed, and the weapon his opponent carried was lethal. Stall for time, he told himself. Stall for time.

"Okay, say you're right," he said. "Where does the progenitor appear?"

Sure, it was stalling for time to the nth degree, but really, how much time did they have? According to the clock on the wall, less than a minute.

"It can appear anywhere in the universe," Markus replied, his eyes hard. "If it were to appear in, say, the Milky Way galaxy, well, I wouldn't be able to reach it in time.

"But this millennia, it's going to appear right here, in this room."

Ed couldn't believe it. "You're serious?"

Markus nodded. "Quite serious. Last millennia, it appeared over Lima, Peru. Before that, it showed up on Mars, and before that, in the spiral arm of Andromeda. For some reason, it's gravitated toward this world, but as for the reason why, I have no idea.

"All I do know is that it appears for the briefest of nanoseconds. Mortals see a flash of white light, as the door opens and closes too fast for the human eye to follow, but we're a little different, aren't we?"

He then leaned forward, his eyes madder than ever, and yet, his voice was calm and almost persuasive — almost. "You know, if you join me, I'll let you and your girlfriend live. You can be my lieutenant. In my new universe, there won't be any angels or devils. There will be only gods, only I'll be the chief one. We've got about thirty seconds. Choose."

Ed had already made his choice, the choice to do some good. He'd done so when he rescued Nell from certain death, and he'd never regretted it. "I've made my choice. I'm playing for a different team."

Markus looked disappointed as the corners of his mouth turned down in a frown. "Too bad, really. You were a worthy competitor."

Unlike the impromptu apocalypse of before, now, the ground began to shake intensely, the sky cracked open with lightning streaking its way through it, and the very fabric of existence seemed to wink out.

It was beyond awesome, beyond terrifying. Ed had never seen this before or even heard about it from the true veterans of Hell. This was it, the possible end of everything. Entropy would reign over everything.

Markus' disappointed expression changed to one of joy. "This is it," he cried. "This is it! Come to Papa!"

As if by magic, the ground in front of the bar opened, and in a burst of slow-motion, a doorway appeared.

Markus stepped out from behind the bar, keeping the gun steady and level, and holding the Colossus under his arm with his free hand. "This is going to be great," he cried and then giggled maniacally as he reached to open the door. "Guess who's going to become the next legend beyond God?"

A trillionth of a nanosecond later, a lightning bolt of pure white came through the ceiling. Another one of pure red shot out from under the floor. Both bolts fried Markus in his tracks, and he disappeared from all existence without so much as a scream. It also fried the Colossus, reducing it to a puddle of metal and melted plastic.

Time resumed its normal course. The shaking stopped, and the door disappeared. The floor reformed. A blessed silence fell.

No voice spoke, but Ed knew what had happened. There was only one God, and he'd been mightily displeased. There was also only one Lucifer, and pissing off the king of the underworld was not a smart idea.

It almost seemed a bit of *deux ex machina*, but that had something to do with the ancient Greek gods, and the rulers of above and below were considerably older.

Only a tiny piece of Markus' clothing remained. Ed fired a blue bolt of energy from his finger to laser it out of existence. "Bye, Markus."

Outside, the sky had resumed its normal dark color, the stars were out and bright, and the world—in fact, three worlds—continued on, as did the rest of existence.

Ed breathed a sigh of relief. It was over, and he couldn't help but smile. With a snap of his fingers, he erased the stains from the couch and rug, and the apartment took on its fresh and clean appearance again, unsullied by Markus' existence.

Nell woke up, moaned, and he quickly untied her and pulled the gag from her mouth. "Are you okay?" he asked.

She melted into his arms. "Never better. What happened?"

He started to explain but stopped as her body began to fade out of existence. In a split-second, she was gone. She didn't even have time to say goodbye.

"Nell!"

Ed's lament echoed over his apartment, and then he heard the voice of his master call him. *Ed, we have to talk.*

Your wish is my will.

And Ed disappeared. He knew that he had to make a report, and if oblivion waited, then at the very least, he'd done his best. He only wished that he could have kissed his one true love once more, but apparently, that was not to be.

Chapter Twenty-Two: Decision

The boardroom was empty, and Ed took his time wandering around, checking out the chairs, straightening one here and brushing off non-existent dust from another over there.

A pop in the air made him aware that someone had arrived. He spun around to find Lucifer leaning over the table, his gaze fixed on the stone. He greatly resembled a corporate executive musing over his latest and greatest acquisition. In this instance, Ed's mental picture of his master wasn't wrong.

Lucifer had reacquired Hell and a new lease on existence, as had everyone else. Things had gotten back to normal. Since it was a new year, the leader had decreed a day of rest for the damned. After that, there'd be new ways for demons to rip souls from mortals as well as new pain to inflict on those damned to the great depths.

On the flipside, the Halos were going to do their best in order to save those they deemed worthy. All in all, the great-above-great-below war would continue.

In the long run, Hell would remain what it was — a jail cell for the damned. Ed could almost sense what would happen tomorrow. The cries of pain and agony, the crack of whips, the smell of sulfur — all of that would signal that Hell was back on track. Annihilation on the eternal scale had been averted, and now, unlife was good.

For now, though, an unearthly quiet settled over the room. Lucifer spoke without looking up. "Ed, approach me, please."

Please? The master had never been so courteous. Ed did as

the master requested. He stood a respectful distance away and kept his head down.

He risked a quick look at the overlord, only to find Lucifer gazing at him with a mild expression on his now-human face. He wore a perfectly tailored black suit with an ebony dress shirt and a neatly knotted black tie. The only indication of his demonic origins was his tail that he lashed back and forth with obvious pleasure.

And why not? The pressure on him was off, and he had another year in which to plan the apocalypse. Anyone would be elated at such a prospect. "Please, be seated, Ed. Relax. You're among your own, now."

The overlord parked himself on his throne, one foot over the armrest, and he snapped his fingers. An obscenely long cigar appeared, already lit, and he puffed on it contentedly. Ed continued to sit up straight in the humble pose as his mentor had taught him, thinking about what would happen in the next few seconds.

On the upside, Markus had been erased forever, the progenitor was safe, and all of existence would continue for at least another millennium.

On the downside, Nell was gone, and he doubted the ones from above would allow her to take her place on Earth again. She'd done everything they'd asked, but if Heaven was as unforgiving as Hell was, well, he could kiss that relationship goodbye.

Whatever. Without her, life, eternal or not, wasn't really worth it. Ed said nothing, though. He waited for what seemed like an eternity for his master to speak, and while every fiber of him wanted to shout say something — he kept silent.

Finally, after more puffing, Lucifer carefully placed his cigar on the edge of the throne and cracked a rare smile, one that was genuine and radiated bliss and utter contentment, both of which seemed out of place in that realm, and yet — not.

"Ed, I want to tell you that I'm pleased. In fact, I'm more than pleased. The world is back on its course, the progenitor is out of harm's way, and all is well."

All is well for you. That thought ran through Ed's head, but he kept up his silent front. Still, the prospect of saying nothing bothered him, and he asked after a few more seconds had passed, "You knew about it? Markus said you didn't."

"Oh, I've known about it for, well, forever." Lucifer offered a somewhat guilty smile.

"Why didn't you tell me about it?"

The lord of all badness actually looked embarrassed, and he assumed a more dignified pose, sitting up straight as if he was a schoolboy being scolded by a teacher. "I told no one. Call it pride," he finally said after scratching his jaw.

"Or, you could call it vanity, if you wish. I didn't want to believe that something else could be more powerful than me or, er, my maker. That's one of the reasons why it's never mentioned around here. People like to believe in me or him."

He pointed upward. "If they stopped believing in us, well, our jobs wouldn't be as much fun."

Lucifer then picked up his stogie to take another drag on it, and a plume of purplish-blue smoke wreathed his face. "So, yes, only the three of us know about the progenitor's existence. Congratulations. You're privy to a great discovery."

Everyone has their pride, Ed thought, and then realized that his master had just swallowed a mega dose of his. He also felt gratified that Lucifer had entrusted him with a special secret, and he did not intend to betray his master's trust. "Okay, I get it. So what did you do with the progenitor?"

His master chuckled softly. "It's not what I did with it. It's what *it* wants to do. It disappeared. I've already told my counterpart."

Lucifer flicked his forefinger skyward once more. "We still communicate, you know. As I said before, usually, he sends

Peter. Sometimes, he sends his accountant, Murray, to talk things over with Irving. I trust Murray as much as I trust my own accountant, and that's saying a lot.

"In my case, either we meet at the walls of Dis, or we meet on Earth. Usually, it's at a ballgame. I'm not much for going upstairs, but to watch the Yankees play, I make an exception."

All right, progenitor problem—solved. The overlord of all evil took another drag on his cigar, tapped it against his thigh, and a fine cloud of ash dropped to the ground. "As for the Colossus Five, I imagine that it was destroyed."

"Uh, yeah, it got fried by, well, both of you."

Lucifer waggled his head back and forth as if weighing the pros and cons of destroying that invention. "I figured as much. It was a marvelous machine, and it would have taught us so much. But, in the wrong hands, it was capable of endowing those with knowledge, and a little knowledge is a dangerous thing, don't you know.

"So, from now on, since we're going to keep files on every-one, then we'll have to do it the old-fashioned way, by ledger. That's how it was done from time immemorial, and that's how it will be done from this point on."

"That's a little slow," Ed pointed out, trying to be helpful.

A shrug greeted his statement. "The dead can wait. It's the eternity thing."

Lucifer drew a deep breath from his cigar, puffed out some purplish-blue smoke, and examined it with a tiny smile. "I love Cuban cigars. They have such a fine smell."

Said smile disappeared, and he shifted his position to one of command. Equally so, his eyes had now acquired a hard-ness and sense of purpose to them. "Now, as to calling you back here."

The moment of truth had arrived. "Yes, sir?"

"Being the magnanimous person that I am, I shall grant you one wish. That's the least that I can do. Think it over carefully. If you need time to come to a decision, that's fine. I'll always be here."

He glanced around the boardroom. "Yes, *we* will always be here."

Ed really didn't have to think about the offer. "I'd like to go back to Earth, sir, as a mortal."

"What?"

This time, the walls of the boardroom shook and almost collapsed. The overlord shot up to a ramrod-stiff position, and for a change, his eyes lost their hardness, replaced by surprise. No, more than that. They registered dismay. "Why?"

"I think there's more to existence than taking souls."

Lucifer recovered from his shock quickly enough, stubbed out his cigar, and far from being angry, though, he adopted a conciliatory tone.

"Ed, you've been a faithful employee. You've never failed in your duties, and you didn't fail this time. I know you and that Halo were close, but still, if it's the eastern seaboard you want, it's yours. In fact, I trust you enough to let you have total control of the country, and —"

"No, sir, I don't want that. I want to go back to Earth — as a mortal. That's all I want."

His master's eyes bugged out. "Do you realize what you're asking? You'd give up all the power, the wealth, the fun . . . oh, wait." His eyes narrowed. "You're doing it for her, aren't you?"

"Yes, sir."

If ever there came a moment where humiliation or degradation entered the picture, this was it, but Ed didn't see his request as humiliating or degrading in any way.

In fact, he picked his head up to lock gazes with his master. Call it defiance or suicide or both — it didn't matter. Nell did.

"I'm also doing this for me. I want the chance to see what life is all about, to do it differently than what I had before, back in Roanoke.

"And Nell, well, if she returns to Earth, maybe she'll take me back. I don't deserve it, but that's what I want. Just a chance."

His words proved most persuasive. The master sat on his throne, stroked his chin, and finally, he offered a very human-type shrug. "You realize that if I send you back as a mortal, you might not find her. She may not be allowed onto that plane of existence."

"I know."

"You also know that your soul is fair game. I have it here, and it can be returned to you."

In all his time downstairs, Ed had never entertained the notion of where the souls of the dead were kept. There had to be a repository, but it would have been imprudent to ask. Instead, all he said was, "Yes, master."

Lucifer's voice hardened. "And you also realize that if my maker upstairs decides to send that girl back, then her soul is fair game, too?"

"I'm prepared for that. Maybe she'll be ready, too."

With a huff, Lucifer got off his throne, paced around for a minute, mumbling something about losing the best person he ever knew, and then he returned to place his hands on Ed's shoulders.

A benevolent smile formed on his face. "Done. I'll . . ." He ducked his head. "I'll have a word with my maker on your behalf."

"Thank you, master."

Lucifer waved him off as if embarrassed at doing something truly good. "I'm only doing what's right. You deserve that, at the very least."

Gratitude was something that couldn't be quantified, yet Ed felt compelled to say, "I'm grateful to you and everyone else. Please say goodbye to Frank and everyone else for me."

Lucifer chuckled. "I most certainly will. Close your eyes."

Ed did as the dark lord instructed. Once he did, a charge ran through him. He gasped, trying to adjust to the energy of that which was so important being returned to him.

Then he heard the three magical words for the last time. "Thou art sent."

EPILOGUE

Twelve-oh-seven AM, January first. Times Square.

Ed emerged out of a pocket of air that shimmered in the darkness to find himself in the middle of a crowd of drunken revelers. They were so hammered that they didn't notice his arrival or smell the sulfur that had accompanied it.

The events of the past few hours had been forgotten. It was as if it had never happened, but it had. That was something Ed would always keep with him, to the end of his days.

Behind him, the portal closed up with a sharp snap of air, and the odor of sulfur and the other smells of Hell quickly dissipated. "Hey, man!"

The voice startled him. One of the party people held a can of beer and proffered it with a hearty, "Hey, man, Happy New Year. Have a beverage!"

"Uh, no thanks," Ed replied, still somewhat disoriented. He shivered in the cold night air. "You see a girl around?"

Everyone laughed. "Lots of girls here, man," another drunken dude said, waving his hand in the air as if the women would suddenly materialize in front of him. "Look around you. Take your pick."

Ed didn't want to choose. He'd already made his choice. "Thanks, anyway."

Suddenly depressed, wondering if he'd made the right decision, he walked around noting the festive mood and taking no joy in it.

Cold, it was cold, but as he examined himself, he found that he'd been clad in a lined gray suit, and he wore a heavy trench coat and a pair of lined slacks that helped keep the warmth in.

A snowflake touched his nose, and then another one landed in his hand. Call this a first-time experience. He'd never known snow as a mortal in his entire life, only when he'd been in demonic form.

Things had totally changed, and there would be more changes, he felt. A laugh, small at first and then larger in intensity, burst from his gut. "Snow. This is snow!"

"What else would it be, man?" someone called. "Dumbass, this is winter!"

"Yeah, it is," he answered, elated to experience the cold and snow and all that came with it for the first time as a mortal. "Happy New Year."

The person who'd called out didn't bother to return the greeting. Ed continued walking, taking in the neon of Times Square, the raucous atmosphere, and the utter joy at being what he was and where he was.

Abruptly, his elation disappeared. "It's not the same without Nell," he murmured. "Never the same . . ."

"Someone call my name?"

At the sound of the voice, Ed jerked his head to the left. Nell stood three yards from him, wearing a stylish white overcoat that was partially open to reveal a white blouse and a mini skirt.

An off-white purse was slung across her body, giving her a distinctive look reminiscent of a woman straight out of the nineteen-sixties.

She made her way over, bypassing a few revelers who'd conveniently passed out in front of her, and decided that the ground was a good place for a nap. She then stopped five feet away, a peculiar smile on her face, one of uncertainty combined with hope. In a quiet voice, she said, "Nice to see you again."

"Yeah."

Immediately, he cursed himself for giving a standard answer, but Nell didn't seem to mind as she returned the greeting. Their talk began slowly, with him trying to pick up the details of their recent adventure, but the longer they spoke, the more confused he became, as he began to forget the specifics. "You know . . ."

I had a little chat with my maker. It is done.

A voice spoke in Ed's mind, and in that nanosecond, the memory of his former life as a minion began to fade. Was this what he wanted? *This is New York. It's cold, it's snowing, and what am I doing out here? I should be home.*

Another voice—familiar, and yet, not—echoed inside his gray matter. *Check your pockets.*

Ed fumbled around in his right pocket and came out with a wallet loaded with money, a gold watch, and identification that said he was Edward Anderson, nineteen, living in a trendy condo in Manhattan.

Another thought popped into his head. He was the son of Brynn Anderson, a wealthy industrialist. "Yeah, that's right. He's my father," he mumbled.

More memories—implanted ones—came to the surface. He'd just graduated from a preppy high school in upstate New York, and he was taking a year off to relax before going to university. That was it.

A millisecond later, his memory of his old life disappeared entirely, but before it did, he heard one final voice, deep and sonorous that he didn't recognize at all. *Take care, Ed. We'll be in touch – someday.*

And then it was gone. Only a vague memory of being somewhere hot and oppressive remained in Ed's mind. He didn't realize that the overlord had blanked out his memory of Hell.

However, that blanking out didn't include erasing memories of Nell, who now faced him with a dazzling smile.

"Do you remember what you used to do?" Nell asked.

Ed scratched his head, puzzled at his faulty memory, but faced with this gorgeous woman, he decided that ... wait, yes, now he knew. "Uh, I didn't at first. Something happened, maybe I drank too much, but ... we met in school, right? I think, yeah, I know, we graduated."

She fluttered her eyelashes, and it proved to be a most alluring gesture. "That's right. We met in school, we graduated together, and you fell in love with me."

High school sweethearts? Call that a trope and then some, and ... he had? Yes, by God, he had. "Yeah, that's right."

"And ... you asked me to move in with you."

Move in? Oh, he could go for that. Her smile warmed him to the depths of his now-restored soul. "Naturally," he replied, still fumbling for the right words. "Yes, I mean, yes, you can move in with me, if you're sure."

"Absolutely and positively, yes."

Her smile, formerly somewhat shy and innocent, now transitioned into a most devilish grin. "Absolutely and positively, yes," she repeated.

And with that, she ran forward to hang onto him, and he embraced his future.

The end

ABOUT THE AUTHOR

J.S. Frankel was born in Toronto, Canada, many moons ago, grew up there, receiving his degree in English Literature from the University of Toronto. After working for three years in that fair city, he moved to Japan to teach English as a Second Language and has been there ever since. In 1997, he married the charming Akiko Koike, and their union produced two sons, Kai, and Ray. Frankel and his family make their home in Osaka where he teaches English by day and writes by night.

All his novels are in the YA Fantasy genre, the best-known among them the Catnip series of five novels, Master Fantastic, Odoru, The Dance of Death, Hoppers, and Twisted, among many others.